D1645665

THE GIRL FROM THE DISCOTHEQUE

Inspired by a true story

*To Caroline
Best Wishes*

Bennett Arron

The Girl From the Discotheque

Published by Silly Papi Ltd 2015

© Bennett Arron

The Right of Bennett Arron to be identified as the Author of this work
has been asserted by him in accordance with the Copyright, Designs
and Patents Act 1988.

All Rights Reserved. No part of this book may be printed, reproduced or
utilized in any form or by any electronic, mechanical or other means,
now known or hereafter invented, including photocopying and
recording, or in any information storage retrieval system, without
permission in writing from the publishers.

This is a work of fiction. Names, characters and businesses are either the
products of the author's imagination or used in a fictitious manner. Any
resemblance to actual persons, living or dead is purely coincidental.

A catalogue record for this book is available
from the British Library

ISBN: 978-0-9933571-1-4

Printed by CPI Group UK, Croydon CR0 4YY

About the Author

Bennett Arron is an award-winning writer, stand-up comedian and BAFTA-shortlisted director. He has written for several television programmes including *Genie in the House*, which was the highest-rated sitcom on Nickelodeon, and the BBC's BAFTA-winning *The Slammer*. He has written and starred in two radio series, *Bennett Arron is Jewelsh* and *Bennett Arron Worries About...*

His first book, *Heard The One About Identity Theft,* is an autobiographical tale based on his critically acclaimed television documentary *How To Steal An Identity.*

He is a past winner of the BBC New Writers' Award and the TAPS Comedy Writer of the Year Award. In addition to this, he came third in an international disco-dancing championship in Tenerife.

Genuinely original and funny
THE TIMES

Hilarious . . . clever wit . . . razor sharp
STANDARD

One of the best on the circuit . . . a Welsh Seinfeld
THE GUARDIAN

For Rosy, Yasmin and Xander

CHAPTER ONE

It wasn't the first time Steve had worn a dress. No, the first time was when he'd worn his mother's favourite blue and white checked one to enter a talent contest. The judges said that he was the best Demis Roussos they'd ever seen. This had upset him somewhat, mainly as he'd gone as Dolly Parton.

So although this was his second time in a dress, it was the first time he had done it for sexual gratification. Not his own of course, but that of his current sleeping partner, Emily. It was, if truth be told, a compromise – although he was beginning to dislike his end of the deal more and more.

It had started when he had subtly, drunkenly, mentioned to Emily that he wouldn't mind having sex with her and one of her friends at the same time.

He'd always imagined how Emily might react to his saying this; angry, upset, angry again. But not in his wildest dreams – including the recurring one in which he is naked, except for a pair of earplugs, and riding a six-legged camel through a busy shopping centre – had he expected Emily to say, 'That sounds like a fantastic idea.'

Five minutes later, as he walked back from the bar carrying more unnecessary drinks, he was still in a state of shock. This shock reached a new level when he sat down at the table and Emily asked him which friend he'd had in mind.

As he hadn't expected to get to this stage, he wasn't quite sure what to say. His knee-jerk reaction would have been to scream, 'Carol! Please, please can it be Carol. She's stunning!'

1

But he realised that it might sound just a bit too keen, and if she said no then in future there would always be that embarrassment if the two of them were ever alone together. He also realised that his second immediate thought – 'Not Beth, she's a trog!' – wouldn't stand him in good stead either.

So he went with, 'You decide. Whoever you would be happier with is fine by me.'

Now admittedly this had been a bit of a gamble. But the way he saw it, Beth was the only unattractive, large bullet in an otherwise babe-packed chamber.

Emily had nodded. 'Okay, Steve. I'll have a think which of my friends I'd feel the most relaxed with.'

When she'd rung him at work the following day to tell him that she'd made her decision he was very excited – physically and emotionally. However what he wasn't expecting were the conditions that followed.

First of all Emily told him that he wouldn't know which friend she had chosen until they actually all met up on the day. Steve was a little hesitant about this but he remembered the Russian-roulette odds and agreed. The second and final condition was the one with which he was going to have real problems. Emily told him that, as she was prepared to carry out one of his fantasies, he would, at the same time, have to carry out one of hers.

He'd hoped that her fantasy was going to involve him sitting and watching her and her friend play nurses and nurses, but he was way off. Emily's fantasy was for him to wear one of her dresses and full make-up. At first he'd laughed and waited for the 'Just kidding. Can you hire some nurses' uniforms?' But that hadn't happened.

Realising she was serious, he said that he wouldn't do it. Purely and simply it was too weird.

'Fair enough,' she'd said. 'Then let's forget the whole thing.'

'Hang on,' he'd said. 'Are you serious? If I don't do this, the whole thing's off?'

'Yes.'

And there it was.

Although Steve hadn't been seeing Emily all that long – an intense eight weeks and three days to be precise – he knew that once she'd decided on something she didn't change her mind.

So he gave it some serious thought. Maybe it wouldn't be so bad. Maybe it was just a way for Emily and her friend to feel less inhibited – by pretending the other person was also a girl. Albeit a girl with the biggest erection of her life.

'Okay,' he'd said, 'I'll do it.'

And now, a week later, here he was, doing it.

He looked at himself again in the wardrobe mirror. It was only a half-size mirror so he had to jump up and down to try and get the full effect.

He shook his head. This would not have been the dress he would have picked had he been given the choice. He then realised he was actually mentally going through Emily's wardrobe to decide which outfit would have suited him better. This really was too weird. He seriously thought about putting his clothes back on and forgetting the whole thing, when he heard the front door open and close.

Emily called up the stairs, 'Steve, are you there?'

Steve thought about answering in a girl's voice but then realised that it might have the wrong effect.

'Yeah,' he shouted back, in his deepest tones.

He heard two sets of footsteps walking up the stairs. Even together they didn't sound heavy enough to be Beth.

He looked at himself once more in the mirror and then

tried to decide where he should be *discovered* when they entered; lounging nonchalantly on the bed? Sitting astride the chair? Standing and leaning in as macho a way as possible?

Too late to think, the door was opening. He quickly sat down on the bed.

Emily walked in. She looked fantastic. She was wearing his favourite outfit. The one he would have chosen for himself.

'Hi,' she said. 'You look great.'

'Oh, this old thing?' he said.

Emily smiled. She then looked out of the door and indicated for whoever was there to come in.

Emily's friend walked in.

Steve immediately realised his error– this was a friend of hers he'd never met, or even heard about. Emily made the introductions:

'Steve, this is my friend . . . Colin.'

Steve looked at the man in front of him. He then looked at Emily. Emily was grinning like a Cheshire cat who'd found a way to have its cake and eat it.

'So,' she said, looking at Steve, 'do you need some help taking my dress off?'

Steve picked up his clothes from the floor and, without saying a word, walked out past Emily and Colin.

'Call me!' shouted Emily.

'Me too!' shouted Colin.

Their laughter followed him down the stairs and only stopped when he slammed the door behind him.

He stood outside the door. He was humiliated. Not only because he was wearing a dress and not only because he had been made to look a fool, but mainly because he had just stormed out of his own flat.

CHAPTER TWO

'I don't know why she did it, Jeff! Maybe she was pissed off with my whole fantasy thing or maybe she was going to split up with me anyway and this seemed like a *fun* way to do it . . .' Steve sighed loudly into the phone. 'Yes, Jeff, I know you never liked her . . . Okay, mate, I'll see you tomorrow . . . really, can't we meet somewhere else? . . . Okay, fine, I'll see you there.'

Steve ended the call and stared at the phone for a moment. He then sat back in his chair and, even though he knew the exact layout, looked around his office.

On The Edge – United Kingdom Division was based on the top floor of a four-storey building in the middle of Soho. It had been converted from what was once a luxury residence into several tiny offices. There was one toilet in the whole building, which was meant to cater for everyone. Most people preferred to use the facilities in the local pubs and hotels. In fact, at the previous year's joint office party, most of the festivities took place in the gents' and ladies' of the London Soho International Hotel.

Steve's office overlooked a cigar and pipe shop, an 'All You Can Eat for Five Pounds' Chinese buffet and a sex shop – or, as Steve referred to them, 'Snuff, Buff and Muff'.

The walls of his office were covered in posters of some of the shows Steve had produced:

'The Fun Guys – Live in the West End.'

'Norman Frogmore and William Glass – Together Again for the First Time.'

'Gareth Ice – No More Mr Ice Guy.'

'Theresa Wild Is Funny Ha-Ha.'

Most of the shows had made money or at least covered their costs and one or two of the acts had made little guest appearances on TV game shows. Theresa Wild had done very well. Steve had always known how talented she was. Talented, quite sexy and a hard worker. He also knew that the minute she started doing well in her career she would leave him for a bigger agent. And he'd been right. She had signed with Donald Watson and Associates and was now hosting her own chat show: *Wild Encounters*. She still sent him the occasional email to see how he was doing. He had yet to reply.

***

Steve, like most people in his profession, didn't set out to be an agent-cum-promoter. He had initially wanted to be a teacher, but after failing to achieve the required qualifications he had decided to go to drama school instead. Although it was a three-year course, he had left drama school halfway through the second year as he hated all the pretentiousness and falseness. Ironically that is exactly what he had been dealing with since starting the agency two years earlier.

The agency idea had happened by accident. Up until then he had been running a lettings company from a small office in Kilburn, north London. He had worked for an estate agent/lettings agent for a while after leaving drama school and saw the potential for making a substantial profit from very little work. So after a succession of jobs he hated, which ranged from telesales to taking part in murder mystery weekends (in which he always felt like the victim regardless of which part he played), he had decided to start up his own lettings company. The business had gone well at the beginning, but, as with *almost* everything in Steve's life, it hadn't taken long for him to lose interest.

Eighteen months after starting Station Lettings (the office was near the station) he had gone with his friend Jeff to the Laff a Minute Comedy Club in the East End of London. They'd been there before. The previous time was at the start of Jeff's bi-annual 'sober month', which usually lasted a week. Jeff always had difficulty going to a place that sold alcohol if he was only having soft drinks. To him, that was like going to a brothel and paying for someone to hold your hand. Steve once asked Jeff if he could have a good time without drinking. Jeff said that he probably could, but didn't want to take the risk.

That night they had seen some excellent comedians and a few weeks later they were very excited to see one of them on TV, although they were disappointed to see him perform exactly the same act.

During the course of the evening, Steve had mentioned to Jeff that he thought there'd be good money in running an agency for comedians. Jeff had thought this was a fantastic idea. However, Jeff had already caved in to his promise of not having a drink and was ready to find any idea fantastic.

The thought had stayed with Steve and was one of the reasons he had suggested going back to the club. Surprisingly, what convinced him even more was when they watched one of the comedians 'dying' onstage.

***

Chuck Ling hadn't done well from the start. His opening line – 'I'm Chuck Ling, which is no laughing matter' – had been met with silence. And things had gone downhill from there. But there was something about him that Steve liked. He liked the oversized three-piece pinstripe suit which made him look like a child dressed up in his dad's clothes and he liked some of the material; not all, but some. So far Steve's favourite line had been: 'I went out for a drink with my oldest friend yesterday. He's 106.' But the audience had decided they weren't going to like him regardless of his material.

'So,' said Chuck Ling, 'I was in the newsagent's, and—'

No one in the Laff a Minute that evening would find out what happened in the newsagent's, as the anecdote was interrupted by a cigarette packet flying through the beam of the spotlights and hitting Chuck on the nose. For the first time in six minutes and twelve seconds, the audience had laughed.

Steve could see the compère at the side of the stage indicating for Chuck to finish his act. Chuck had turned to the audience.

'Well, that's all from me' . . . a huge cheer . . . 'enjoy the rest of the show' . . . a loud cry of 'we will now' . . . and Chuck Ling was off the stage and replaced by the compère.

'Well . . .'

The audience had waited. Was there honour amongst fellow artistes or would the compère go for the easy laugh?

'Looks like he picked the wrong night to record his live DVD!'

The audience had cheered. The compère, no doubt feeling a bit cheap, quickly continued;

'Okay, we'll have a beer and toilet break for, say, fifteen, twenty minutes, and then we'll be back with your headline act, Billy Topp. So please put your hands together for the last act: Chuck Ling.'

But the noise of the audience leaving their seats drowned out whatever pitiful applause there might have been.

***

8

'Two pints of lager, please'.

Steve had ordered the drinks and then turned to Jeff.

'Well, that was embarrassing.'

'Really?' said Jeff. 'I thought you ordered the drinks pretty well.'

'Oh that's brilliant. Really, you should be up there. Oh, and should I remind you that it's really your round?'

'Er . . . I'll get the next one.'

Steve smiled. 'You know *you* should be the comedian, you're the one with the catchphrase.'

Jeff felt slightly uncomfortable. But didn't show it.

Steve continued: 'I actually felt sorry for him. I mean, some of his stuff was quite funny.'

'What, like. "Any Greek people in? . . . Corfu? Yes, loads of them!" You're right, it's a modern classic. Who knows, this time next year he could be hailed as yet another unique comedy genius.'

Steve then saw Chuck Ling walk towards the end of the bar. He was now wearing normal clothes.

Steve turned to Jeff. 'I'll be back in a minute.'

As Jeff walked back to the table in as straight a line as the alcohol would allow, Steve went over to Chuck.

'Hi. I enjoyed that.'

'Ah, you were the one.'

Chuck had dropped the high-pitched 'comedy voice' he'd used on stage and spoke instead with a slight Scottish accent.

'No, really. Have you been doing this a while?'

'Couple of years. I'll be giving up any day now.'

'I really think that would be a shame.'

Chuck Ling looked at Steve. 'Is this a wind-up?'

'No, not at all. I just thought that some of your stuff, most of it actually, was really clever. I think it just went over their heads.'

Chuck shrugged. 'What can you do? Of course, I could try to change my act but that's not—'

'No, don't do that. Just change your audience.'

Chuck frowned.

Steve continued: 'I think you'd be great on TV.'

Chuck smiled politely. This bloke must be drunk. He'd humour him for a couple of minutes and then make his exit.

'The thing is,' Steve went on, 'I've been thinking about starting an agency for comedians; you know the old saying: "Those who can't, represent those who can." Or something. Anyway, here's my card.'

Steve handed over a business card.

Chuck looked at it.

'You do know it says "Station Lettings" on this?'

'Yes, I know. That's the company I'm running at the moment. But I hate it. Lettings! All I do is deal with scummy tenants and even scummier landlords. I've wanted to get out of it for ages. That's why I want to start this agency.'

'Oh. Okay. Well, I'll give you a call then.'

But he never did.

However, just talking about the idea was enough to make Steve want to take the risk. The following day he looked for a new office space, in central London and slowly started to wind down Station Lettings while simultaneously starting up On The Edge. He later added the 'United Kingdom Division', thinking that people would believe the company was international. They didn't.

Steve's first client was Gareth Ice.

***

Gareth Ice is what is commonly known as a 'mainstream act' – although the boundaries between what was once mainstream and is now considered 'alternative' have become less and less clear.

Steve saw Gareth doing a surprise guest spot at Laff a Minute a couple of weeks after he had seen Chuck Ling. The audience, at least those over the age of thirty, knew Gareth and were excited by having a 'celebrity' perform for them – even one that was doing virtually the same routine he had done on almost every *Saturday Night Special* they had watched with their parents. The younger audience members, who had never heard of him, were not so lenient. However, it was when the heckling started, forcing Gareth to break away from the persona that had made him his first fortune – a dim-witted policeman from Birmingham – and begin improvising that Steve saw a side to Gareth that he believed had potential. Steve had given Gareth his card – a newly printed one – and invited him for coffee the following week.

***

'I'll be honest with you, mate. I'm in my fifties – although for the press I'm forty-five – and I can't make a living from playing the working men's clubs any more. There aren't that many of them still around for a start, and the ones that are don't have much money. So I've got to branch out a bit, you know. I've got to play to a wider, younger . . . wealthier audience.'

He took a mouthful of his skinny latte. Steve had actually laughed when Gareth had said what coffee he'd wanted – which had momentarily caused an awkward atmosphere in the cafe.

Gareth wiped his mouth with his sleeve.

'I'll be honest with you . . .'

Steve had noticed that Gareth started most of his sentences this way and wondered whether this was something he did to hide the fact that he actually wasn't being honest.

'I've had one or two agents over the years, but they've all been, you know, older. Stuck in their ways really. So I'm happy for someone like you who's new, young, hungry, full of energy, to look after me. And I'll be honest with you, I'm very easy-going.'

***

Steve's first real coup was to get Gareth a guest spot on the satirical quiz show *Read All About It*, and although the appearance wasn't exactly a triumph – Gareth had tried to crowbar in a few of his stock gags and trademark phrases and had been promptly ridiculed by the regular team captains – it did bring him back to the minds of the public. And, more importantly, producers. He was offered, and readily accepted, two pilot shows for the independent production company Peak Bananas.

The first was an adult version of *Blind Date,* in which the contestants had to guarantee that they would have sex if they were chosen. Gareth was the host and his coarse humour fitted right in. However, none of the broadcasters wanted to pick it up. If truth be told, they all wanted to, but none of them wanted to be seen wanting to. The second pilot, which was commissioned as a six-part series by the digital channel Fun & Games, was a hidden-camera show set in a doctor's surgery. The idea was that the 'Doctor' (Gareth in heavy make-up . . . well, as heavy as the budget would allow) would give appointments to unwitting patients and either carry out bizarre examinations or tests, or prescribe very inappropriate, yet harmless, medication. The patients would be told the truth at the end and, providing they agreed and signed the acceptance forms, their 'appointment' would be on TV.

The programme was not surprisingly criticised by GPs and patient groups and didn't go to a second series – although this could have been due to the tiny viewing figures as opposed to the complaints.

Gareth had been delighted to be back on television and pleased with the way Steve was handling his career. However he was frustrated that he had to start proving himself all over again. It was this frustration that led to his ill-fated appearance on *You Can't Stop the Music*.

Gareth had watched the programme and always enjoyed the banter between the host and guests. However, when Steve rang him to tell him that he was going to be a guest the following week, he was genuinely nervous. He hadn't had a drink before appearing on *Read All About It*, and he felt that if he had, he would have been more relaxed and therefore funnier.

So he decided to have a drink this time. After all, what's hospitality for if not for taking advantage?

So he drank. A lot. And got drunk. Very.

If the producers had had any compassion they would have stopped the show and allowed him to sober up. But of course, having a drunken 'has-been' on a youth-orientated music show is great television.

Steve, who had arrived late at the studio, having taken public transport that had broken down en route, was watching the recording from backstage. He knew there was a problem from his client's first words. Gareth had been asked the question 'Who had a hit with *"The Right Type of Love, the Wrong Type of Woman"*?' To which Gareth had replied, 'Dunno. Probably some paedo.'

Later Steve would beg the producers to cut the line. They had agreed, but only if they could use it on the outtakes section of the DVD.

'Good afternoon, On The Edge, Steve Connors speaking ... Hi, Kev ... yeah, I'm fine. Sorry, it was just that the phone made me jump!'

As Steve said it he realised that it didn't sound very positive. But the truth was the phone hardly rang any more. There was the occasional call from comedians/ventriloquists/magicians – sometimes a combination of all three – looking for representation. He was always pleasant; after all he didn't have a secretary to deal with them. He used to have a secretary, but lack of finances and the threat of sexual harassment made that very short-lived. The allegations would never have stood up in court, but it was a way for Steve to let her go without having to pay her redundancy. And the truth was she *had* made several passes at him and once grabbed his crotch to see how he measured up to her boyfriend. Normally Steve would have been flattered, but not only did he not fancy her but her boyfriend was built like the proverbial outhouse of the third little pig.

Steve actually *did* have vacancies on his books for new acts. Several vacancies. But he no longer had the enthusiasm for the work. He was happy ... no, happy was too strong a word, he was *content* to look after the few clients he had and live off his percentage from their live work and the occasional royalty cheques from the cable and satellite channels. Most of this money came from Gareth. Gareth's last agent had died (they said it was old age but Steve reckoned starvation had a lot to do with it) and Steve had said that he would be happy to handle all outstanding monies and royalty payments. Well, why wouldn't he?

The other occasional calls to come in were, like this one, from clients asking about work.

'No, sorry, Kev – nothing's come in at the moment . . . yeah, of course I sent your DVD to the producers . . . no, nothing at all . . . yeah, of course. Speak soon. Bye.'

Steve put down the phone. He picked up a small remote control and turned the radio back up. He had pressed mute just after he had jumped in shock when the phone had rung. As Beyoncé's *Crazy in Love* played from the middle of the track, Steve opened a drawer in his desk and took out a DVD. The smiling face of Kevin Summer looked hopefully, trustingly, at him. Steve opened a second drawer and took out a padded envelope. He put both items onto his desk. He then picked up his large collection of bills and flicked through them. He thought about putting them in order of priority-to-be-paid until he realised they were all final demands and therefore all had equal priority. 'Beyoncé there with "Crazy in Love",' proudly announced the DJ, with the same uniform voice as airline pilots. 'And now the final song in today's "My Favourite Three", suggested by Helen Sanderson from Oxford is, "The Way You Make Me Feel" by Michael Jackson. Steve suddenly stopped. He turned and looked towards the radio. Although he'd heard exactly what had been said, as far as he was concerned the DJ might as well have shouted, 'Hey, Steve, remember this? This is when things started messing you up!' Steve put the bill collection down, put his feet up onto the side of the desk and pushed his chair backwards against the wall. This was his favourite position; the toes of his shoes resting on the lip of the desk and the back of his head against the wall. He took up this position so often that the wood on the lip of the desk was worn and there was a perspiration mark on the wall from his head. As he listened to the song, he stared at the posters in front of him. As he stared he began to lose focus. As though he were looking at one of those annoying Magic Eye drawings, Steve started to gaze beyond the poster. And even though he had promised himself he would try to stop, the memory once again flashed across his mind.

CHAPTER THREE

Steve had managed to roll most of the C60 cassette tape back in. Annoyingly the pencil he had been using was just that fraction too small for the spool and had therefore frequently kept slipping off. He ran his fingers along the remainder of the tape in an attempt to iron out the last of the crinkles. He then continued turning the pencil until all of the tape was back inside the cassette. He put the cassette back in his Walkman and pressed play.

The song, 'Wishing Well' by Terence Trent D'Arby, started playing. He sang along, trying to ignore the occasional wobble where the recently chewed-up tape ran along the cassette head. No amount of Dolby was going to improve that.

This was his and Debbie's song, which was the reason she had put it on the compilation tape. She had given him the tape, along with a new Walkman, as an eighteenth birthday present two month's earlier. Steve looked at his digital watch. 17.17. He would have to leave soon to meet Jeff. Although he was looking forward to seeing his friend, it felt a little strange that he wouldn't be seeing Debbie. This would be the first Saturday night they had spent apart in the six months they had been dating. They had of course planned to see each other, but Debbie had called him at the last minute to say that her best friend had been dumped by her boyfriend and she had to be with her. She had suggested that Steve come as well to show support, but he kindly refused, explaining that he would prefer to douse his testicles in paraffin and limbo-dance naked under a burning bar.

So Steve had planned instead to go to a disco with Jeff. This had annoyed Debbie, mainly because Steve had not gone dancing with her in a long time. Steve had told her that it was because he preferred their evenings to be just the two of them, but the truth was he believed taking a girlfriend to a disco was like taking a four-pack of cheap lager to a party – you're guaranteed to be having something, but you might be able to get something better.

Even though Steve wasn't actively looking that night, he still put on his old 'scoring' pants (the ones with a hole in the shape of a heart) and his most expensive aftershave, the one he told Debbie that he'd finished; well, there was no point in wasting it on her when they were already dating.

***

Steve had planned to meet Jeff at Bar 7 as it had happy hour from six to eight. Steve had never quite understood how the term 'happy hour' had changed to describe any period of cheap drinks. They arranged to meet at six, so Steve arrived at a quarter past, knowing that Jeff wouldn't be there until after half past. He ordered himself a bottle of Mexican lager with a glass and asked the barmaid not to stick a wedge of lime into the top of the bottle. He then picked up two paper napkins from the bar and put them into his pocket. The drink arrived; he paid half the normal price, put the wedge of lime he'd asked not to have into an ashtray and walked over to a table.

Although there were several smaller tables with two chairs at them, Steve went for the last remaining larger, four-chaired table. The reason for this was that his somewhat active imagination had quickly offered him the following scenario: he and Jeff would be sitting at the table a little later in the evening when all the other tables would be full. Two incredibly beautiful girls would then come into the bar looking for somewhere to sit. Steve would coolly and nonchalantly indicate the two spare chairs at his table. The girls would then join them. The four of them would then spend the rest of the evening drinking and chatting together before going back to the girls' flat.

As Steve accepted the unlikelihood of this happening, he removed one of the napkins from his pocket, wiped the top of the bottle and poured the lager into his glass. Although he preferred to drink straight from the bottle – the lager stayed colder for longer that way – he had been told that bottles are sometimes left outside the back of the bars overnight and animals, primarily rodents, had a tendency to urinate over them.

'Need You Tonight' by INXS was playing on the jukebox as Steve drank his lager and looked around the bar. As it was early evening a high percentage of the clientele were couples. They would leave as the bar filled with pre-disco single-sex groups out on the pull.

Another bottle of lager was suddenly placed on the table in front of Steve. He looked up to see Jeff smiling down at him. Steve checked his watch.

'You're early. For you.'

'Well, we've hardly gone out since you've been seeing Debbie so I didn't want to waste any time.'

Steve nodded. Jeff was right. He'd always promised himself that he wouldn't be one of those people who stopped seeing their friends when they started seeing someone. But of course he *had* become one of those people. He would have liked to blame it on Debbie, but the truth was Steve actually preferred to have a Saturday night at Debbie's place (providing her parents were out) with a couple of beers, takeaway pizza and a guaranteed snog and grope, than moving from pub to pub with Jeff. However, now, six months down the line, he realised he had missed their fruitless drunken wanderings.

Jeff put his jacket, with its rolled-up sleeves, onto the back of his chair, turned the chair so that it was now facing towards him and placed his short, stocky body onto it. He put his hands behind his head, undid the band which was keeping his hair in its ponytail, ran his fingers through his hair and then reattached the band.

Jeff hadn't really liked Debbie from the outset. Although he could see the physical attraction and would gladly have taken a weekend off just to play with her breasts, he just found her company dull. He especially hated the fact that when he and Steve would clown around together she would give them a 'shouldn't you two have grown up by now?' look. She would follow that look by saying, 'Shouldn't you two have grown up by now?'

'So, what's the plan of action for tonight?'

'Well . . .' said Jeff, 'we'll have a couple of drinks here and then move on to The Bear and Whistle, see if there's anything around, and then go to Angels.'

'Sounds good to me.'

Jeff took out a box of small cigars.

Steve frowned. 'What are you doing?'

'I'm going to smoke a cigar.'

'You don't smoke.'

'They're only cigars.'

'It's still smoking. And, as I previously mentioned, you don't smoke.'

'Well, perhaps I do.'

'Do you?'

'No.'

Jeff put the box back inside his jacket pocket.

'Do you want to hear my new chat-up line?'

Jeff's chat-up lines were legendary. That he did actually use specific lines was remarkable in itself. He had tried to convince people that he was the first person to ever come up with 'What's a nice girl like you doing in a place like this?'

Steve sighed. 'Go on then.'

Jeff put on his *cool and suave* face, which was like his normal face except fatter.

'Hi. Do you have a map of your face, because I'm lost in your eyes.'

Steve looked at him. 'Are you honestly going to say that to someone?'

'Oh yes. And you just wait to see what happens.'

'I think I can guess, but I won't spoil the ending for you'.

***

After visiting several pubs and one burger van – just to line their stomachs – Steve and Jeff arrived at Angels.

The owner of Angels had obviously watched the film *Saturday Night Fever* and decided to make a copy of that nightclub. Unfortunately he had probably seen a badly out-of-focus pirate copy of the movie.

Maybe, just maybe, when it had first opened it had been in some way *classy*, but now, and at least since Steve and Jeff had been going there, it was run down and smelt of sick. The carpet was tacky – in every sense of the word – and most of the lights under the glass panels on the dance floor were broken, which meant that you could hardly see anything but the array of handbags and matching stiletto-heeled shoes. Steve and Jeff hated going there, but the drinks were cheap and there was every chance of scoring.

While Jeff went off to get the drinks Steve waited in the queue for the cloakroom. It was while he was standing there, waiting to exchange their coats for two raffle tickets, that he saw her. Albeit briefly, but enough to recognise her as being the most beautiful girl he'd ever seen. She saw him at the same time, and she smiled. No, not just smiled. As far as Steve was concerned, she had managed to make everything around them stop while simultaneously lighting up the whole room.

'Two?'

And then louder. 'Two?!'

Steve turned to the girl at the cloakroom desk. Well, not so much a desk as a stable door with the top half opened.

'Oh, er, yes. Thanks. Although one is really a jacket, so . . .'

'One hanger per item.'

'Of course.'

Steve handed over the money, took the tickets and turned back. But she had gone.

He looked around. Maybe she'd gone inside. He walked over to the two large black doors that wouldn't have been out of place at the start of a ghost-train ride, pushed them open and entered the heart of the club.

Soft Cell's version of 'Tainted Love' was playing loudly. Steve walked past the dance floor, narrowly avoiding the swinging arms of the girls who had decided to mime the actions to the song lyrics, and looked around for her.

'I thought you were going to meet me at the bar?'

Jeff was holding two doubles of whisky and ginger ale. He gave one to Steve.

'Sorry. I was looking for a girl.'

'Already? They're nowhere near drunk enough yet.'

'No, a particular girl. She was really attractive. And she looked at me.'

'She looked at you! Oh the shame! How could you possibly face Debbie again?'

'Sod off.'

They drank for the next two hours, breaking off occasionally to be rejected by a girl or to dance together to 'You Give Love a Bad Name' and 'Don't You Forget About Me' and 'The Final Countdown'.

At half past twelve Jeff decided that he couldn't be bothered to wait another fifteen minutes for the slow snog songs to come on to see if he could get a last-minute score. So, as Michael Jackson's 'The Way You Make Me Feel' started playing, they downed the remainder of their drinks and prepared to leave. That's when Steve saw her for the second time. She was walking towards the cloakroom.

Steve ran over across as she disappeared through the ghost-train doors. He banged through the doors and found himself face to face with her.

'Hi.'

She smiled.

'Er . . . I . . . er . . . I have a map of your eyes.'

She looked confused.

Steve spoke again. 'Sorry. Look . . .'

Suddenly Steve was propelled forward. He shot past the girl and ended in a heap on the carpet. He tried to get up, but the weight of the two blokes fighting on top of him pinned him down.

Steve looked up at the girl. The girl's friend, who was standing next to her, looked down towards Steve.

'Come on, leave him, he's not worth it!'

Steve was about to say something when his face was pushed down into the carpet as the two men continued their fight over his head.

Steve eventually managed to wriggle free and stand up. Several cigarette butts had, thanks to discarded chewing gum, managed to attach themselves to his face. He looked around for the girl. Again. But she had gone. Again.

And that was the last time he had seen her.

Over twenty years ago.

And he'd hardly thought about her since. Save for his every breathing moment.

A month after this encounter, Steve broke up with Debbie. He told her that he'd met someone else. It was true, but only in the most literal sense.

***

Steve was so engrossed with his memory that at first he thought the ringing telephone was a part of it. Then, as he heard his voice announce that there was no one at the office to take the call, he realised where he was. He picked up the telephone and interrupted himself.

'Hello, hello? . . . Yes, it is . . . really!?'

Steve looked at the *Time 4 A Laugh* competition clock on the wall. Hilariously the numbers were the wrong way around; although as Steve had looked at it so often, he didn't really notice any more.

'I'll call him now!'

Steve put down the phone and dialled a number from memory. He'd gone past the shock of having two phone calls in one day.

'John? Where are you? . . . What?! You're supposed to be doing a corporate gig for Telephone Express . . . I reminded you yesterday . . .'

He looked again at the clock.

'You'll never get there in time. I'll call someone else . . . No, of course you can't split the fee with them!'

Steve put down the phone and picked up his address book. He flicked through the list of numbers.

'Hi, Paul, it's Steve from On The Edge . . . Yeah, not bad. Look, John Bush has . . . er . . . broken down in his car on the way to a gig in Cambridge – do you have anyone who could get there in an hour or so? . . . Okay, thanks. Call me back when you know.'

Steve then made the same call to three other agents. He knew where his own acts were and knew that none of them could get there in time. Five minutes later, the substitute act was on his way to entertain the staff and management of Telephone Express, Cambridge, and Steve, who had organised the whole thing, wouldn't get a penny out of it.

CHAPTER FOUR

'Make a wish first!'

Lucy closed her eyes. 'I wish—'

'No, don't tell us or it won't come true!'

Lucy stopped talking and concentrated. She quietly mouthed the words of her wish and then blew out the five candles on her Barbie cake.

Her sister, mother, father and uncle all sang a loud out-of-tune rendition of 'Happy Birthday'.

'I wished for a rabbit.'

'Lucy!' Hayley, her sister, sighed loudly. 'Now it won't come true!'

'Doesn't matter,' replied Lucy. 'I didn't want a rabbit anyway.'

***

While Steve and his sister Sheila (Lucy and Hayley's mother) sat in Sheila's kitchen, drinking coffee and eating birthday cake – making sure not to eat Barbie's head – Lucy excitedly opened the present her uncle had brought her.

'A Bad Girl!'

Lucy ripped open what was left of the princess wrapping paper. 'It's a Pyjama Party Bad Girl! I don't have this one!'

She ran to her uncle and threw her arms around him. 'Thank you, Uncle Steve!'

Steve smiled.

'Look, Mum!' Lucy proudly showed the doll to her mum.

'That's great!' said Sheila. She turned to Steve; 'What a clever uncle you are, knowing exactly what she wanted.'

Steve smiled sarcastically.

'I'm going to put her with the other ones!' Lucy ran out of the room and up the stairs.

'Can I watch TV?' Hayley asked her mother.

'No, not now; you have your homework to do.'

'Great! Lucy gets to play with her presents and I have to do my homework!'

'You're right, that is unfair,' said Steve.

Sheila stared at him.

'After all,' continued Steve, 'you're a little girl as well. You should be playing with dolls too. What are you now – six? Seven?'

'I'm eight!' said Hayley a little annoyed.

'Oh, are you really? Well . . . in that case, as you are so much older – I mean, almost a teenager – then maybe you *should* do your homework. After all, I'm sure that the boy you like in school would prefer to have a girlfriend who's clever than one who likes to play with dolls.'

'Steve, she's eight! There isn't any boy in school that she likes! And I don't think—'

'Actually, I will go and do my homework.'

Hayley smiled at her uncle and walked out of the room.

Steve smugly took a sip of coffee.

'Well . . . don't expect her to come to you for relationship advice when she's older.'

'Of course not. She has you. And you've had, let's see, how many boyfriends? Er . . .' Steve counted on his fingers, '. . . oh yes. One. Whom you married.'

'Well, at least I'm not a . . .' she spoke more quietly, 'what's the male equivalent of a slag?'

'A stud.'

'Ha-ha. Anyway, do you want to stay for dinner? I'm probably going to do Chinese.'

Steve looked at her. '*Doing* Chinese is a little misleading, isn't it? You mean you'll be *ordering* Chinese food.'

Sheila scowled back. '*I'll* be deciding on which dishes compliment each other the best, then *I* will personally ring the number and eventually *I* will pay for it. To me that's virtually the same as making it.'

Steve nodded. 'Yes, to you it really is. Anyway I won't, thanks.'

Sheila stood up, walked over to the sink and opened the drawer underneath. She took out a handful of takeaway menus.

'Your recipe book?' suggested Steve.

His sister ignored the remark. She closed the drawer, put the menus on the table and sat back down.

'So, *stud*, how's it going with your latest girl? What's her name – Mandy?'

'Emily. I'm . . . er . . . not really seeing her any more. It didn't work out. We wanted . . . different things.'

'Of course you did. Just like the one you were seeing before her. The singer.'

'Who? Oh, Jane. Yeah. No, the problem with her was that she just got a bit too . . . heavy.'

'Really? Doesn't she realise you're still only seventeen?'

Steve greeted this remark with another sarcastic smile.

Even though he had heard them many times, the sound of heavy footsteps on the stairs made Steve jump slightly. He turned as Dave, his brother-in-law, walked back into the room. This time in his full police uniform.

PC Dave bent down and kissed Sheila on the lips. 'I've said goodnight to the girls. I'll call you later.'

'Be careful.'

'I will.'

Dave shook Steve's hand. 'Sorry I have to go. I'll see you soon.'

'Actually,' said Steve, 'I'll walk out with you. I want to ask you something.'

***

They stood on the front steps outside the house. Steve made sure that he stood on the step above Dave's so that he didn't look so short next to him.

'Er . . . is it true that sometimes people have hypnosis to remember things about crimes?'

'In some circumstances, yeah, it does happen. Why?'

Steve ignored the question and continued. 'How far back can they remember things? And in how much detail?'

'I don't know much about it, but I know it depends on the person and on the hypnotherapist. Why the interest? Are you planning on hypnotising someone? You know that's an illegal way to get girls to go out with you.'

Steve smiled. 'Just curious.'

They started to walk down the steps when Dave suddenly stopped and turned to Steve. They were now on the same step and Dave was looking down.

'It's not that girl again? Please don't say it's that girl again!'

'What girl?'

Steve might have trained as an actor, albeit for a short time, but no one would have been convinced by his feigned confusion.

Dave continued: 'If you are seriously thinking about having yourself hypnotised so you can remember about a girl you met, what, twenty years ago, then you are madder than I thought you were when I first met you. And I thought you were borderline insane then.'

Steve looked towards the house to make sure Sheila wasn't listening.

He hadn't spoken about this girl to Sheila in almost five years, mainly because the lecture she gave him then had made him feel pathetic and puerile.

He had mentioned her to Dave during one rare drunken night they'd had together a few months earlier.

'It was just a thought, that's all. You know, a bit of a laugh.'

Dave stared at him.

Steve forced a ridiculous, hopeful grin; 'Ha-ha?'

CHAPTER FIVE

Jeff listened and nodded as he drank from his bottle of lager. If there was one thing you could say about Jeff, it was that he was a good listener. He might not understand all the words, but he at least gave them one-hundred-per-cent attention. He suddenly mistimed his nodding and ended up banging his teeth on the rim of his lager bottle. He put the bottle onto the shiny metallic round table in front of him and leant closer to Steve.

'Hypnosis?'

'Yeah.'

Jeff slowly nodded and picked up the bottle again, this time making sure he stopped nodding before taking another swig.

Jeff was still Steve's best friend – not that Steve would ever say that to him. Steve believed that telling someone they were your best friend was like telling a girl that you loved her; it would only cause problems and undue pressure. Suffice to say, if Steve were ever to get married, Jeff would be his best man. Providing Jeff's wife, Francine, would let him.

Francine was not attractive. At all. In any sense of the word. Even the proverbial 'beholder' would pretend to have myopia. And it wasn't just her looks – although her beauty spot should really have been removed under the Trade Descriptions Act – it was the fact that she was so incredibly unpleasant. Francine patronised Jeff at every given opportunity. This had been going on from the day they met and therefore Jeff was by now almost immune to it. In fact, if there were an opportunity to put him down and Francine didn't seize on it, Jeff would ask her, genuinely, if there were something wrong.

Admittedly Jeff had his own flaws and he was no great stunner either: five foot six in heels, now completely bald and with a slightly crooked nose as a result of a drunken disagreement with a ladder. However, girls did seem to find him attractive. Especially since he'd lost his hair. And it had to be said, and Steve had subtly said it on a number of occasions, he could certainly have done better than Francine. They had absolutely nothing in common; apart from the *F* and *E*.

They had met on a flight from London to Glasgow. Jeff was on his way to see an elderly aunt in the hope that he'd be left something in her will and Francine was going back home after meeting a potential investor for her latest internet venture. Jeff had been struck by her assertiveness and breasts. Not necessarily in that order.

Jeff had always liked to be dominated. Not in the dressing-up-in-rubber-and-having-women-walk-over-you way – well, at least not the dressing-up-in-rubber bit. His mother had been a domineering woman. She had died two years earlier from breast cancer. Jeff said it was the only time anything had ever got the better of her. His father was totally lost when she died. She had made all the decisions; from sorting out which plumber to call, to how they should invest their not insubstantial funds. Jeff's father followed her six months later. Even in death she had led the way.

You would have thought that, seeing how his father had had such difficulty coping when he was left on his own, Jeff would have wanted to make sure he was more in control of any relationship. But apparently not. He was happy for Francine to organise everything from where they lived to what they watched on TV. He had let her completely arrange their wedding and honeymoon as well. He felt it was the right thing to do, considering she was the one who had proposed in the first place.

The odd thing was, however much Jeff liked to be dominated by women, when it came to his friends he was the one who had to make all the decisions and organise everything. And if he didn't want to do something that his friends wanted to do, well, he just wouldn't do it. No room for compromise. So you'd wonder why anyone would want to be friendly with him.

Well, the truth was, Jeff was actually good fun to be with (as long as the place where you were with him was one of his choosing). He had a subtle sense of humour and could prove beyond all doubt that sarcasm was actually quite a high form of wit.

'So when . . . ?'

'Hi.'

Jeff had been interrupted by a pretty twenty-year-old girl.

Jeff smiled. 'Hi. How's it going?'

'Good. Would you like a dance?'

'Sure. Do you know the lambada?'

The girl forced a smile.

Jeff took a ten-pound note from his pocket and handed it over.

The girl took the money and immediately went into 'dance mode'. With her knee, she parted Jeff's legs and moved one of hers between them. Pushing her bikini-clad chest into Jeff's face, she gyrated her torso, occasionally 'accidentally' rubbing herself against his crotch.

As the girl began to remove what little there was of her clothing, Steve looked around the room.

He had never really liked coming here. He found the whole experience quite uncomfortable. But he knew Jeff enjoyed it, although he didn't like going there on his own. And at least most of the girls knew Steve now and knew that there was no point in asking if he wanted a lap dance. It wasn't that he thought it was degrading. How could it be? Here were women being paid a minimum of ten pounds to dance for three minutes. Even at that rate it was two hundred pounds an hour (minus time spent for all the superfluous chit-chat). That was eight thousand pounds for a forty-hour week. Of course he realised that no one actually worked like that, but still the money to be made was staggering. No, the thing he found uncomfortable was the actual dancing. He, literally, never knew where to look. It seemed rude not to look at the girl's eyes, especially as she was looking at you while she danced, but if you did that, well, then it was pointless. After all, the whole point of being there was to look at a girl removing her clothing and showing you her naked body. And surely if you didn't look at this offered nakedness, then the girl might feel hurt.

'She's new,' said Jeff, as the dancer left him and approached another table, 'and to be honest with you, I think I might be in there.'

Steve looked at him and shook his head.

'Ow!' said Jeff. 'What are you doing?!'

'Just seeing if it's actually possible to shake some sense into it.'

Steve stopped shaking Jeff's head and looked at his watch. 'I'd better get back to the office soon.'

'Why? It's your own business. You can go back when you like. That's the advantage of being self-employed. You're your own boss.'

'In theory, yes. But I do occasionally have to be there to

take any calls that might come in. And to water the plants.'

'Well, I don't have to leave for another hour at least.'

Steve looked at him. 'And that's the advantage of being unemployed.'

'As I've told you before, we've both chosen our separate paths.'

'Yes. Yours is the one that goes round the back of the cemetery to the dole office.'

'At the end of the day I make more money than you, literally.'

'You don't *make* money Jeff; it is *given* to you.'

'Look, I've worked. My parents worked. We've all paid our taxes. I've got the money they left me, which I dip into when needed, but I don't know how long I've got to live. I probably won't make it to pension age. So I'm taking my pension early. Enjoying the money in my youth.'

'You're thirty-eight.'

'I'm not embarrassed by what I'm doing.'

'I can see that. I'm pleased you're able to stand tall. For you. I'm happy that you don't find any stigma attached to someone who is voluntarily leeching off the state.'

Jeff smiled. 'Thank you.'

'My only question,' continued Steve, 'is why does Francine believe that you're an independent mortgage advisor?'

Jeff ignored the question.

'So how's the business going?'

Steve shrugged. 'What can I tell you?'

'Well,' suggested Jeff, 'you could tell me how your business is going.'

'It's the same,' sighed Steve. 'It's all the same.'

'Yeah,' said Jeff, as he picked up a napkin from the table and wiped his head with it, 'nothing changes.'

CHAPTER SIX

Jeff, leaning against a telephone box, was eating a crusty roll stuffed full of crisps. He looked at his watch and then knocked loudly on one of the windows.

From inside, Steve held up his index finger and mimed 'one minute'. He then finished sticking the poster onto the wall above the telephone.

'Were you the girl in the white top who smiled at me in Angels on June 10th? If so, please call Steve on this number . . .'

Pathetic. He knew it himself. Yet the thing about obsessions is that you can't be rational about them. Knowing that your obsession or addiction is bad for you isn't going to make you stop.

Steve had been putting these posters up for over a month. Ever since he'd finished with Debbie. In fact Debbie had seen one of the posters, recognised Steve's number and called him with a torrent of abuse. Steve had expected this to happen. What he hadn't expected were the hundreds of calls he received each day from people just laughing at him or pretending they were the girl. His parents weren't very happy, and after failing to persuade him to stop putting up the posters and to forget about the girl, they relented and gave him his own line and telephone in his bedroom. They didn't see it so much as encouraging his obsession as keeping them out of it.

Steve came out of the phone box.

'Shll w goo smwr dfrnt ths wwknd?'

Steve watched the mix of bread and crisps fall from Jeff's mouth as he spoke.

'What?'

Jeff swallowed. 'I said, "Shall we go somewhere different this weekend?"'

'Why?'

'Oh, I don't know. Maybe because I am sick to death of Angels. Some of the staff are convinced I work there. There are other discos around. We could try Cinderella's. Skids said that him and Nobby both scored there. And if Skids can score with his spots and breath, then I reckon even I can.'

Steve started to walk off.

Jeff followed him.

'I also heard that Tracy Brown goes there.'

Steve faltered. Just for a moment.

Before Debbie, and the girl at the disco, Tracy Brown had been the object of all Steve's desires. She was a year above him in school. Steve had first noticed her when, at thirteen, she had played the part of Wendy in the school's version of 'Peter Pan'. The only time they had ever spoken was three years later when, now a prefect, she had told him not to run in the corridor.

'So what?' said Steve.

Jeff sighed, blowing out a stream of bready crisps. He finished what was in his mouth and then spoke slowly and calmly. 'Look, Steve. There's every chance this girl's never going to be in there again. She could have been an exchange student who's gone back to her own country. She could have had a sex change. She could have a boyfriend. She could have had a sex change *and* got a boyfriend. She could have—'

'All right, I get your point! Fine, we'll go to Cinder-fucking-rella's.'

Jeff looked at him.

Steve sighed. 'Sorry.'

Jeff smiled. 'It's okay.'

Steve looked up at the sky. It was meant to be summer, but the dark clouds wouldn't have looked out of place in the middle of November. 'You know I wish I'd never seen her. It was such crap timing. Just before the exams, just when things were going okay with Debbie.'

'No, they weren't.'

Steve ignored him and continued. 'I mean, what am I doing? Posters in phone boxes, postcards in shop windows, ads in the local papers . . . If I'd spent this much time revising, I'd probably have got all *A*'s.'

'How do you know you haven't?'

Steve turned to him. 'Because I walked out halfway through the English exam, because I spoke Spanish in my French oral and, as I could hardly remember what had happened that morning, history was never going to be a high scorer.' He looked down at the posters in his hand. Then, to Jeff's amazement, he ripped them up, walked over to a bin and threw them in.

'Wow. Well done.'

'Come on, let's go to the amusements before we get too old for them.'

Jeff dropped the remainder of his crisp butty into the same bin and followed after Steve.

'Er, Steve, the amusements are the other way.'

'I know. I just have to get some more posters done first.'

CHAPTER SEVEN

Steve had actually bumped into Tracy Brown a couple of years after he'd moved to London.

He had been taking yet another day off from his drama academy and had got onto a tube at Pimlico station. As he'd sat down, he'd seen her walking along the platform towards the exit. Instinctively he'd jumped up, run to the closing doors and stuck his foot between them. He'd waited, much to the annoyance of the other passengers, until the doors opened. Then, as the 'voice' was telling everyone to stand clear of the doors, he ran along the platform calling her name. It was only when she stopped and turned around that Steve realised he had no idea what he was going to say next. You can't really use a chat-up line after you've screamed a person's name and chased after them.

Tracy looked at him. He had hoped that there might be some glimmer of recognition. But there was nothing. He was going to pretend that he had mistaken her for someone else, but he realised that mistaking someone with the same name seemed a bit far-fetched. It was about as likely as ringing a wrong number and getting the person you wanted.

'Hi.'

He had tried to say the word in as friendly a way as possible.

'Er . . . hello?'

Yes! Apart from the telling-off when she was a prefect, this was officially the longest conversation they'd ever had. He was ecstatic. Now if he could only think what to say next.

'We went to school together.'

He was shocked. Stunned. This was the last thing he'd expected her to say. Well, actually the last thing he'd expected her to say was, 'I don't know who you are but I'd like to sleep with you', but this was still pretty unexpected.

'Er . . . yes. Yes, we did. That's why I called after you, because . . . we went to school together.'

'Simon, isn't it?'

'Yes. Yes, it is,' said Steve.

'So where are you off to?'

He looked around quickly. There was a poster advertising an exhibition at the Tate.

'The Tate,' he said.

'Really!' She smiled. 'That's where I'm going.'

As they walked off together, Steve allowed himself a little clenched fist of celebration.

However, his sense of accomplishment quickly faded when he realised what he'd let himself in for.

***

The only thing Steve knew about art was that he was scared of it. An odd emotion admittedly, but one which stemmed back to the only time he had ever been to a gallery – on a weekend trip to Madrid with his parents when he was seven. To escape from the blazing heat, they had gone to El Prado. He had never been so bored – until he had seen the war paintings of Goya. That was when his boredom had turned to fear. He would never forget the horrified, horrifying and horrific faces in those paintings. That night, in the hotel room, he'd had a nightmare about being trapped inside one of the paintings. In the dream, people were looking at the painting. He tried to scream at them to help him, but he couldn't move and they couldn't hear him. Whenever he was feeling particularly down or insecure, this dream would come back to visit. So, pretty often really.

He and Tracy had spent that afternoon together walking around the Tate. Tracy had pointed out her favourites and Steve had pretended to share her interest, when really all he had been doing was focusing on anything that wasn't paintings; other visitors, gallery staff, exit signs . . . He had also been to the toilet so many times that Tracy wondered if he had a bladder problem or a bad masturbatory habit. Coincidentally he had a bit of both.

When they eventually left, they had gone to one of the local pubs. It was there that Steve had fully relaxed (three pints had helped) and where they really had a chance to talk.

Tracy had recently come out of an eighteen-month relationship. Steve realised that she was probably on the rebound – and decided to take full advantage.

They had arranged to meet up again that weekend and from there a relationship had started. He even told her his real name.

The morning after they had slept together for the first time, Steve telephoned all his old school friends to tell them. They'd all congratulated him and asked him not to call again.

Steve idolised Tracy. In his eyes, everything she did and everything she said was perfect. There was nothing they wouldn't do for each other – she had even dressed up as Wendy again and he had played the part of Peter Pan (although he had found this a huge turn-on, he had also been slightly disturbed by it.) To Steve, Tracy was his ideal girl and he truly felt this was the person with whom he could spend the rest of his life.

So he'd finished with her.

CHAPTER EIGHT

A large, bald, bearded man with a ring through his eyebrow was standing on a chair singing 'I Will Survive'.

Although this was funny in itself, the fact that he had his trousers around his ankles gave it that extra touch.

Sitting on a chair next to him, a woman in her sixties was dealing imaginary cards to an imaginary group of poker players.

On the floor in front of them, a girl in her late teens was sucking her thumb and holding a teddy bear.

Greg Rutland, a middle-aged man dressed in a suit with the sleeves rolled up, smiled broadly as he looked at the activities around him. He shouted, 'Sorry, but did anyone say *fire!*?'

At this, a young man who had been sitting quietly, suddenly jumped up and started to put out imaginary fires.

'They won't stop!' he screamed. 'Someone call the fire brigade!'

'Stripper' music then started to play. Another young man stood up from his chair and slowly and seductively started to remove his clothing.

The audience in the packed theatre screamed and cheered.

Greg Rutland walked over to the bald, bearded man who was still singing. He put his hand onto his shoulder and spoke quietly into his ear. The man immediately fell silent, climbed down from the chair, sat on it and fell asleep.

Greg did the same thing to each of his participants until

they were all back sitting on their chairs, on the stage, fast asleep.

Greg turned to the audience to receive their applause. They didn't let him down.

'Thank you very much. Thank you all for coming. And before we go, let's say a big thank-you to all our volunteers.'

He then turned to the quietly sleeping group and told them to wake up. As one, they opened their eyes and looked around, calm now. They all seemed in a relaxed, if slightly bemused, state as they each walked off the stage to a round of applause.

As the last one left, Greg said, 'Didn't they all do a good job? If I was their boss, none of them would be *fired*.'

At that the young man from earlier ran back onto the stage and again started to put out imaginary fires.

The audience screamed their approval. Greg spoke into the young man's ear. The young man stopped what he was doing and looked around, puzzled. He then slowly walked back to his seat in the audience.

***

'So, is it like a trick or something?'

Greg looked at Jeff.

'No. I really have the power to alter people's minds. I can also fly and turn back time.'

Before Jeff had time to retort, Steve spoke. 'Thanks again for seeing me.'

'No problem. So, how's Gareth Ice doing? I haven't seen him for a while?'

'Er . . . yeah, he's doing okay. Not as busy as he should be, but it's getting there.'

'He's a funny bloke. Shame he keeps fucking up. Nice of him to recommend me to you though.'

'Yeah.'

The dressing room, with its traditional mirrors framed in spotlights, was shabby. Fading 'good-luck' cards were stuck to a corkboard, and graffiti which included 'The policeman did it' and 'She's in the attic' adorned the back of the door.

'I'll be honest with you . . .' said Greg.

Steve wondered whether Gareth had picked this phrase up from Greg or vice versa. Maybe it was a phrase that all mainstream acts used.

'I'm not really looking for a new agent. I've been with Tony for . . . well, forever really and — '

'No, that's not why I wanted to see you. I . . . er . . . well, it's a bit odd really . . .'

'He wants to have a memory regressed to remember a girl he met at a disco in 1988.'

Greg looked surprised.

Jeff smiled. 'So now you have a chance to use your turning-back-time power.' He was pleased with this comeback.

Greg ignored him and turned to Steve. 'Regression. Mmm.' He took a sip from a bottle of water. 'Well, there's a couple of things. First, it might not work. I have done this type of thing before but I'm not really a clinical hypnotherapist. Second, you could come across memories that you had intentionally hidden away in your subconscious. I once had someone who thought they wanted to remember an incident in their childhood that no one in the family would tell them about. It turned out it wasn't a good memory. And he's now trying to sue me for emotional damage.'

'Well, I don't mind signing something to promise that I won't take legal action or anything.'

'And if he doesn't, you could always make him think that he had!' Jeff was enjoying himself.

Greg turned to him. He held up his hands in a wizard

stance and dramatically shouted: 'You will take off all your clothes!'

Jeff stared at him. 'Nice chat-up line. I might use it myself. But I really don't think it'll work on me.'

Greg looked at him. 'Maybe not just now. But it will.' He smiled as he continued: 'Let's just hope it's not at an inopportune moment.'

Jeff suddenly looked worried.

Steve sighed. He turned to Greg. 'So can you do it?'

Greg nodded. 'Sure.' He took out a diary. 'Can you come to my place next Tuesday? I live just outside Oxford.'

'Yes, of course. That's great. And I won't expect you to do this for free.'

'That's good, because that wasn't going to happen.' He handed over a card. 'Here's my address. Three o'clock okay?'

'Yeah, sure. I'll see you then. Thanks.' Steve walked out.

Jeff was about to follow him when he stopped at the door and looked back nervously.

Greg looked at him and smiled again. 'Take care. Don't do anything I wouldn't do.' He paused for effect. 'Unless of course you can't help yourself.'

Jeff quickly left the room.

CHAPTER NINE

There was an uncomfortable silence.

Eventually Jeff spoke.

'How?'

'Well, if I must explain it to you – you put your penis inside my vagina and ejaculated semen, which impregnated me.'

'But . . . I mean. But . . .'

'Don't worry Jeff, take your time. We've got just under seven months.'

'I thought . . . you know . . . pill.'

'Oh, I see, you're giving me some words and I have to make the sentence up myself. Well, yes, I am on the pill, but I can only assume it didn't work for some reason. Maybe the antibiotics I took for that throat infection stopped it.'

Another silence.

'So . . . what do you . . . ?'

'What do I want to do? Did I want to have a baby? No, of course not. That's why we used *protection*. However, I am . . . getting older and perhaps this is the only chance I'll have to be a mother.'

'But . . . But I thought you didn't want children.'

Francine hesitated for a moment. She needlessly rearranged the magazines on the coffee table in front of them, put the selection of remote controls on top of them and then sat back on the sofa. 'Well, now I'm not sure.'

Jeff was more shocked by this than by the news of the pregnancy. 'Not sure? You're never *"not sure"*. Yesterday when I asked you if you wanted a takeaway pizza, you said, "No". You didn't say, "I'm not sure."'

'So, I assume you're not so keen on having a baby then?'

'To be truthful, no. Again, like yesterday, I'd be happy to settle for a curry.'

'So what if I decide to have it.'

It was Jeff's turn to hesitate. 'Er . . . well . . . first of all, shouldn't it be *our* decision?'

'No.'

'Okay – you seem pretty *sure* about that. Well, in that case then I'd . . . support you. Of course.'

'Could you? Do you mean emotionally? Financially?'

Jeff thought; 'Erm, I'd probably go with—'

'It's not an either/or.'

'Oh.'

Jeff had everything going through his mind. He suddenly pictured himself sitting at the lap-dancing club giving the baby its bottle. He saw himself pushing the pram into the benefit office and asking how much extra he could now get. He saw Francine pregnant. He saw himself surrounded by nappies. He saw himself standing outside a pub, rocking the baby in his arms while Steve and his new friends were drinking inside.

'You're going to have to get a job.'

Jeff stared at her. 'Er . . . what?'

'You're going to have to get a job. You can't continue to *sign on* if we're having a baby.'

Jeff didn't know what to say. There was obviously no point in lying. How did she know? How long had she known? What else did she know?

'Oh. Okay.'

And that was that.

CHAPTER TEN

'Well, say something. Call me a bastard at least.'

Steve shrugged.

'I'll pay you for the upcoming gigs you've got me, and you'll still get commission on repeat fees and that.'

Steve eventually spoke. 'And what about commission for the new jobs you'll get because of me?'

Gareth Ice looked at the floor of Steve's office. He then looked up and sighed. 'Look. Steve, it's show *business*. I am just making a good business decision. Anne Blackman is one of the biggest agents around. She contacted me the minute they saw me doing that *100 Greatest Movie Vomit Scenes* and—'

'Really? That job I struggled to get you when you were the last person they wanted. How ironic.'

Gareth again looked at the floor.

Steve knew that this type of thing happened all the time and he really couldn't have any complaints; after all he hadn't really worked that hard to get Gareth that job. The production company had rung to ask for Theresa Wild and he had said that she was unavailable (well, she was for him anyway) and he had suggested Gareth instead. He did have to persuade them a bit, and accept less than the normal fee, but at least he'd got him the gig. 'Don't worry.' He held out his hand. 'Seriously. It's okay. Good luck.'

Gareth shook the hand. 'Thanks. And thanks for everything you've done for me. I'd still be working my way around the clubs if it wasn't for you.'

'Yes, you probably would.'

Gareth started to walk out of the office. He stopped at the door and turned back. Framed in the doorway, he was identical to the way he looked in the poster on the wall above him. He was even wearing the same shirt. 'By the way, how did it go with Greg?'

'Fine, thanks. I've got an appointment with him tomorrow.'

'Hope it goes well.'

Gareth left.

Steve stared at the empty doorway for a while. He then looked around the office. Was it time for a change again? Was this the push he had needed? Maybe, after all these years he would find and stick with a career he actually wanted.

The telephone rang.

'Good afternoon, On The Edge, Steve Connors speaking.'

Although he had said this so many times in the past, it suddenly felt odd. Almost unreal. As if he were just temping for someone and they'd return any minute to take back their job.

'. . . no, I'm sorry, my books are completely full at the moment. But thanks for thinking of me . . . Sure, no problem . . . Okay, bye.'

Steve put down the phone, leant back on his chair and stared at the poster of Gareth Ice.

'Hi.'

Steve jumped and kicked the rim of the desk with his shin. 'Jesus!'

'Sorry mate, didn't mean to scare you.'

Jeff walked in and sat down.

Steve sat up and rubbed his ankle. He looked at the backwards clock on the wall.

'You're early again.' He then thought and looked puzzled. 'Hang on. We didn't plan on meeting up today.'

Jeff smiled. 'No, I know. I just thought I'd pop in and surprise you.'

Steve was still rubbing his shin. 'Well, you obviously did that. It's good to see you're achieving all your goals.'

Jeff looked around the office. 'I haven't been here for a while.' He looked at Steve. 'So, how are things?'

'Well, my main source of income has just left me, I'm obsessed by a girl I haven't seen for over half my life and I believe I may have broken my shin. You?'

'I'm going to be a dad.'

Steve immediately forgot about the pain. 'You idiot! You always said you wouldn't do it, but I knew you would. That whole "I don't mind touching or kissing another woman, but I'd never be completely unfaithful nonsense". I don't blame you of course. I mean, Francine can be hard work and quite cold, so—'

'Shut up.'

Steve did.

'The baby is mine and Francine's.'

Steve looked at him. He thought, This makes no sense.

'This makes no sense.'

It was impossible to have kept it in.

'I know.'

'What happened?'

'Well, I put my . . . oh I can't be bothered. It was a mistake, that's all. We rarely have sex and when we did . . . this.'

'And Francine wants to have it?'

'Apparently so.'

'But you two have always said that you didn't want kids.'

'I know. Apparently we've changed our minds. Oh, and by the way, I'm supposed to wait three months to tell you for some reason, so don't let on that you know.'

'Okay. Wow. Wow!'

'Yeah.'

They sat quietly.

'Oh, and she knows that I've been signing on.'

'How?'

'I have no idea. I can only assume she doesn't know about the club as well or she would have mentioned it.' He thought for a moment. 'Unless of course she's keeping it for a special occasion.'

'So . . . what are you going to do?'

'I don't know. My initial reaction is to run.'

'Of course.'

'But I won't.'

'Of course not.'

'So I'd better start looking for a job. And getting a pension. And life insurance. And a people carrier.'

CHAPTER ELEVEN

There was silence, save for the distant muffled sound of dogs playfully barking.

Greg looked at Steve. He felt he'd waited long enough and so asked the question again.

'Steve? What do you see now?'

There was no response. Greg spoke once more, slowly and clearly.

'Steve, tell me, what do you see now?'

'My name's not Steve, it's Victoria.'

Jeff, who was sitting on a chair a couple of feet away, looked at Steve. He then looked at Greg. He then looked back at Steve. He wished there were more people he could have looked at. 'What's going on?!'

Greg turned to Jeff and spoke sternly; 'Shh!'

Jeff didn't like being told off, although Francine did it on such a regular basis you'd think he'd be immune to it by now. He briefly looked out of the conservatory window and saw Greg's two Alsatians chasing each other through the large landscaped garden.

'This sometimes happens,' explained Greg quietly, aware of his previous tone. 'You can never just go back to a particular time. We've obviously gone back quite far.'

Jeff tried to speak quietly, which he'd always found difficult. 'Back to when? I've known him since he was five. He's never been called Victoria. What's he on about?'

'He's gone back to a previous life.'

Jeff stared at him. 'Oh shut up!'

Greg looked annoyed. 'Look, I have no interest in what you do or do not believe. I didn't want you here in the first place, but he insisted.'

'So you're telling me that, in a past life, Steve was . . . a woman?'

'Yes.'

'I see.' Jeff made a note in the spiral pad on his lap.

He turned back to Greg. 'So, was he . . . sexy?'

Before Greg had the chance to reply, Steve spoke. 'Has anyone seen my baby?'

Jeff looked shocked. 'What the . . . ?'

'Shh!' Greg turned to Steve. 'Listen to me, Ste— Victoria. You are going to leave where you are now.'

'What about my baby?' Steve was getting upset. 'I can't find my baby!'

'Your baby is fine. Just listen to me. Listen to my voice. Your baby is fine. We're going to go back to Steve now. So just sleep. Sleep.' He waited a moment. 'Steve, can you hear me?'

Steve spoke calmly. 'Yes.'

Jeff was relieved – although he knew he'd be having nightmares about this for months.

'We are still going to try to go to 1988. You are eighteen. Do you remember?'

A long pause.

'Yes.'

'Good. You are in a nightclub—'

Jeff interrupted. 'A disco.'

Greg looked at him. He then continued: 'You are in a *disco* called . . .' He looked at his own notebook. The name wasn't there. He reluctantly looked at Jeff.

Jeff smiled smugly. 'Angels.'

'Angels.' He again looked at his notes. 'You are about to check in your jacket when you see a girl. A beautiful girl. Can you see her?'

They waited again.

'Yes.'

'Describe her to me.'

The wait was longer this time.

'She has . . . hair.'

Jeff sighed. 'Brilliant.'

Greg glared at him and then turned back to Steve.

'What else? Describe her face.'

Jeff watched as Steve frowned and twitched his nose. He wasn't sure if this was part of the remembering process or whether he had regressed to a rabbit.

'Pretty.'

That was it.

Greg wasn't quite sure what to do now.

Jeff attempted to whisper: 'He saw her later as well. When we were leaving. Tell him to remember seeing her at the end of the night. Before he got pushed to the floor or something.'

Greg turned back to Steve. 'It's later the same night. You're about to leave.'

'Where's Jeff?'

'Aaaw.' Jeff was touched by the concern.

Greg scowled at him and continued: 'Jeff is coming in a minute. You are about to see the girl again. Can you see her yet?'

'No. She's probably gone. I'm just going to get my coat.'

Greg was about to say something else when . . .

'There she is!'

'Look at her,' said Greg. 'Hold that image in your mind.

Now, what does she look like?'

Behind his closed eyes, Steve looked.

'She's beautiful.'

Greg and Jeff nodded impatiently.

'She looks like . . .'

Greg and Jeff waited.

'Like . . . Olivia Newton-John.'

CHAPTER TWELVE

Jeff screwed up his eyes. He moved closer and peered intently. He frowned and squinted.

'No.' He shook his head. 'Nothing.'

'What are you talking about?' Francine asked irritably.

'I can't see anything. Just . . . a blob. It looks like a lava lamp that's overheated.'

Susan the midwife smiled. 'Look. Let me show you.'

She took out a pen from her top pocket and used it to point at the screen.

'Here's the baby's head, its feet, hands . . .'

Jeff nodded as each of the shapes on the screen in front of him became defined by their names.

'So . . . what is it?' Jeff asked, after the point-and-tell had ended.

'Jeff!!'

Francine's scream made both Jeff and the midwife jump. The baby's heartbeat, which was pulsing through the ultrasound speaker, suddenly doubled in time.

'You can't just ask like that!' continued Francine. 'We haven't discussed if we even want to know the sex!'

'I'm afraid we can't tell you anyway,' explained the midwife. 'Oh, and by the way, it's a good idea to avoid any undue stress while you're pregnant. It can affect the baby.'

'Isn't it better to acclimatise it early on?' suggested Jeff.

The midwife looked at him.

'So why can't you tell us – if we *did* want to know?'

The midwife lowered the volume on the ultrasound.

'Well, some people, some cultures, only want a particular sex. And we've found out that if we tell them and it's not what they want, they . . . terminate the birth. Even at this stage.'

'Oh.'

They sat in silence listening to the now quieter and more stable sound of the baby's heartbeat. For a moment the three of them were each lost in their own thoughts.

Francine thought about what the midwife had said. She looked at her baby on the monitor.

The midwife thought about the faces of those parents – mainly the fathers – after she'd informed them that their new offspring would not be their son and heir.

Jeff thought about the overpriced pay-and-display in the hospital car park.

***

'Do you remember when we first met?'

'Of course I do. It was the happiest day of my life.'

'Shut up!'

Jeff, as usual, did as he was told. He turned the volume up slightly on the car radio.

Francine looked at the succession of shops along the high street. Although it wasn't that warm a day, she was feeling hot and so had the passenger window wound halfway down. As she looked at the ladies' clothes shops, she wondered how long it would be before she would have to change her wardrobe. She had always hated maternity clothes. She actually found them depressing. Yet that's what she would be forced to wear before long. Not that all women wore it of course. She remembered the woman, or rather the young girl, in the hospital waiting area. *She* hadn't followed convention. She'd dressed as though she were going to the beach or out clubbing – it was difficult to know the difference any more. Either way, Francine had felt that a pair of denim shorts and a cropped T-shirt was surely not the correct dress code for pregnancy. And the belly-button ring on her huge stomach made her look as if she was carrying a large beach ball with a ring-pull.

'When we first met, did you think that one day we would have a baby together?'

Jeff turned the volume back down again. 'If you remember correctly, we could have started making a baby eight hours and twenty minutes after we first met!'

'Well, at least this time it wasn't fuelled by alcohol.'

'Yeah.'

Francine stared back out of the open window. For the first time ever she became aware of the number of prams there were around. All different shapes, colours, sizes. How did anyone know the right one to choose? Was there a right one? And what about cots? Car seats? Baby monitors?

'And this time it was in a bed, not a toilet cubicle. And—'

'Yes, Jeff, you've made your point.'

Jeff continued to drive.

More silence. Jeff was missing the sound of the heartbeat.

'I have an interview with an ad agency next week. Just a small one. I mean a small agency, not a small interview.'

Francine nodded.

'Although I suppose it might be a small interview as well.'

More nodding.

'Be good if I got it. Be nice to have something to celebrate.'

Francine looked at him.

'I mean, something *else* to celebrate.'

Francine turned back to the high street.

CHAPTER THIRTEEN

The face of the blonde girl, aged about seventeen or eighteen, stared at him. All the features were there – eyes, nose, mouth – yet it was lifeless. It wasn't how he remembered her. Not in his conscious mind anyway.

Steve looked at the face from different angles. It was true, from a certain spot the image did look like the character Olivia Newton-John portrayed in the film *Grease* – the naive high-school girl, not the slut she turned into at the end to get her man. What a lovely moral tale for young girls that was.

'What do you think?'

Steve sighed. He turned and looked at his brother-in-law.

'I don't know.' He shrugged. 'I mean, it sort of looks like her. At least the memory I have of her, but it's . . . different.'

'Well,' said Dave, 'we've just gone by the notes Jeff gave us. And if he did write down everything you said, then this is as close a match as we're gonna get. And that hypnotist bloke did say that your subconscious memory of her would be stronger.'

'She's quite good-looking.'

Dave and Steve looked at the young 'facial composite artist' who was sitting at the computer.

The artist continued. 'I'm just saying, you know, I would.'

Steve wanted to shout, 'Leave her, she's mine!' but realised how ridiculous that would have sounded. She wasn't his. At this moment she wasn't even real, just a computer-generated Photofit.

'So are you ready for the next bit?' asked the artist.

Steve took a breath.

'Not really.'

'It's been over twenty years,' said Dave. 'She will have changed quite a bit. Unless she's Peter Pan.'

'Or Dorian Grey,' said Steve.

The facial composite artist looked at Dave and they both shared a puzzled frown.

'Right,' said the artist, 'here goes.'

He moved the mouse along the control panel and double-clicked. The face on the screen became highlighted.

'You're lucky – we couldn't have done this so well last year. This is a new system. It's based on the original FACE, the "Facial Automated Composition and Editing" system.'

Steve wasn't quite sure what to say. 'Wow!' he suggested.

As the artist continued with his work, Steve turned to Dave. 'Thanks again for doing this. You're sure you won't get into trouble?'

Dave smiled. 'It's okay.' He nodded towards the artist. 'We all do each other favours.'

'Well, I really do appreciate it,' said Steve, then quickly followed this with, 'You haven't said anything to Sheil, have you?'

'Are you kidding?! She'd kill me for encouraging this. I'm only doing it because . . . well, because I actually feel sorry for you.'

Steve sighed. 'Don't worry. I know how pathetic it is. To be truthful . . .'

He looked at the artist. He then took Dave to one side and spoke more quietly. 'I actually asked Greg, the hypnotist, if he could . . . erase that particular memory.'

Dave looked shocked. 'What?'

'I know. Anyway, he wouldn't even try it.'

'Good. You can't just go getting memories erased. That could be really dangerous.' He paused and thought for a moment, 'Although, if you could, I'd probably get rid of my stag night.'

Steve smiled. 'All of it? Surely you'd want to keep the bit with the blow-up sheep and the bottle of Tequila.'

Dave shuddered at the memory.

'There you go,' said the artist.

Dave and Steve went over to the screen.

'Wow,' said Steve. He was going to have to find a new expression.

'So that's what she looks like now?' asked Dave.

'Well, you can never be sure,' said the artist. 'I've had to guess what her hair would be like and whether she's put on a lot of weight or not, and of course I don't know if she wears glasses now. But going by the average, then, yes, it's probably fairly accurate.'

'That's . . . incredible,' said Steve, who was still struggling to find a substitute for 'wow'.

'Yes, I know,' said the artist. He looked at the picture. 'And I tell you something . . . I still would.'

CHAPTER FOURTEEN

Jeff watched the barmaid top up his pint of bitter. He'd recently stopped drinking lager in the belief that, as bitter was a heavier drink it would mean he drank less, which would therefore, as Francine had 'suggested', help him lose some weight. It hadn't worked so far.

'And two packets of crisps, please.'

The barmaid put the bitter next to the pint of lager in front of Jeff. 'We don't do crisps, only olives, pistachios or nachos.'

'I'll have a packet of nachos then, please.'

'They don't come in a packet. They come in a large bowl with cheese, salsa, jalapeno peppers, guacamole and sour cream.'

'And how much are they?'

'Seven pound twenty-five.'

Jeff laughed. The barmaid didn't.

'Just the pints, thanks.'

The barmaid tapped the order into the till.

'Nine pound ninety-five.'

Jeff handed over a ten pound note.

'I honestly don't know how you can make a profit.'

The barmaid ignored the comment and put the money into the till. She looked at Jeff. He stood his ground. She handed him the five pence change.

Jeff smiled, picked up the two pints and walked away from the bar.

At their table, Steve was texting.

Jeff put down the two pints.

'Since when did olives become a pub snack?'

'Since everyone went on holiday to Spain.'

Jeff sat down. 'Yeah, but they give them free over there.'

Steve finished sending his message and put his phone back into his pocket. 'Cheers!'

They knocked their glasses together. Some of Jeff's pint spilled onto the table.

'Hey, careful – that's about twenty pence worth there!'

Steve drank some of his pint and put the glass back onto the table. He turned and put his hand into the inside pocket of his jacket, which was resting on the back of his chair. He took out a folded piece of paper and handed it to Jeff.

'Er . . . thanks,' said Jeff, taking the paper. 'Sorry, but I didn't bring you anything.'

Steve watched as Jeff opened up the paper.

Jeff looked at what he'd unfolded. He frowned. He looked at Steve.

He was just about to ask what he was looking at when it dawned on him.

'Is this . . . her?' He stared at the picture, 'I always thought she'd be younger.'

'She was, you idiot. This is what she looks like now – well according to the police facial composite computer bloke. To be fair, she might not look anything like this at all. But then again, she might.'

Jeff lay the picture down on the table. Steve looked at it upside down.

Seeing the face from this angle sent him into an immediate flashback.

***

Angels disco. 1988.

He had just been knocked to the ground by the two guys fighting. He was looking up into the face of the girl. The angle was the same as the face in the picture. He could see her upside down. The image froze in his mind. Then the girl's face changed. It changed to the face in the picture. The face smiled at him. Steve smiled back.

'Steve? . . . Steve!'

Steve blinked. He suddenly saw Jeff's worried face right in front of his own.

Instinctively Steve moved back.

'Are you okay?'

'Yes. Fine. Why?

'What do you mean, "why"? You were just sitting there staring at the picture for ages. You didn't answer me or anything. I've seen some ways of trying to get out of buying a round, but that's a bit extreme!'

Steve looked at Jeff's glass. It was now almost empty. He then looked at his own full one.

'I . . . I don't know what happened.'

'Do you think that hypnotist has put a curse on you?'

Steve looked at him. 'Yes, Jeff. That's what I think. He's put a curse on me. Because that's what happens in real life.'

He looked back at the picture. He looked puzzled. 'I don't remember her having a beauty spot on her cheek.'

'Oh, sorry,' said Jeff; 'I think that's the spilled beer on the table coming through.'

'Don't worry,' Steve said. 'I have other copies. Loads. And there'll be some in magazines too.'

'What are you talking about?'

'Why do you think I've done this? I'm trying to track her down. I've sent the photo to the lonely-hearts pages of magazines, the 'Have You Seen This Person?' pages, the 'Are You This Person?' pages.'

'I've never heard of those.'

'You know what I mean.' He sighed. 'Don't you see, Jeff? This is it. This is my last attempt before I give up. Or go mental.'

Jeff shrugged. 'All I ask is that you don't put any in telephone boxes.'

Steve smiled. 'I don't even think they have telephone boxes any more.'

'Well, here's hoping. Good luck. I would make a toast to your success, but . . . I don't seem to have a drink.'

Steve took a mouthful of his pint and stood up.

'Same again?'

'Of course.'

Steve set off towards the bar.

Jeff called after him. 'Oh, and get me some olives.'

CHAPTER FIFTEEN

The elderly man attempted to breathe normally. How odd, he thought. This was something he did naturally thousands of times a day, but now that he had been asked to do it on demand, it felt strange.

'And again.'

He breathed again. It was as though he were fighting a normal impulse as opposed to going along with it.

'Well, that all sounds fine. You can pull your shirt back down now.'

The elderly man lowered his vest and shirt and tucked them both into his trousers.

'You don't smoke, do you?'

'Not in seventy-nine years,' replied the elderly man as he adjusted his tie, 'and I'm not going to start now.'

The doctor scrolled through the notes on the screen. 'Well, I can't hear anything. Your lungs seem clear; your blood pressure is one-thirty over eighty-five, which is fine.'

The doctor looked back at the notes. 'Show me again where the pain is.'

The elderly man rubbed an area on the side of his chest. 'Here, and then it sometimes goes under my arm and to my back.'

'Have you done anything strenuous recently?'

The elderly man thought. 'Not really. Bit of gardening, that's all.'

The doctor thought for a moment. 'Gardening? Have you done any raking?'

'Of course. The garden is always covered in leaves this time of year. They look nice on the trees, but not so nice when they're rotting on my lawn!'

'Are you right- or left-handed?'

The elderly man was surprised by the question, and more surprised by the fact he had to think about the answer.

'Right-handed. Funnily enough, my brother is ambidextrous. I used to say that I'd give my right arm to be ambidextrous.'

The doctor smiled. 'Show me the movement you do when you're raking.'

The elderly man stood up and mimed his raking movement. 'I haven't played charades for years.'

The doctor watched the movement. 'I think that's the problem. You've strained a muscle doing the raking. Just take it easy for a while. No exercising. Nothing too strenuous.'

'Oh, does that mean I have to cancel the bungee jump this weekend?'

The doctor smiled again. 'I'm afraid so.'

The elderly man started to put on his blazer.

'You have a lovely smile, you know.'

'Thank you,' said the doctor.

'You have a boyfriend?'

The doctor looked at him. 'So as I said, just take it easy. If it does get worse, then come back and we'll try and fit you in with a physiotherapist.'

The elderly man smiled. 'Thank you, doctor.'

***

The waiting area was deserted. Magazines, mainly women's fashion or gossip publications, towered on a small occasional table. In the corner of the room, a selection of children's toys, virtually all broken, were piled into a red plastic crate.

The receptionist was switching off the computers as the doctor walked up to her and handed her some notes and a Dictaphone.

'Just a couple of referral letters and a scan request.'

The receptionist took them. 'Okay. Anything exciting planned for the weekend?'

The doctor thought for a moment. 'Not bad– a friend's fortieth tomorrow night and the usual weekly visit from my parents on Sunday.'

'Sounds fun. Apart from the parents bit, obviously. See you Monday.'

'You too.'

The doctor started to walk out.

'Oh, Kimberley?' The doctor stopped and turned.

The receptionist continued: 'That sales rep called again; the one who came in last week with the new glove samples. He only wanted to speak with *you*. I think he's taken a bit of a shine to you. Anyway, I said you'd call him back on Monday.'

'Oh goody – something for me to look forward to all weekend. Thanks, Becky.'

***

Kimberley walked to her car, which was parked in her designated spot outside the surgery, by the sign which had initially read 'Dr K. Richardson' but now, after a *hilarious* vandal attack, simply read 'Dr.... hard...'. Kimberley opened the boot of the car and put her medical bag inside. She closed the boot and looked at the large dent facing her. She sighed. It really hadn't been her fault. What was the point of putting small cement posts on the pavements of a residential area? No one was going to ram-raid a house. It had been late, she had been tired and she'd just finished a rare house call to a small semi at the end of a tiny cul-de-sac. Her attempted three-point turn had ended up being a seven-point-turn, with the penultimate point reversing her into the post. She couldn't be bothered to have it repaired. She'd just put up with it until it was time to sell the car.

She opened the driver's door, got in and placed her handbag on the seat next to her. As she put the key into the ignition her telephone rang. She leant over to the passenger's seat and opened her bag. The James Bond theme grew louder and louder as she rummaged around, trying to find her phone. One day she'd get around to changing it. She eventually found the phone, looked at the name on the display and pressed the green button to answer.

'Hi, Ness . . . Yeah, just finished . . . No, what are you talking about? What picture? . . . No, I don't know anything about it . . . What do you mean, it looks like me?'

CHAPTER SIXTEEN

Steve liked to watch the rain. When he was a child he used to watch it running down the back window of his father's car as they went on their weekly Sunday run. He'd choose two drops and watch them race down. He always felt sad for the losing drop.

Here he was, thirty-odd years later, doing the same thing again. Only this time it was on the window of his office. And this time he felt sorry for the winner.

The phone rang. Steve answered it before it finished its first ring.

'Good morning, On The Edge, Steve Connors speaking.'

His face dropped when he heard the voice at the other end. As he listened his facial expression changed from annoyance to shock, via confusion.

'But it can't have! I checked the account before I sent it. There's no way it could have bounced!'

He listened again while the person spoke at him. He eventually managed to interrupt.

'Look, give me five minutes and I'll call you back. They must have made a mistake . . . No, I did *not* say that last month; you're obviously mixing me up with another tenant! I'll call you back.'

Steve hung up. He opened the diary on his desk, turned to the address-book section and looked at the telephone numbers. He pressed the speaker button on the phone on his desk and dialled a number.

'Hello,' said the automated voice. 'Please key in the first digit of your security pass code, followed by the star key.'

Steve did as he was told.

'Thank you. Please key in the fourth digit of your security pass code followed by the star key.'

Steve again followed the robotic instruction.

'Thank you. To help us deal with your call more efficiently . . .'

'We'll put a member of staff straight on?' suggested Steve.

'. . . please make your selection from the following nine options.'

Steve sighed. He leant his forehead onto his hand and rubbed his temple. He listened to the list of options until he heard the one that said, 'To speak with a member of staff, press seven.'

Steve pressed the number seven.

'Thank you.'

There was a long pause. Then . . .

'Due to an unexpected increase in call volume, your waiting time may be longer than usual.'

'How's this for an increase in call volume!?' shouted Steve.

As Steve listened to the annoying 'hold' music, which wouldn't have sounded out of place on a Westlife album, he looked through his small pile of outstanding invoices.

'We are sorry to keep you waiting. 'Please be aware that your call *is* important to us and will be answered shortly.'

The boy-band music resumed. However this time it had a new intermittent high-pitched tone coming through it. Steve looked at the phone. *Call waiting*. What should he do now? He didn't recognise the number. It could be to do with work. More importantly, it could be an emergency – maybe something had happened to his sister or one of the kids and they were calling from the hospital. He should answer; but then he might lose his place in the bank phone queue.

Beep.

Steve pressed the key to switch between callers.

'Hello?'

'Hello, mate,' said Jeff's echoing voice through the loudspeaker.

'Jeff? What number are you calling from?'

'My new work number. Is everything all right?'

Steve sighed. 'Yeah, fine. Just a bit of a problem with the landlord. I'm on hold on the other line with the bank so I can't . . .' It suddenly dawned on him. 'What do you mean, your new work number?'

Steve could hear Jeff smiling as he spoke. 'I have a new job. Or rather, *a* job. In an ad agency. I'm on a three-month trial, and if that goes well they'll keep me on.'

'That's . . . great. I bet Francine's pleased.'

'What do you think? Of course she's the one who got it for me in the first place. Friend of a friend of . . . you know. Anyway, Francine wants to invite you around for dinner on Saturday night. To celebrate.'

'Really? Oh . . . er . . . well—'

'Do you want me to give you some time to make up an excuse? I can call back.'

They knew each other too well.

'No. I'd love to come. Thanks. Look, I'd better go; The bank . . .'

'Okay. Call you later.'

Steve switched the call back to the other line – just in time to hear the phone click off and be replaced by the long, monotonous disconnected tone.

Steve slammed down the phone. 'Apparently my call wasn't that important to you!'

He was about to redial when the phone rang again;

'Good morning, On The Edge, Steve Connors speaking . . . Hi, Kev . . . no, sorry, nothing's come in at the moment . . . Yeah, of course I sent out your DVD . . . No, nothing at all . . . Yeah, of course. Speak soon, bye.'

Steve looked at the DVD of Kevin Summer, which was still sitting on top of the pile of bills on his desk.

Steve looked back at the rain.

CHAPTER SEVENTEEN

Kimberley, wearing a white T-shirt and shorts, ran backwards. She squinted as she watched the ball fly up in front of the sun before making its descent.

Although she thought about going for the volley, she decided to let it drop. Taking it just before it bounced for the second time, she hit a hard forehand towards the right-hand corner of her opponent's baseline.

Her opponent however had anticipated the shot and had run to the net.

'Urgh!'

Her opponent had blocked the shot and, angling her racket head, had used the ball's pace to send it across the court, almost parallel with the net. Kimberley hadn't had a chance.

'Nice shot. Well done.'

Vanessa, the opponent, looked satisfied. She'd pleased herself with that one. And with the match in general.

Kimberley walked towards the net, hand outstretched.

'I'd forgotten how noisy you are.'

Vanessa smiled. 'PP says the same thing!'

***

'So you're really not going to get in touch with him?'

Kimberley put the tray onto the table. 'What? No, of course not!'

She took the cappuccino and muffin from the tray and put them in front of Vanessa, who was already seated.

'Why?'

Kimberley placed a bottle of fruit juice and glass of ice in the table and then, after leaving the tray on an empty chair behind her, turned to her friend.

'Because, Ness, I am hardly going to contact some stranger who put a photo of someone who vaguely looks like me, in a magazine.'

'Oh, come on. It's so romantic. He's obviously been looking for you for years.'

Kimberley stared at her. She spoke slowly and clearly. 'It. Is. Not. Me!'

Vanessa tried to open the packaging around her muffin. She knew she shouldn't really eat it, not with the diet she was supposedly on, but she felt she'd earned it after the tennis game. And she had lost weight recently, not all the weight she'd put on since the pregnancy, but enough to make her feel better about herself.

'It looks exactly like you. And it's not just me who thinks it. Ruby and Sarah rang me.'

'Yeah, they rang me too.' Kimberley took the muffin from her, pulled the packaging apart and handed it back. 'Oh, by the way, I had a patient last week who looked like your dad. But, guess what, it wasn't him!'

Kimberley unscrewed the top of her juice bottle and poured it over the ice. She watched as the pieces cracked and fell apart from each other.

She looked around the leisure centre cafe. It had changed a bit. They used to come here regularly. Game of tennis, quick swim, shower, then coffee and muffin. However, since Vanessa had had the twins their games had been less regular.

Vanessa's mobile beeped.

And less relaxing.

Vanessa read the message. She looked at Kimberley.

'It's PP. Charlotte won't stop crying. Sorry, I'll have to go as soon as I finish this.

'Okay, no problem,' said Kimberley. Although what she really wanted to say was, 'I bet she miraculously stops crying as soon as you get home – just in time for your husband to go to the pub.'

***

Kimberley had never liked Vanessa's husband, PP. Well, that wasn't strictly true. She had liked him when she had been dating him herself.

As a couple Kimberley and PP were absolute proof that opposites attract. Of course PP wasn't his real name. His real name was Phillip Peter Fowler, but he insisted on everyone calling him PP. He wouldn't answer to anything else – even though a lot of people wanted to call him something else, and did so behind his back. PP was a 'lad'. If he were a character in a sitcom he would be regarded as unbelievable and two-dimensional. Yet this was him. He'd had a succession of girlfriends, although ironically none had been a success. He had one child from a previous relationship – whom he always turned up to see, laden with presents, two or three days after her birthday – and a string of near-misses.

Kimberley had actually met him through Vanessa. Vanessa and PP had been friends since they had worked together for a time-share company in Tenerife. For Vanessa it had been a temporary job after university while she tried to decide what to do after failing her degree. As far as PP was concerned, it might be the only job he'd ever do.

Although nothing had happened between him and Vanessa, they had remained in touch and always sent birthday cards. Well, Vanessa had always sent a card. PP invariably forgot and would call a week or so later with an apology and a joke.

Kimberley was introduced to him at Vanessa's thirtieth birthday party and they had hit it off immediately. PP was one of life's genuine charmers, although the word 'genuine' was not really in PP's vocabulary, along with the words 'truthful', 'honest' and 'onomatopoeic'.

Kimberley could see what he was like, yet was still taken with him. She didn't know if that was down to his charm or the fact that she had been single for the previous two years; she guessed it was both.

They slept together the night of the party. They both said that they had never slept with anyone so soon after meeting them. They had both lied.

A few weeks later PP had called her and asked her out on a date. It was three dates before they slept together again. They had dated, all in all, for three months, although they did break up four times during that period. The eventual final break-up, from which there was no return, was when PP and a couple of his friends went out for a drink one night and came back a week later. He tried to convince Kimberley that he had told her he was going way. She had ended their relationship.

And now he was married to her best friend. The girl who had introduced them in the first place.

Kimberley was happy for them – at the start. She had been surprised when they first moved in together. She was shocked when they announced they were getting married, then amazed when the wedding actually went ahead. It was during the wedding that Kimberley stopped being happy for her friend and started to worry. Admittedly PP had drunk too much – he slurred most of his groom's speech – but that couldn't excuse the fact he had made a pass at her.

She had been helping Vanessa to take some of the presents to the honeymoon suite of the hotel where they were having the wedding. As she put an armful of gifts on the bed and turned around to leave, she came face to face with PP. He had smiled and thanked her for all her help, especially for organising Vanessa's hen night. He then pecked her on the check. Kimberley congratulated him for the twentieth time. That's when PP had moved in to kiss her – at the same time attempting to lie her down on the would-be nuptial bed. Kimberley had twisted away, thrown PP onto the bed and stormed out.

She had never said anything to Vanessa and had never spoken about it again to PP.

Vanessa and PP had eighteen-month-old twin girls, Charlotte and Amy. PP hadn't been there for the birth. Kimberley was amazed he'd actually been there for the conception. And since the children had been born, PP had found more and more excuses to spend less and less time with them and Vanessa. If it wasn't work or football, it was having-a-drink-with-mates evening. Kimberley couldn't believe that Vanessa actually put up with it. But Vanessa was smitten. Still. And he did bring in the money, working as the area manager for a chain of mobile-phone stores.

Kimberley hardly ever saw Vanessa any more. This was only their second tennis game since the birth of the twins. They'd been out for a drink a couple of times and once to the cinema. Each time PP had called at least three times throughout the evening with one *dilemma* or another: 'Amy has diarrhoea', 'How do you record two channels at the same time?', 'Charlie's got hiccups.'

***

'Anyway, I think you should get in touch with this guy.' Vanessa put down her cup and patted the sides of her mouth with her serviette. 'It could be fun.'

'Unlikely.'

Vanessa took out a folded piece of paper and opened it up on the table in front of them. Kimberley looked down at it.

Staring up at her was the photo which everyone, except her, thought was her.

'You brought it with you?!'

'Listen.' She read from the page in front of them *'Is this you or do you know this person? She is in her mid-thirties, blonde (or at least was in 1988), approximately 5 foot 6, slim build (again, was in 1988). On a Saturday in June 1988 she went to Angels disco in Reading, Berkshire. She left at 1.15 a.m. That's all I know. If this is you, or if you think you know who this person is, please get in touch. It's not a matter of life or death, but it will help to keep me sane. Please send an email to . . .'*

Vanessa stopped reading. She looked up at her friend.

'You used to go to that place, didn't you?'

Kimberley was a little surprised. 'Well . . . yes. I mean, I went once or twice, if there wasn't much happening in Bracknell, but I can't remember if it was in 1988, let alone in June of that year!'

'But I'm sure you could work it out. Have a look through old diaries or something.' Vanessa picked up the photo. She put it next to Kimberley's face. 'It's just too much of a coincidence.'

'But it *is* a coincidence . . .'

Kimberley turned sideways and looked at the picture.

'. . . it must be.'

CHAPTER EIGHTEEN

Steve looked at the stacked shelves in front of him. It was all meaningless. Why couldn't they just have two bottles: one red, one white. He glanced along the labels. What exactly was a Cabernet Sauvignon? And how did it differ to a Shiraz or a Chardonnay? And why were they all different prices?

'Can I help you?'

Steve didn't take his eyes from the array of bottles. 'Er . . . I'm just trying to decide.'

'What type of wine are you looking for? Something dry? Fruity? Sweet? Any particular region?'

'Yeah, the region of . . . eight quid.'

The salesperson nodded. He then went over to the *Offers* section, picked up a bottle of white wine and handed it to Steve.

'Here, try this. It's a Sancerre. French. Very good. It's normally around fifteen pounds, but we're doing it at half price until the end of the month.'

'Great,' said Steve. 'And I'll take a small bottle of whisky as well.'

'The cheapest?'

Steve nodded.

***

Steve stood around the corner from Jeff and Francine's house and opened the bottle of whisky. Normally he'd have gone to the pub for a pint or two before arriving, but he'd been running late – another fracas with his landlord – and therefore had to make do with a couple of quick nips before going in. The spirit warmed him up yet made him shiver at the same time. He re-screwed the bottle, put it into his inside pocket and walked towards the house.

He wondered what type of mood Francine was going to be in. The last time he'd been there, which was now over four months ago, she wasn't too bad. She'd drunk more than normal and she'd actually relaxed a little and let her hair down – not literally though; she'd never do that. They'd even talked about her brother and his boyfriend. Something she rarely referred to when sober.

However, the time before, she had been the proverbial nightmare. She'd had a bad day at work; one of the newly recruited applicants she'd sent to a company hadn't turned up and no one knew where they were. Eventually, after multiple messages, the applicant had texted to say that she had changed her mind and had decided to go to Australia with her boyfriend. This had annoyed Francine and had infuriated her client, who threatened to use another recruitment agency in future. Francine had eventually managed to persuade them to stay with her – by offering a reduced rate on any future candidates. But that hadn't stopped her from bringing her bad mood home with her.

Steve stood at the door. It was then that he remembered. Francine was pregnant! So she wouldn't be drinking!! It was going to be hell!!!

He contemplated doing a runner, but it was too late. Francine had spotted him through the opaque glass panels and opened the door.

She was smiling. Maybe she had decided to drink after all and stuff the consequences – the kid would just have to cope.

'Hello, Steven.'

She kissed him. On both cheeks. Steve couldn't stand it when people did that – unless they were foreign and that was their custom. When British people did it, he just found it pretentious.

Steve handed over the wine.

'Oh, Sancerre, my favourite, not that I can have any!' Francine laughed. Steve was suddenly reminded of *The Wizard of Oz*. He wondered if there was a bucket of water nearby.

'In you come.'

Steve walked into the house. This wasn't normal. He began to wonder if parallel universes actually existed.

He saw Jeff in the kitchen. 'Hi, Jeff.'

'Hi.'

Steve frowned. There was obviously something going on. Jeff usually greeted Steve with some kind of insult, but tonight he gave him a look that was almost apologetic.

'Go on in,' said Francine, still smiling unnaturally and pointing towards the dining room – as if Steve didn't know where it was.

'Er . . . thanks,' said Steve.

He walked in. It looked different. He was expecting, or rather hoping, to find the PlayStation on the floor – ready for Jeff and him to have a post-dinner game. But it wasn't there. In fact hardly anything was there. It all looked . . . tidy. Like the majority of the 'new money' couples and families who'd moved into the Muswell Hill/Crouch End parts of north London, Jeff and Francine had bought a house that was bigger than they actually needed and they found maintaining it and keeping it clean and tidy an impossible chore. They'd had numerous cleaners, all of whom had eventually quit due to Francine's impossible demands. So they were currently having to cope on their own which, up until now, had proven unsuccessful.

Steve looked at the large framed mirror on the wall. That's when he saw someone sitting on the sofa against the wall behind him. Steve turned around. At first he thought it was Natalia, their last cleaner – or 'home help' or 'domestic aid', Steve wasn't sure of the current politically correct title – but he quickly realised that this person wasn't anywhere near as attractive or young enough to be Natalia.

'Oh,' said Francine, as though she too had only just become aware of this other person in her house. 'Steve, this is Susan. Susan, Steve.'

Susan got up from the sofa and held out her hand.

'Hi, nice to meet you.'

Steve shook the hand. 'Hi.'

It was a blind date!

That's why Jeff had looked so uncomfortable. Francine must have done this without telling him – knowing that he would have put a stop to it. Or at least tried to. Maybe he had tried to stop it and Francine had ignored him. After all, that was the way their marriage worked. Or failed. No, surely if Jeff had known about it he would have warned Steve.

It had happened once before, about six months earlier. Just as he was about to arrive he had a brief text message from Jeff: 'blnd date don't cum'.

Susan smiled. 'Francine's told me a lot about you.'

Steve smiled back. 'Well, she's told me fuck all about you.'

***

Steve stayed for dinner. He was tempted to leave immediately, but he didn't want to abandon his friend to his wife's wrath. And he was hungry. And after all, as he realised, it wasn't the girl's fault – Steve always referred to females around his age or younger as 'girls' and the ones older than him as 'women' – it was Francine who had set this up. And Steve knew why. It wasn't a kind gesture; she was hoping he'd find someone so that he wouldn't bother them so much. She tended to blame Steve for being a bad influence on Jeff, when the truth of the matter was it was actually the other way around.

***

An hour later and Steve was helping himself to more fruit salad and refilling his own wine glass. This was his third full glass and, on top of the whisky he'd had earlier, he was feeling pretty drunk. He'd actually spoken with Susan quite a bit during the course of the meal, throughout all three courses in fact. He'd found out that she was one of the midwives working at the hospital where Francine was due to have her baby. Steve liked her. She seemed fun and had a good sense of humour. He just didn't fancy her.

'So do you know loads of famous people?'

It was the question he was always asked when he told people what he did for a living.

'No, not really. Oh, I used to look after Gareth Ice.'

'Oh, really?' said Susan.

Steve looked at her. 'You have no idea who that is, do you?'

'No,' said Susan.

'Tell her about the time you nearly met Bruce Willis.'

Steve turned to Jeff. 'Surely the fact that you said "nearly met" shows how dull a story it really is.'

Jeff gave Steve an 'excuse me for trying' look.

'Anyway', said Steve, 'Jeff is the one who's going to start meeting famous people. He just has to write an advert for them to be in.'

'And offer them enough money.' Jeff got up and walked over to one of the cabinets. He opened the door and took out a bottle of whisky.

'Oh,' said Steve, 'talking about money, don't forget to use some of my clients in your campaigns.'

'Sure,' said Jeff, opening the bottle on the way back to the table. 'If you have any left by then!'

Steve knew it was joke, and laughed. But the truth was, the way things were going, he actually might not.

His thought process – clients, money, television – reminded Steve that he hadn't told Jeff about a phone call he'd had earlier that day. 'I forgot to tell you – a TV production company contacted me. They want me to go on a chat show to talk about my *quest*.'

'Steve!'

It was one of the few things Francine had said all evening. She was still being appalled at Steve's initial comment to Susan.

Steve turned to her and frowned. 'What?'

'Do we have to talk about that now?'

It suddenly dawned on Steve; Francine hadn't told Susan *everything* about him.

'Oh. Sorry, Fran,' he said. Steve then took the glass of whisky Jeff had poured for him and turned to Susan. 'I'm trying to track down a girl I met over twenty years ago.'

Francine got up and started to clear the table.

'Really?' said Susan 'That's interesting. Who is she? An old school friend? Childhood sweetheart?'

'No one. I don't know her. Never met her – not properly anyway. I just bumped into her at a disco in 1988.'

Susan looked at him. 'Gosh. Right. Well. Good luck.'

Susan got up, picked up an empty wine bottle and the bread basket and followed Francine into the kitchen.

Jeff turned to his friend. 'Sorry, mate.'

It was the first time he and Jeff had had a moment to themselves.

'It's okay. I assume it was nothing to do with you?'

'Of course not. I knew about it when she arrived, five minutes before you. And Francine took my phone away.'

'Don't worry about it. She's actually very nice.'

'No looker though.'

'No.'

Jeff drank some whisky. 'So are you going to go on this talk show?'

'No, of course not.'

'Really? I think it's a good idea. You want to find this girl, TV is the best medium.'

'I'll just come across as some pathetic loser.'

Jeff looked at him.

Steve narrowed his eyes. 'Leave it!'

'Consider it left.'

They sat in silence for a moment, both contented and able to do that without feeling uncomfortable. The sign of a good friendship. They listened to the sound of the wind echoing through the chimney.

'So, what's going on with the landlord?'

Steve sighed and put down his glass.

'Just a bit of a cash-flow issue, that's all.' He raised his glass and held it out. 'Anyway, congratulations on the job.' Steve finished off his whisky as Jeff prepared to refill his glass.

CHAPTER NINETEEN

The red light of the LCD seemed to almost burn into his eyes. Was that a five or an eight? He hoped it wasn't a five. He squinted as he tried to focus. It was a five. Of course it was a five. He closed his eyes but he knew the chances of going back to sleep were very remote. That was the annoying thing about alcohol; well, one of the annoying things. It helped you fall asleep yet woke you up just a couple of hours later to punish you. He knew it was dehydration, although he could never understand how you became dehydrated from drinking too much.

Over the years he'd tried every hangover-avoidance remedy: drinking a lot of water before going to bed, taking a couple of paracetamol, putting a wet sock on his forehead. He was convinced this last one was one of Jeff's wind-ups, although it had seemed to work once. But he hadn't tried anything before going to bed this time. Or as far as he knew he hadn't. He couldn't actually remember very much at all. His last clear recollection – and even that was a bit fuzzy – was Jeff suggesting that they opened the bottle of single-malt Scotch he'd taken from his parents' house after his dad's funeral. And that was about it. He remembered arriving, talking to Jeff, meeting Susan . . .

Susan.

There was another memory. Or was this a dream? No, it was a memory. Leaving Jeff's house. With Susan. They walked. No, they shared a cab . . . who got out first? Where did she live? Who paid for the cab? Did he leave his phone in the cab again? He opened his eyes and looked at his bedside table. No, his phone was there . . . next to a packet of condoms.

A packet of condoms.

Opened.

Empty.

It was probably the pulse pounding in his head which had blotted out the sound initially. But now he could hear it. Loud and clear.

Breathing.

And it wasn't his.

He slowly lifted his head from the pillow and turned it 180 degrees.

Yep. There was Susan.

Then flashes: coming into his flat, looking for a drink – a drink! What was the matter with him? – then remembering the whisky bottle in his jacket pocket, sharing it with Susan. Another flash: opening the fridge, suggesting he make something to eat and wondering what culinary delights he could rustle up with an egg, a couple of cheese slices, some coleslaw and a bottle of balsamic vinegar. Emily had brought this bottle over when they had started dating, but he'd never opened it. He didn't even know if it was meant to live in the fridge.

One more flash – this was like a trailer for a bad film – having his offer of a cheesy one-egged omelette with a side order of stale coleslaw and balsamic vinegar turned down. Then kissing. Then the bedroom. Then . . . then . . . he couldn't remember having sex. How could he not remember having sex? Wait . . . Nakedness. He had flashes of nakedness. His. Hers. Neither was great. He felt sick. It was the drink more than the memory. And the constant flashes weren't helping the pounding headache.

He quickly got out of bed. Too quickly. He hadn't had this bad a hangover for a long time. He attempted to walk in a straight line to the bathroom, but the bedroom apparently had other ideas. As though he were in one of those large revolving tubes in a Fun House, he had to rebalance himself with each step to avoid falling over.

He eventually arrived at the bathroom, lifted the toilet seat – why was it down? It was never down. Oh, yes . . . he wasn't alone. He then leant forward and brought back most of what he'd eaten and drunk the previous night.

After he'd finished for the third time, he cleaned his teeth, washed his face and walked back into the bedroom.

'And there's no better compliment.'

He looked at Susan.

'Sorry. That was nothing to do with you.'

'I know. I was joking.'

The silence that followed was short yet still uncomfortable.

'I know it's a cliché, but I really don't do this. I drank too much. And mixed it.' She breathed out deeply.

'It's okay,' said Steve. He wasn't really sure what else to say.

'Is there any chance you could not tell Jeff about this?'

Steve took a couple of baby steps and sat on the bed. 'I could lie to you and say that I won't tell him. But I will. Of course I will. He's my friend. I'm a bloke. That's what we do.'

Susan shrugged. 'At least you're honest.'

'But I promise I won't go into any . . . details.'

Susan looked at him. 'Details? Like what?'

Steve was surprised. 'Like . . . you know . . . what we did. In bed.'

Susan slowly smiled. 'You don't remember, do you?'

'Of course I remember. I mean, I admit I was a little bit drunk, but—'

'You couldn't get an erection, I assume because you were too drunk. I tried to . . . help. We both did. But . . . nothing. I'm pleased really. It would have been a mistake.'

Steve looked at the empty box of condoms. Then he spotted the three little square packets, unopened, on the floor.

'Oh.'

She smiled brightly. 'Still sure you want to tell Jeff?'

Steve looked at her. 'Maybe not.'

'There is one thing I need to know though.'

'What's that?' asked Steve.

'Before we went to sleep last night, why did you put a wet sock on your forehead?'

CHAPTER TWENTY

'I'm not your father. I ain't never been your father. I'm . . .
I'm your brother!'

The shock was palpable.

The young girl stared at the man sitting in semi-profile to
her. The man who, for the past seventeen years, she had
considered to be her father.

'What are you talking about, Dad?'

Tears welled up in the man's eyes. 'I'm sorry, love. I
wanted to tell you before, but . . . There was never the right
moment, was there?'

The young girl started to cry. She shook her head. It didn't
make sense. How could this be happening? Was it some
dreadful joke? Was this really a hidden-camera TV show?

'This is crap! This is fucking bullshit!'

Some of the audience also started to cry. They knew that
her swearing would be bleeped out so they felt pleased to
have been there to hear it live.

'So how did this all come about, Derek? Why have you
been lying to Kylie all these years?' Charlie Race, the host,
took a couple of steps forward as he asked the question.

The guest, Derek, looked at the floor. He then wiped his
eyes on his sleeve, looked at his daughter/sister and turned
to Charlie.

'What happened was—'

Charlie interrupted him. 'Sorry, Derek, you'll have to tell
us when we get back after the break.'

He turned and looked dramatically straight into the camera. 'And you won't want to miss it!'

He stayed in place, facing the camera.

'Okay, we're out.'

Once the floor manager had spoken, Charlie's dramatic stare was replaced by a look of indifference.

A make-up girl walked onto the studio floor and dabbed Charlie's face with powder.

'Thanks, babe,' said Charlie.

Kylie turned to her brother/father. 'What's going on? What are you talking about?'

Charlie turned to her angrily. 'Don't talk about it yet – wait until the cameras are back on!'

'But—'

'Just save it.'

***

Steve could not quite believe what he was watching. This was without doubt one of the worst programmes he had ever seen.

'Steve, you'll be on after the next segment.'

And he couldn't believe he'd agreed to be on it.

The young floor manager walked onto the studio floor and clapped her hands. The Pavlovian audience joined in with her.

Charlie looked into the camera.

'Welcome back to *Charlie Race*. Coming up later: *"I've been thinking about you for almost half my life, but I don't even know your name"*. How one man's quest has ruined his life.'

Steve looked at the monitor in the greenroom and shook his head. 'It hasn't ruined my life. I never said it had ruined my life!'

'Yeah, but it's good telly, innit?'

Steve looked at the woman sitting on the sofa opposite

him. 'But that's not why I came on this programme. I just wanted to . . .' He stopped himself. He sighed loudly.

'Don't worry about it,' said the woman. 'It's just a laugh, innit?'

She leant forward towards Steve. Steve was worried that her breasts were going to fall out of her tracksuit top. She spoke quietly.

'Do you know why I'm here?' She didn't give Steve time to say no, or even attempt a guess. 'I'm going to tell my husband that I'm sleeping with his best mate and I want to marry him.'

'But . . . why?'

The woman looked genuinely puzzled. 'Why what?'

'Why . . . ? Why . . . ?' He didn't know which question to ask first. Eventually he went with 'Why are you coming on here to tell him instead of doing it in private.'

'Well, it's good telly, innit?'

It was like a mantra.

'And . . .' she continued, 'they put you up in a nice hotel and stuff.'

***

Steve could only make out the first two rows of the audience. He knew there were at least another six raked rows behind them, but the lights shining into his eyes darkened everything. He moved uncomfortably on his chair. He hadn't given the chairs much notice when the other guests had been sitting on them, but now he realised how uncomfortable they were. Maybe this was part of the psychological torment, to heighten the emotion of being on the programme. Or maybe they were just cheap – in keeping with the theme of the programme.

How had he agreed to this? Had Jeff's argument really been that persuasive?

He of course knew the truth. This was really a last stab at putting this behind him, a final attempt to get on with what was left of his life. If the girl contacted him through this then fine, great, wonderful. If not, he vowed to himself that he would give her up. Maybe he could find another hypnotist who would be prepared to erase the memory. He'd read a bit about it. It could be done. Yes, there might be side effects: other memory loss, headaches, disorientation, but he felt it was worth the risk. Surely whatever the consequences, they wouldn't be as bad as what he was about to go through.

***

'So let's all hope and pray that Chantelle manages to persuade her sister to give up her life of drugs and prostitution and goes back to being a lollipop lady.'

The audience applauded.

Charlie Race continued talking to camera; 'Now, have you ever met someone and then couldn't stop thinking about them for days, maybe weeks, maybe even months later? Well, how would you feel if you met someone and then thought about them constantly for the next twenty-odd years? And worse, you knew nothing about them – not even their name!'

The audience gasped on cue.

'Our next guest has done that. And now he's had enough. This is his final plea to find the girl of his dreams – although it's really been a living nightmare. Please welcome . . . Steve.'

The audience applauded. The red light on top of the camera directly in front of Steve lit up. Out of the corner of his eye he could see himself on the monitor. Did they have to come in that close?

'So, Steve,' said Charlie, 'tell us your story.'

CHAPTER TWENTY-ONE

The crying was, at last, slowly fading away. Although there was still the odd burst, just as a reminder, it was now generally being replaced by the soothing sound of constant sucking.

Trying to control her breathing – she didn't want anything to break the rhythm she had set up – Vanessa slowly leant forward and, putting all her weight onto her toes, eased herself up from the sofa. However, before she had become vertical, while she was still in a semi-squat position, the crying started again.

She quickly sat back down on the sofa and continued the rocking motion she had been using earlier. The crying once again gave way to the sucking.

'Why can't you be more like your sister?' Vanessa looked at her restless daughter in her arms. 'She's fast asleep in her cot. No crying. No dummy. Nothing.'

Baby Charlotte responded by sucking on her dummy at an increased rate – as though she understood and just wanted to show how defiant she was able to be. As Vanessa looked down at her, already forgiving her for everything, the telephone rang. Charlotte wriggled, irritated by the noise, and sucked harder. Stretching out her left arm, the one that wasn't supporting her daughter's head, Vanessa picked up the telephone.

'Hello? . . . Oh, hi, Sarah . . . What? . . . Really? Okay, I'll have a look now!'

Vanessa switched off the phone, picked up the TV remote

control and aimed it. The red standby light on the television went off, and as the screen crackled and hummed to life, she immediately saw a face she recognised. Kimberley's face! Or at least the Photofit she had shown Kimberley after their tennis game a couple of weeks earlier.

The picture was then replaced by the face of Charlie Race.

'So if that is you, or you know, or think you know, who this person is, then you can contact Steve here through the website *www.girlfromthedisco.co.uk*.

The picture again changed. This time to a shot of Steve.

Vanessa looked at him intently, as though studying someone who might be bluffing at a game of poker.

Then back to Charlie.

'Thank you for watching. See you again next time.'

As the credits for the programme rolled, the voiceover suggested that if anyone watching had a personal or family problem they'd like to discuss and share, they should contact the studio. The telephone number, email address and postal address all came up on the screen. The voiceover read the details out as well. Just in case.

***

Vanessa looked at her daughters sleeping side by side in their matching cots. They looked so different. They *were* so different. She questioned, as she often did, whether she would be a good mother. She wondered, as she often did, what the world would hold for each of them. She worried, as she often did.

Vanessa walked out of the bedroom and went back downstairs. She sat at the desk in the living room and switched on PP's computer. It seemed like years since she had done this, yet in truth it had only been a couple of months. Since the weekly baby-group newsletter had finished, she hadn't bothered checking her emails. Most of her friends now called her, or at least texted her. Not that she had that many friends any more. There was Kimberley of course, and Ruby and Sarah – although they were really Kimberley's friends – and Catherine, whom she'd met at the baby group. And that was about it. Once the baby group had disbanded, no one else had kept in touch. At least not with her. And the rest of her friends, none of whom had children, hadn't really been in touch since they had sent congratulations cards. Maybe they all had secret meet-ups and no one told her. She smiled at her paranoid thought.

***

She clicked the internet icon. The home page opened – showing the company for which PP worked. She typed *www.girlfromthedisco.co.uk*. Immediately the Photofit filled the screen. Vanessa looked at it. She was positive that this was her friend. She moved the mouse to the 'Contact' button. And then stopped. Should she really do this? What if it were the other way around? How would she feel if Kimberley were going to contact a random stranger on her behalf?

She clicked the mouse and was instantly taken to an email link.

'Hi,' she wrote, '*I think you are looking for my friend Kimberley. I could be wrong, but I don't think so! Anyway, here is her email address: drkimberleyrichardson@hotmail.com. Drop her a line and introduce yourself. She might not want to meet you at first, but I'm sure you'll be able to persuade her!*'

Vanessa then wrote *LOL* – and immediately erased it.

She smiled to herself as she remembered a story one of the women at baby group had shared. This woman – Vanessa couldn't remember her name – had never had or wanted a mobile phone. However her husband had insisted when the baby was born that she had one. Being new to phones and the concept of texting instead of speaking, the woman had thought that it stood for *lots of love*, not *laugh out loud*. So, on receiving news that the mother of a friend of hers had died, instead of calling as she normally would, she sent a text message so as not to disturb her. The text message read: *'Just heard about your mum. LOL.'*

They were no longer friends.

Vanessa finished typing the message: 'Anyway, good luck. Vanessa. P.S. Here is a photo of Kimberley.'

She sent it immediately, without giving herself time to think whether or not she should.

She sat back.

She looked at the clock. PP had said he was going to be home late that night, for a change. Vanessa leant forward and typed in her email URL. She entered her name and password and clicked on the inbox.

She had seventeen messages, all from someone called Sean. The subject line read 'Cheap Viagra'.

She erased them. That was something PP certainly didn't need. She closed her eyes and sighed. She regretted sending the email to that man 'Steve'. Why had she done it? She realised that she was tired and not thinking straight. Kimberley was going to be furious. But what could Vanessa do about it now? She decided to send another email. She would explain the situation and ask him not to contact Kimberley – not until she'd spoken to her anyway.

She clicked on the 'History' tab to see the list of all the website addresses recently visited. She'd intended to go back to the website address and press 'Contact' again. However, what she saw under the previous visited sites made her forget her plan.

She knew PP stayed up late most nights. He said he always had orders or invoicing to organise. Apparently that wasn't all he'd been organising.

There, under History, was a list of pornographic sites he'd visited. They ranged from *Adorable Asian Girls* to *Weird Watersports*. She wasn't sure exactly what the last one referred to, but she guessed it wasn't anything to do with jet-skiing.

She felt . . . well, she wasn't sure how she felt. Upset? Disappointed? She knew they'd not had much sex since the twins had been born but, well, was this really necessary? She shrugged. It wasn't the end of the world.

But the next link she saw might well have been.

There, halfway down the list, was a site named . . . *Dating Yet Married*.

She froze. She felt her stomach contract. She coughed – more of a nervous action than to clear her throat. She moved the mouse until the pointer hovered over the link. She clicked on it. It opened up several new links. One called 'My Profile'. She clicked *www.datingyetmarried.com/myprofile*.

There was PP's photo. It was the shot she had taken of him on their honeymoon in Barbados.

She read the profile: 'Big Guy. Male. 37. Married. Looking for fun. Will travel. Box no. 4497672.'

Vanessa first thought was to laugh at the words *Big Guy*; that and the photo, which was now a couple of years old, and the waist size then meant that anyone who contacted PP was in for a disappointment.

Vanessa didn't know how long she'd been staring at the screen when she suddenly became aware of Charlotte crying again.

This time Vanessa wanted to join her.

CHAPTER TWENTY-TWO

The applause echoed as twenty-five-year old Michael Dutch walked onto the stage.

'Good evening, you bunch of fucking retards.'

The sound of a *click*, and the screen went blank.

Steve stared at the portable combined television/DVD player in front of him. He leant over and ejected the DVD. He looked at the cover. What had he expected? Here was a picture of a guy wearing a 'Make War Not Peace' T-Shirt and holding a severed hand with the index finger sticking up. His material was never going to be subtle wordplay.

There was no point in his watching any more. Steve knew it wasn't for him. Even if this was what audiences wanted, and Steve wasn't sure if that were true or not, he knew he couldn't represent someone he didn't respect. No, that wasn't quite true. He didn't have to respect them as a person, but he did at least have to respect their act.

Steve flicked through the other DVDs on his desk. 'Roy J. Wall', 'Louise McDavidson', 'Norfolk and Good'.

This was a monthly ritual for Steve. It used to be weekly, then fortnightly. He used to feel that if people had taken the effort to send him their showreel he should at least look at it.

When he first started the business he used to send the showreels, on video as they were then, back to the comedian, usually at his own expense, along with some advice and comments. But now it was just a pain in the arse. He knew he should keep up with what was going on, what the new trends were, but he just didn't have the interest any more. He picked up 'Norfolk and Good' and read one of the quotations: 'The best and funniest double act since Morecambe and Wise – *Two Months Magazine*'. Although he'd never heard of the act, or the publication, he knew for a fact that the statement was a lie.

He put the case back down and looked around the office. He suddenly noticed how quiet it was. He knew the phones didn't often ring, but it still seemed quieter than usual; even the noise from the street below seemed clearer. There wasn't even the occasional *ping* announcing the arrival of another email.

Email.

His computer.

He swivelled in his chair and looked at the screen. That's why it was so quiet; he hadn't switched on his computer and was missing the soothing sound of its cooling fan. He walked his swivel chair backwards, switched on the monitor and then turned on the tower case. He watched as the computer welcomed him and then proudly displayed the icons on his desktop. He logged on to his email account and watched as his inbox racked up all his incoming mail.

Thirty-five.

He went through them, deleting the spam – the ones the filter had annoyingly missed – and then opened the others. A couple of representation requests (he'd reply to these later), a YouTube link from Jeff called 'When not to light your farts', and . . . a message forwarded from *www.girlfromthedisco.co.uk*.

He opened it.

Dear Steve, I saw you on the Charlie Race programme. I'm sorry but I'm not the girl you're looking for. However, I am also single and looking for someone and I thought you looked very nice. So if it doesn't work out with the girl, or if you don't find her, please drop me an email or give me a call on this number. I am attaching a photo of myself. Look forward to hearing from you, Barbara x

Steve had received quite a few emails via the website. Some had insisted they were the girl – even though they looked nothing like the Photofit – one had said he knew the girl and would pass on the details for a small fee, and one had asked him to leave the girl alone. That one had upset him for a short while as he realised that he could, in a way, be defined as a stalker; although he wasn't really sure if you could stalk someone when you didn't know their name, didn't know where they lived and didn't even know exactly what they looked like.

Steve looked at the attachment icon next to Barbara's email. Might as well have a look, he thought. Before opening it, he scanned it with his antivirus software. 'No virus found.' Steve clicked on the photo. It opened to reveal a woman – older than Steve – completely naked save for a Burberry trilby.

Steve looked at the photo – for quite a while. He wasn't quite sure what to do now. He had been sent a few photos by women, as well as one or two by men who suggested that he gave up the whole 'looking for girls' thing. Although one or two of the photos had been a tad raunchy, this was the first fully nude one.

Should he reply? If so, how? *'Thanks for getting in touch. I will let you know what happens. Nice breasts by the way.'*

He decided to leave it for the time being.

He checked the emails again. Nothing else. Not even any more spam. He suddenly felt hungry. Maybe it was because he'd been thinking of spam. He looked at the backwards clock. Not even twelve thirty. He guessed the hunger pangs were more down to boredom than anything else. What should he have for lunch today? A sandwich, packet of crisps and some kind of fizzy drink? Why not. Why change a ritual. And anyway, this popular combination was now referred to as a 'Meal Deal' in most places, which meant he could save anything up to a pound!

The phone rang. Steve looked at it for a couple of seconds before picking it up.

'Good morning, On The Edge, Steve Connors speaking . . . Yes, that's right . . . I see, and what type of event is it? . . . Okay, and how many people will be there? . . . And how long would you like the act to do? . . . Well, to be honest I've found that there's no point in an act doing more than thirty minutes and . . . Yes, they could do an hour, but . . . Yes, all my acts are of a high standard and . . .' He listened and sighed. 'Yes, a couple of them have been on TV, but it's not always the most talented that go on television. Some of my acts . . . Yes, yes, I understand that *you're* paying, but I was just saying . . . Of course, don't worry, I'll send you a suitable act. I'll fax over the contracts and . . . No, I won't *rip you off* . . .' Steve looked at the DVD of Mike Dutch and his 'Make War Not Peace' T-shirt. He smiled. 'In fact, I have the perfect person for you.' He looked at his combined TV/DVD player. 'And he has just been on TV.'

After putting down the phone, Steve opened a drawer in his desk and hunted around for something to eat. Anything. Amongst the envelopes, paperclips, stamps and dried-out felt pens he managed to find a piece of chewing gum and an extra strong mint. As he tried to decide in which order to consume these delicacies, there was a *ping*.

Steve looked at the email. It was another one from the website. He wondered if it was another naked middle-aged woman.

He started reading and it made him sit up – until then he'd been lying back in his chair.

'*Hi, I think you are looking for my friend Kimberley. I could be wrong, but I don't think so! Anyway, here is her email address: drkimberleyrichardson@hotmail.com. Drop her a line and introduce yourself. She might not want to meet you at first, but I'm sure you'll be able to persuade her! Anyway, good luck. Vanessa.*'

Steve read it twice. It seemed genuine. Of course it wasn't from the girl herself, but at least this Vanessa wasn't asking for money.

Steve opened the photo.

It was a close match. Definitely a close match. She looked a little older than the Photofit, and her hair was longer, but there were real similarities.

Steve looked at the photo for almost ten minutes.

Eventually he started typing:

'Dear Kimberley, your "friend" *Vanessa sent me an email as she believes you are the girl I have been looking for.*'

He stopped typing.

He erased the message.

He started typing a new one.

'*Hi, I know it sounds weird but I met a girl a few years ago and I wanted to see her again. Your friend Vanessa thinks this girl might be you. Of course it might not. But it might . . .*'

He deleted, he rewrote, he deleted again.

For the following half an hour Steve tried to find the best way of introducing himself to the girl who, as he was about to say, might or might not or might be the one he was looking for.

Eventually he wrote something he was satisfied with. Not pleased, but satisfied. And so he sent it.

CHAPTER TWENTY-THREE

The group of young children listened intently. To them, nothing else in the world was as important as the instructions currently echoing around the walls of the small scout hut.

'Simon says sit down . . . Simon says put your hands on your head . . . Simon says . . .'

'Simon says can you explain how you're charging a hundred pounds for this?!' whispered Sarah, the mother of the birthday girl, from the back of the room.

Kimberley and Vanessa laughed.

'Seriously,' Sarah continued, making sure her voice was only loud enough for her two friends to hear, 'a hundred quid just for doing some dreadful "magic" tricks, playing games and giving out sweets.'

'Don't forget the rabbit.'

Kimberley frowned. 'What rabbit?'

Vanessa explained. 'Right at the end, he puts the word 'RABBIT' into a box, taps the box, opens it, and lo and behold out comes a real rabbit. The kids go wild. Even though most of them have seen him at other parties and know it's going to happen. Then they all queue up to stroke the rabbit, after which they go home with a packet of Mr Birthday sweets, a Mr Birthday business card and no doubt some rare rabbit disease courtesy of Mr Birthday.'

Kimberley watched the children as they listened to whether or not Simon had actually 'said' that they should perform the next task. He hadn't. Another two children were sent to sit against the wall.

'When we were kids,' said Kimberley, 'our mums would do this themselves. They'd organise games, make the food . . .'

Sarah smiled. 'Cheese and pineapple on sticks . . .'

Kimberley cut in: 'Neatly presented, courtesy of a foil-covered grapefruit.'

The three of them laughed, a bit too loudly.

Mr Birthday looked over towards them. He didn't look happy.

Kimberley spoke quietly, trying not to move her lips: 'Simon says shut up!'

Vanessa adjusted baby Charlotte in her arm. She moved her head so that she was able to feed her more comfortably. She looked across at Amy fast asleep in her section of the double pram.

'How can she sleep through all this noise?'

Vanessa smiled. 'She can sleep through anything, that one. This one on the other hand . . .' She shifted Charlotte in her arm again, still trying to find a comfortable position.

'Anything I can do to help?' asked Kimberley.

'Not really, unless you want to breastfeed.'

'No, I've eaten, thanks.'

'You know PP hates me doing this in public. He says that showing everyone my breasts is embarrassing.'

'What?! This from the man who wanted to send topless photos of you to a Reader's Wives' page?'

'I know.'

Kimberley looked around the room. Sarah was now with Julie, her three-year-old daughter – the birthday girl. The other three and four-year-olds were eating, throwing their food or running around after balloons.

'I'm still not sure why Sarah invited me. Or, more to the point, why I came. I don't have children and I'm not that keen on other people's. Apart from yours obviously.'

'Obviously. Of course, mine aren't old enough to enjoy this anyway. It's just an excuse to get out of the house. And I'm happy with that.'

A balloon floated over to Kimberley, quickly followed by an out-of-breath small boy. Kimberley knocked the balloon with the palm of her hand and it floated back towards the boy.

The boy, thinking Kimberley wanted to play with him, knocked it back to her.

'You've made a friend,' said Vanessa.

'Well, he seems more mature than Robin was!'

Vanessa laughed. 'That's true.'

Kimberley went to return the balloon once more. This time she used the back of her hand. As she did, her ring, a square diamond in a gold setting which had been given to her by her grandmother while literally on her deathbed, burst the balloon.

Silence followed the explosion.

The children, mothers and the one father all looked towards Kimberley. The silence was broken by the sound of a cat being strangled. At least that's how it sounded to Kimberley. The little boy ran back to his mother, wailing, tears streaming down his face.

'Remind me not to invite you to their parties,' said Vanessa, nodding towards her daughters.

Kimberley nodded.

They sat in silence for a short while.

'Is everything all right, Ness?'

'Yes, why?'

'I don't know. You just seem . . . I don't know . . . not yourself.'

'I'm fine. Tired, that's all. Charlotte kept me up most of the night.'

'I bet PP was happy about that. Or did he sleep through it all again?'

Vanessa didn't answer. She adjusted Charlotte again, yet she still felt uncomfortable. In every way.

Kimberley wasn't sure how to play this. There was clearly something going on, but maybe Vanessa just didn't want to talk about it.

'I think PP's cheating on me.'

Kimberley looked at the floor. She looked at the children running about. She looked everywhere apart from at Vanessa's face.

'Did you hear what I said?'

Kimberley suddenly realised she was staring at the feeding child. She looked up. She didn't know what the correct response should be. With any of her other friends it would have been 'I don't believe it!' or 'Are you sure?' but with Vanessa . . . all that had come into her head was: 'And . . . ?'

She eventually went with: 'How did you find out?'

It seemed like a compromise.

'He's been meeting girls on the internet. He calls himself "Big Guy".'

Kimberley laughed out loud. The children all turned around. The mothers and the one father stared at her. To them, the evil childless woman who had burst the balloon was obviously enjoying herself.

Vanessa continued. 'I know. He could be sued for false advertising.'

'So . . . what have you said to him?'

'Nothing. Not yet. I'm not quite sure what to do. Knowing PP, he'll already have an excuse ready. He'll probably say that he just plans the dates but never turns up. Just does it for a laugh or something.'

Kimberley thought for a moment. 'Of course, there is one way you could find out if that's true.'

'How?'

'Contact him yourself.'

Vanessa looked puzzled. 'But . . . he'll know it's me.'

Kimberley sighed. 'I'll put it down to lack of sleep. Let me explain: you will pretend you are someone else – false photo, fake name, email address, etc. You will plan to meet somewhere, then you turn up and confront him.'

Vanessa looked for a flaw. She couldn't find one.

'That's brilliant!'

Kimberley started to take a bow.

'Although . . . he will know it's me when I turn up.'

Kimberley stopped mid-bow.

Vanessa smiled. 'I'm kidding. It's a brilliant idea. Oh, and talking about emails – I'm sorry again about giving that guy your email address. I don't know why I did it. He just seemed like a nice guy and—'

'And probably a nutter!'

'Is that your professional opinion, doctor?'

Another balloon floated over. The little girl who was chasing it stopped when she saw it reach Kimberley. Kimberley gently picked it up and carefully handed it to the girl. The girl tentatively reached for it. As soon as she grabbed it she ran off.

'Look, Ness, I appreciate that you think this bloke is searching for me. But he's not. He's just some sad, lonely guy. Do you really think I need someone like that in my life?'

Vanessa opened her mouth to speak.

Kimberley interrupted. 'That was rhetorical.'

CHAPTER TWENTY-FOUR

'Hi,' said Steve.

'Er . . . hi,' said Kimberley.

'Er . . . I'm Steve,' said Steve.

'Oh. Right,' said Kimberley.

Steve waited. He quickly realised that she wasn't going to say anything else. He wasn't quite sure what to say next. He looked down at her glass. It was full. He felt he should ask anyway and so pointed towards the bar.

'Er . . . can I get you a drink?'

'No, I'm fine, thanks.'

Steve frowned. It was an odd time for her to be playing hard to get.

He looked at the empty chair opposite her, which was currently occupied by Kimberley's coat and handbag.

'Can I . . . ?'

'Sorry,' said Kimberley, 'I'm waiting for someone.'

Steve frowned again. He went to speak and then stopped. Surely this was her. It must be. She looked like the photo. And she was sitting on her own. Waiting for someone. Wasn't it him?

'I'm Steve,' said Steve. He wasn't quite sure what else to say.

'So you said,' said Kimberley. 'And it's nice to meet you, but I really am waiting for someone.'

'But . . . aren't you Kimberley?'

It was Kimberley's turn to frown. 'Sorry, have we met before?'

'Er . . . no.'

They were now both confused.

'So . . . how do you know who I am?'

Steve didn't know what was going on. He wanted to walk out and come back in again.

The music in the bar changed from 'I Bet You Look Good on the Dancefloor' by The Arctic Monkeys to 'Push The Button' by Sugababes.

'I'm Steve,' said Steve for the third time. He suddenly became aware of how boring his name was. He wished he'd chosen to use his middle name instead. Troy had much more of a macho ring to it – even though his dad had actually named him after the captain of *Stingray*.

He ploughed on. 'You asked me to meet you here this evening.'

Kimberley frowned once more and suddenly became aware how wrinkled her brow must be. She quickly lifted her eyebrows.

Steve thought she had suddenly remembered.

'I'm sorry,' said Kimberley, 'you must be mixing me up with someone else. I'm meeting a friend.'

'Oh,' said Steve. 'Right. Well . . . that's all a bit of a coincidence really. Not to mention embarrassing. Anyway, I'm sorry to disturb you. Enjoy your evening.'

'Thanks.'

Steve, completely bemused, walked away from the table.

'Wait a minute!'

Steve turned around.

'What did you say your name was?'

You've got to be kidding, thought Steve.

'Steve,' said Steve. He really wished he'd gone with Troy.

Kimberley thought for a moment.

'And you came here to meet someone called Kimberley.'

'Well . . . yes.'

'At what time?'

'Seven o'clock . . . I'm pretty sure it was seven.' Steve put his hand into his pocket and took out a folded piece of paper. He opened it up and looked through it.

'Yes, seven o'clock.'

'May I have a look at that?'

Steve handed over the printout of his email.

Kimberley read it.

'*Dear Steve. Thanks for your email. Vanessa told me she had sent you my address. To be truthful I wasn't all that happy about it at first, but I know she did it with the best intention. I'm really not sure if I'm the girl you've been looking for. I know that some of the details match: age, location, sort of looks etc., but I really don't think it's me. However, if you would like to meet for a drink, I'd be willing to do that. What about the Three Horseshoes next Wednesday at 7? Look forward to hearing from you. Kimberley x. PS Please note my new email address.*'

Kimberley handed back the paper.

'I'll kill her.'

'Sorry?'

Kimberley sighed. 'My friend. Ex-friend. Enemy. Vanessa. She set me up.'

'Then you didn't send . . .' He waved the printout. 'This isn't you.'

'No. Although I do know who you are. Now. But to be honest, I had no intention of ever meeting you.'

'Oh.'

'Sorry.'

'No, don't worry,' said Steve. 'It's fine. Really. In fact this is one of the best dates I've ever had. They rarely last this long.'

Kimberley smiled. 'Sorry. It's just, you know, you're

looking for this girl – who definitely isn't me by the way, even though all my friends think it is – and, well, I just thought it was a bit . . .'

She paused.

Steve decided to help her out. 'Weird, strange, sad, pathetic?'

'Well . . . Yes. Although you missed out insane.'

'Damn, I always forget that one!'

Kimberley smiled again. 'Look, do you want to . . . sit down, for a minute?'

Steve looked at her. 'Are you sure. I mean the whole "I had no intention of ever meeting you" is slightly off-putting.'

Kimberley leant across the table and moved her coat and handbag.

Steve took their place.

CHAPTER TWENTY-FIVE

Jeff and Steve looked at the rows of cots in front of them. They turned and looked at the rows of prams behind them. They then turned back to the cots.

'Well, good luck.'

'What do you mean, "good luck"?! You're supposed to be helping me.'

Steve slowly turned and looked at Jeff; 'No, I am not meant to be helping you. I have just come to keep you company. You are meant to be doing this yourself. This was the task Francine set you.'

'But what do I know about cots and prams?'

'The same as Francine knows.'

'Rubbish. She's a woman.'

'Oh, of course,' said Steve, 'and as we know, women are born with the instinct to know which cots and prams are best for their unborn child!'

'May I help you?'

Steve and Jeff jumped. The sales assistant had appeared from nowhere. Like the shopkeeper in *Mr Benn*.

'Hi. I'm looking for a cot. And a pram. For a baby. Mine. My baby. Well, he's not born yet. Or she.'

'Excuse my friend,' said Steve. 'He rarely gets the chance to speak and tends to get a little over-excited.'

The assistant smiled. 'Have you any idea what you'd like?'

'Well, I'd prefer a boy, but apparently I'm not allowed to say that.'

'I meant, which pram and cot.'

'Oh, right. Sorry.'

'Would you like a complete pram and car-seat system? Just a pram? Would you prefer a three-wheeler? Or do you just want a buggy?'

Jeff stared at the assistant. He then turned and stared at Steve. He attempted a smile.

Steve sighed. 'His wife has ordered him to choose two potential prams and cots. She will then come in and tell him which of those two they'll buy. So what would you recommend? And no, a divorce isn't an option.'

**

'Jo has got a message! Jo has got a message!'

Steve and Jeff looked up from their coffees.

The girl on the table next to them was busily replying to the text message she had just noisily received.

'Should we let her know when that becomes annoying?' suggested Jeff.

Steve smiled.

'Anyway,' continued Jeff, 'as I was saying, when do you think you'll see her again?'

'I doubt if I ever will.'

Steve picked up his spoon and played with the piece of biscuit which had fallen into his cup and was now floating in the remainder of his coffee.

'Will you call her?'

'I don't have her number,' said Steve. 'I gave her mine – well, I gave her my card, but she didn't offer her number in return.'

He squashed the piece of biscuit with the back of the spoon.

'I have two choices—'

'Options,' corrected Jeff.

'Sorry?'

'You have two options. You only have one choice.'

Steve thought for a moment. 'Really? No, that can't be right. I mean, if I wanted to buy, say, a new car—'

'You can't drive; it would be pointless.'

'It's an example. If I go to a car showroom, then they have loads of choices of cars.'

'No, they have various *options*. It doesn't matter how many options you have, you're still only making one choice between them all. For example, tomorrow Francine will come and choose one of two prams and cots. Those are the options I gave her. Because, ironically, I had no choice.'

'Fine. My *options* are to never contact Kimberley again, or stalk her and beg her to see me again.'

'Both of which will lead to at least one of you being unhappy.'

'Jo has got a message! Jo has got a message!'

They both turned and looked at the girl. Oblivious to them and to the other people in the cafe, the girl read the text message and then replied.

'Whatever happened to baked-bean tins and string?' asked Jeff.

'But I can't just let it go, obviously. I mean this is the girl I have been searching for. I can't now go, "Great, found her, what shall I look for next? The Holy Grail? The Temple of Doom? Nemo?"'

'Why don't you ask your brother-in-law what the rules are on stalking? Maybe you can semi-stalk – just evenings and weekends.'

Their conversation was interrupted by loud rap music. Everyone in the cafe looked up. The girl at the next table answered her phone.

'Hi, you all right? . . . Yeah . . . Just got a text from Bigsy, everything's book with him . . . Yeah, wicked. Laters.' She switched off her phone.

Jeff turned to Steve. 'And they say the British can't speak a foreign language.'

'I know.'

'What is "book" anyway?' asked Jeff, 'I've heard them use it quite a lot recently.'

'It means "cool".'

'Eh?'

'Cool. It started when predictive text came in. If you write the word "cool" in predictive text, it comes up as "book". So they, and by "they" I mean the lazy youth of today, decided it was just easier to use the word "book" instead of having to select a whole new word.'

The rap music played loudly again. The girl answered her phone. 'Hey, dude, Liz just rang . . .'

Steve leant over to the girl.

'Excuse me . . .'

The girl looked at him. She spoke into her phone; 'Hang on, hun.' She turned to Steve. 'Yeah?'

'Would you mind speaking a bit quieter? It's really disturbing.'

The girl stared at him. She then spoke into her phone. 'I'll call you back in a minute. There's some rude old bloke in the cafe.'

She switched off her phone and finished what was left of her iced mocha.

'I wasn't the one being rude,' said Steve. '*You* were!'

The girl ignored him, got up and walked out.

'And I'm not old!'

Jeff smiled.

They both continued to drink their coffees. This was interrupted by a loud beeping sound. The people in the cafe looked around. It was Jeff's turn to get angry.

'You're right, this is ridiculous! I mean, we just wanted a quiet coffee. Whose phone is that now?'

Steve didn't reply. He was reading the text message he'd just received.

'You are kidding me!' said Jeff.

Steve looked embarrassed. Then, as he read the message, his expression changed to one of shock and then delight.

'It's from her!'

'Who, Kimberley?'

'No, the girl in the pram shop! Yes, of course Kimberley.'

'That's a shame. I quite liked the girl in the pram shop. She was cute. And young. Mainly young.'

'She'd like to see me again!'

'Really? That's great. Well done, mate. Don't reply to her text immediately though. Give it a couple of hours. Don't seem too keen. Or desperate.'

'Okay.'

Jeff looked at him. 'You've already replied, haven't you?'

Steve nodded.

His phone beeped loudly again. A couple of the other customers tutted.

'People are so rude,' said Jeff.

Steve read the message. He then turned to Jeff.

'I'm seeing her on Saturday night.'

CHAPTER TWENTY-SIX

Vanessa and Kimberley stared at the computer screen.

'So, where do we start?'

'Well, we'll have to set up a profile for you. What name would you like?'

'What's wrong with my own name?'

'Nothing. Except that if PP sees a profile for Vanessa Hicks, he might get ever so slightly suspicious.'

'Ah. Yes. Of course.' Vanessa thought for a moment. 'I could always use my middle name.'

'Good idea.'

Kimberley waited.

'What?' asked Vanessa.

'What is it? What's your middle name?'

Vanessa looked shocked. 'We've known each other for almost fifteen years. We've shared several top-and-tail nights in bed together. We've discussed our most intimate secrets, and you don't know my middle name?!'

'No. Is it Patrick?'

'It's Laura.'

'Very nice. Right, Laura it is then. Laura69.'

'Sorry?'

'Laura69. That's going to be your nickname. It can't just be Laura; it's too dull.'

'Thanks.'

'Anyway, there's probably a Laura on there already. And Laura69 leaves no doubt as to the kind of woman you are.

We'll just check to make sure no one else is using it.'

Kimberley typed *Laura69* into the nickname checker.

'It's available. So Laura69 it is. Now we need to work on your profile.'

For the next hour and a half Kimberley and Vanessa created a profile for Laura69. They decided that she would be thirty-two, married for five years, with one child and a husband who is no longer interested in sex. Laura69 however does like sex. Loves it in fact. And recently discovered that she is bi-curious. Kimberley had to explain this to Vanessa, who had thought she had said 'bike curious'.

They put her place of residence as Leeds – just to make meeting up that little more difficult. They set up an email address but didn't put down a telephone number. Although getting a new phone number would be easy, Vanessa knew there was no way she could disguise her voice from her husband.

'Now we need a photo,' said Kimberley. 'What's PP's type?'

'I thought I was,' murmured Vanessa quietly.

Kimberley turned away from the computer screen. She put her arm around her friend's shoulder.

'Shall we not do this? I mean, maybe it's not such a good idea. Wouldn't you prefer to confront him? Or just ignore it and hope it goes away – which I'm sure it will.'

Vanessa looked at Kimberley. She was determined not to cry.

'You're a doctor. You know that ignoring ailments doesn't cure them.'

Kimberley didn't respond. She wasn't sure what to say.

Vanessa took a breath. 'Brazilian.'

'Sorry?'

'That's his type. Brazilian. You know, dark, exotic-looking.'

Kimberley turned back to the computer. She typed *Brazilian girls* into the search engine.

'Well, there are almost two million pages. We should find something here.'

Kimberley clicked on *Images*. A page opened showing twenty pictures.

Vanessa and Kimberley stared.

'Right, well . . .' said Kimberley. 'That obviously isn't what I was looking for.'

'Surely that must itch after a while,' said Vanessa, staring at the pictures. 'You know, when the hair starts to grow back.'

'Probably, 'said Kimberley, who was already typing in a new search. 'Let's try *women from Brazil*.'

This time the result was what they wanted. They chose a picture of an attractive but not stunning Brazilian girl in her late twenties/early thirties, and uploaded it to the profile page. Once they had finished, they posted the profile on the *Dating Yet Married* website.

***

Vanessa poured the tea into Kimberley's cup. As she tipped the teapot back to a horizontal position, some splashed onto Kimberley's saucer.

'Sorry' said Vanessa.

Kimberley shook her head. 'I still don't know why you do it. I mean . . . teapot, cups and saucers. What is wrong with sticking a teabag into a mug? It tastes the same.'

'Not to me it doesn't. And it doesn't to my mum or to my mum's mum or—'

'Okay. Sorry I mentioned it.' Kimberley took a biscuit from the ones layered neatly on the doily-topped plate.

'So where are you going to go on your date?' asked

Vanessa. 'Maybe you should go back to the place where you first met, you know, for nostalgic reasons.'

Kimberley swallowed the remainder of the biscuit and wiped her mouth. 'Ha-ha.'

Vanessa smiled. 'I'm just pleased you're seeing him again. Now all I have to do is set up two other couples and I guarantee my place in heaven.'

'You're mad,' said Kimberley. 'And we're not a couple! This will be our second, or rather our first proper date. I hardly know anything about him – apart from the whole "searching for the girl of his dreams" bit.'

'You.'

Kimberley ignored the comment. 'Anyway, he's taking me to a comedy club. That's one of the few things I know about him – he's an agent for comedians. There's this new act he wants to see so he's asked me to go with him.'

Vanessa topped up her tea from the pot. 'So not only is he taking you somewhere where you won't be able to talk, but he'll also be able to write off the whole evening as a business expense! And they say romance is dead.'

'You cynic,' said Kimberley as she lifted up her cup. 'You're the one who . . .'

Before Kimberley could finish her sentence, her saucer, which a second earlier had been stuck to the bottom of her cup by the welding agents of tea and soggy biscuit, fell onto the kitchen table with a clatter. The two women looked at each other and waited for the inevitable.

Right on cue, from upstairs, the twins started to cry.

'Sorry,' said Kimberley. 'But that wouldn't have happened with a mug!'

CHAPTER TWENTY-SEVEN

The loud, predominantly female, laughter resonated around the club.

'And I'm not saying that my boyfriend is small, but you shouldn't have to ask him if he's put it in yet!'

The women laughed again.

'Just the women laughing there!'

More laughter of recognition.

'Why don't you fuck off and bring a comedian on?!'

The room went silent. One or two of the women in the audience quietly booed the heckler.

'What's the matter, handsome?'

The crowd all turned from the stage and looked at the man who had decided to heckle.

'You're not funny!'

'Yes, she is,' shouted one of the women in the audience.

'She's funnier than you!' said another one.

'Thanks for that,' said the comedian. 'But I'm not sure how great a compliment that is!'

The audience laughed.

The comedian turned back to the heckler. 'Well, it seems that the rest of the audience finds me funny.'

The audience, as one, cheered and applauded.

The heckler wasn't deterred. 'Well, I think you're shit!'

More booing. The room then waited for the comedian to respond.

'I'm sorry you feel that way. Although we both know

this is just your way of flirting with me.'

A laugh. This time from most of the men as well.

'Fuck off!'

'Wow, you're as good-looking as you are eloquent!'

A big laugh.

'Look, you're not going to win this,' continued the comedian. 'I'm a professional – but not like the type you sleep with.'

A huge laugh, together with cheering and a round of applause.

As the comedienne left the stage to sounds of appreciation, Kimberley leant over to Steve. 'She's the best one so far.'

Steve nodded in agreement.

'Let's hear it one more time for Lady Langley!' said the compère. The audience clapped and cheered again.

'Right then, keep that applause going and welcome onstage your next act . . . Mike Dutch!

'Is this who you've come to see?' asked Kimberley over the noise of the applause.

Steve nodded again.

Mike Dutch came out onto the stage. He was wearing the same 'Make War Not Peace' T-Shirt as on the cover of the DVD in Steve's office.

Mike Dutch grabbed the microphone from the stand and put the stand behind him.

'So, any disabled people in tonight? I mean real ones – not the ones who have a disabled badge because they're too fat to walk!'

There was laughter, but it was strained. The audience wasn't sure whether to laugh or not.

Kimberley looked surprised; not only at the material but

also at the fact that Steve was here to see this particular comedian.

Mike Dutch performed his material. It included, amongst other subjects, disabilities, cancer, AIDS and the mentally handicapped. Incredibly, although these subject matters were usually taboo and not an obvious source of comedic material, Mike managed to make some valid and funny observations. And he only alienated a minority of the crowd.

Towards the end of his set he turned his attention towards the audience. He looked at a man and a woman sitting together, stage left. 'So how long have you two been together?' he asked the man.

The man looked at the woman.

'Don't look at her for the fucking answer. I'm asking you!'

The man thought for a moment. 'Three and a half years.'

Mike turned to the woman. 'Is he right?'

'Just about,' said the woman.

'What type of fucking answer is "just about"? He's either right or he's not right. It's like saying, "I'm sort of a virgin."' This got a laugh. 'Not that you've said that – well, not since you were fourteen!'

This got a mixed response.

Mike then turned to the table next to them.

'And how long have you two been together?'

'Er . . . not long.'

'Another crap answer. How long, a month, a year, two years?'

'Er . . . well . . . this is our second date. Well, actually the first one.'

'Aaaaaw,' said the audience.

In retrospect Kimberley knew she shouldn't have answered, but she hadn't expected to be asked a question and she felt nervous and under pressure.

'What is it with you people?! So what is it – your first or second date? Surely you should know!'

'It's our first proper date,' said Kimberley.

Mike turned to Steve. 'So, mate, do you reckon you'll get your leg over tonight? Reckon she gives it up on the first date?'

Steve smiled uncomfortably.

'Don't talk much, do you?' said Mike. He held out his hand to Steve. 'What's your name, my friend?'

'Steve. Steve Connors.'

Mike looked at him.

'Fuck.' He turned to the audience. 'This is an agent who's come to see me perform. And I've just picked on his date!'

The audience laughed.

'Hang on a minute,' said Mike, turning back to Steve, 'I put two free tickets on the door for you. Are you telling me that you brought a girl on a date where you haven't had to pay anything? You cheap bastard!'

The audience and Kimberley laughed loudly.

***

'I'm sorry about that. I didn't know.'

'That's okay,' said Kimberley, 'The audience enjoyed it – even if I wasn't so keen on being a part of the show!'

Mike finished off the remainder of his water and put the empty bottle on top of the dressing-room fridge.

'So is it really your first date with him?'

'Well . . . yeah. Sort of. It's quite a long story.'

The door opened and Steve walked in. He was carrying

a pint and a half of lager and a glass of red wine. He gave the wine to Kimberley and the half-pint to Mike.

'Are you sure that's all you want?'

'Yes, thanks, Steve, I've got to drive to another gig in a minute.'

They each took a sip of their drinks.

'I know acts always say this, but you should have seen me last night. It was a much better gig.'

Steve smiled. 'I thought it was great. I'll be honest – your type of material isn't usually my cup of tea, but the audience really went with it and I can see why. You have good stage presence and you come across as really confident. And those people at the corporate gig I sent you to loved it. They want you for their annual dinner dance.'

'Hmm.' Mike shook his head. 'Those aren't my kind of thing.'

'They're paying two grand.'

'But I can adapt.'

Mike looked at his watch and finished his drink.

'I'd better make a move or I'll be late for the next gig.'

'Okay. I'll give you a call in a day or so.'

They all shook hands. Mike picked up his bag and left the dressing room.

After he'd gone, Kimberley turned to Steve. 'He's much quieter and nicer offstage.'

'A lot of them are,' said Steve.

'So are you going to take him on?'

Steve nodded. 'I wasn't going to, but . . . he's going to be big. I used to only book acts I liked, but I have a business to run so I know I also have to offer what others like. I doubt if Mr Cadbury likes *all* the chocolates he makes.'

The dressing-room door opened and Lady Langley walked in.

'Oh, hi,' she said. She was surprised, and not particularly pleased, to find people in the dressing room. Especially people she didn't know.

'Hi,' said Steve, holding out his hand; 'I'm Steve Connors from On The Edge agency.'

'Oh, yeah, hi. Mike mentioned you were coming along.'

There was a brief pause. Kimberley gave a sideways glance at Steve. She then held out her hand. 'I'm Kimberley. I thought you were terrific.'

Lady Langley shook Kimberley's hand. 'Thanks very much.'

Kimberley was a little annoyed that Steve hadn't introduced her himself.

The thing was, Steve had thought about it but didn't know quite how to do it. He couldn't say, 'This is Kimberley, my girlfriend,' as it was only their first date! And 'This is Kimberley, my friend' sounded like he had no interest in her other than friendship. And saying the truth – 'This is Kimberley, the girl I have spent half my life tracking down' – was probably a bit too much information.

'Who looks after you?' asked Steve.

Lady Langley opened the door of the fridge and took out a bottle of water.

'No one. I book my own gigs. I was with the ACK Agency for a while but they weren't really getting me anything I couldn't get myself – and still taking fifteen per cent for it.'

Steve nodded. He'd heard this several times from various comedians. He knew he had actually been guilty of it himself. Once a comedian had reached a certain level, they didn't need an agent to get live work for them. They needed someone who could get them other things, like television and radio slots.

Steve handed over a card. 'Give me a call sometime. I was really impressed with what you did. The material as well as the way you dealt with the heckler.'

Lady Langley took the card. 'Okay, I will. Cheers.'

Steve and Kimberley said their goodbyes, left the dressing room and walked back out into the club.

The tables and chairs had been moved away and a disco was now in full swing. About a third of the audience had remained behind to drink, chat and dance. A hen night was dancing to 'YMCA', complete with acronym arm movements.

As they walked towards the exit, 'YMCA' segued into 'The Way You Make Me Feel' by Michael Jackson. Steve stopped. He turned to Kimberley.

'I can't believe they're playing this! This is the song that always reminds me of you!'

Kimberley look surprised; 'When did you have the chance to make that memory? That night in the pub?'

'No,' said Steve, 'it was in the disco. *Angels*. In 1988. It was playing as I left the club and saw you for the second time. It just sort of stuck in my head. Every time I hear it I think of that moment.' Steve stopped. He realised how ridiculous he sounded. 'I'm going to stop talking now.'

Kimberley smiled.

Steve opened the door of the club for her and watched her for a moment as she walked up the stairs towards the exit. He wondered what the future held for them, if anything. He then followed after her, letting the door to what was now a nightclub swing close behind him.

The song faded into the distance.

CHAPTER TWENTY-EIGHT

Steve looked at the tiny newborn baby sleeping in Kimberley's arms. He looked so full of peace. Steve then looked at Kimberley.

'He's . . . perfect.'

Kimberley smiled. 'Yes. Yes, he is.'

Steve looked back at the baby. 'Although, he does he look a little . . . yellow.'

'A touch of jaundice, that's all,' said Kimberley. 'That'll go.'

Steve nodded – as though he knew what Kimberley was talking about.

They both looked down at the little face, peeping out from its blanket cocoon.

'I want to call him Norrin.'

Kimberley looked up. So did Steve. They both turned to the door, where Jeff was helping Francine into the room.

'Norrin?' repeated Kimberley. 'I've never heard that name.' She turned to Steve. 'Have you?'

Steve sighed and nodded.

'It's apparently the real name of the Silver Surfer,' explained Francine. 'And no, we're not considering it.'

Jeff helped her to sit on the bed. She tightened up the bathrobe that was covering her regulation hospital backless gown.

'Well what about Clark Kent? Or—'

Francine stopped him by speaking louder. 'How many

times do I have to tell you? We are not naming our son after a comic-book character!'

Jeff muttered to himself, 'It's not like I wanted to call him Wolverine.'

Kimberley passed the as-yet unnamed baby back to its mother.

Francine took him. 'We'll probably go with Daniel.' She lay him down in the plastic crib next to the bed.

Jeff looked confused. 'Why Daniel?'

Francine turned to her husband. 'After your father.'

Jeff frowned. 'My father's name was Eric.'

'But I don't like the name Eric.'

There was a confused silence. Steve and Kimberley exchanged a look.

Steve got up. 'Well . . . we'd better make a move.'

Kimberley almost jumped out of her chair.

'Yes. Congratulations again.'

They all exchanged kisses – except Jeff and Steve who just exchanged a brief nod.

***

Steve and Kimberley walked out of the hospital building and across the car park.

They were both thinking the same thing.

'Do you . . . er . . . do you ever want to have . . . er—'

Kimberley interrupted. 'Maybe. One day. You?'

'Mmm. Sure. One day.'

The remaining walk to the car was in silence.

As Kimberley approached, she pressed the button on her key fob to unlock the doors.

'So, what do you fancy doing tonight?'

Kimberley shrugged.

'We could go to the Thai Castle.'

'Again? We're there more often than the chef!'

They got into the car, Kimberley on the driver's side.

'What about the cinema then?' suggested Steve.

She pulled her seat belt across her body and clicked it into place.

'What's on?'

'I don't know.'

Kimberley turned to him.

'You know, we don't *have* to go out. We can just stay in and watch a film or something.'

'But it's a Saturday night. You're not on call and I don't have to go and see any acts.'

Kimberley peeled off the pay-and-display sticker from the inside of the windscreen and folded it into the spotless ashtray. 'Then that's a good reason to stay in. We're not eighteen. We're not going to go clubbing, and anywhere we do go will be busier and noisier than the rest of the week.' She started the car and reversed out of her parking space.

'We're getting old, aren't we?'

Kimberley smiled. 'Yes, we are. It's another disease that has no cure.'

'Happy thought. Okay, we'll stay in then. My place or yours?'

'Mine!' said Kimberley.

They both realised how quickly she had said it.

'What's wrong with *my* place? We hardly ever stay there,' said Steve.

'There's nothing wrong with it. Nothing at all.'

She put the car into first gear and drove off.

'It smells a bit, doesn't it?'

'A bit.'

Steve sighed. 'I don't know what it is. I've tried Shake n' Vac and everything. Okay. I'll come to yours. Again. I just feel like I'm there all the time.'

'Well, either there or the Thai Castle.'

'Yes, but I can't see me moving into the Thai Castle.'

Not for the first time in his life, Steve wished he had the ability to reverse time. Not a great amount, not like to go back and stop wars or anything, but just enough to stop himself saying some words. Or sleeping with a particular girl.

In this instance it was the words.

'I didn't mean . . . I wanted to move in. Obviously.'

'I know.'

'I just meant . . . I didn't want to move into the Thai Palace.'

'I know. I know what you meant.'

Steve looked awkwardly out of the window at the passing houses.

'You're going to hurt your neck like that.'

Steve sat up straight.

'And I wish you'd wear a seat belt.'

'I've told you why I don't.'

'Yes, you have. And it's the most puerile reason I have ever heard.'

'No, it's not! I would be happy to wear one if it wasn't a law. I don't mind the government *suggesting* I do things for my own good, but I don't expect them to make a law about it. What's next – a law to stop me from putting my finger in the fire?!'

'And if there were that law, would you then do it every day?'

'No, of course not.'

Kimberley opened her window.

'Oh, I'm sorry,' she said. 'I just opened my window and now your argument has flown right out.'

'Oh, very clever,' said Steve. 'And stop looking so pleased with yourself.'

He put on his seat belt.

They sat in silence for a short while.

As Kimberley came to a set of traffic lights, she stopped, put on the handbrake, put the car into neutral and turned to Steve.

'Steve, would you like to move in with me?'

CHAPTER TWENTY-NINE

As usual the cafe in the leisure centre was almost full. Most of the women there had become members just to socialise and weren't interested in the state-of-the-art gym facilities on offer in the rest of the complex.

Although Kimberley and Vanessa did use the tennis courts and pool occasionally, today they were also meeting just to use the cafe. Vanessa had wanted to leave her house for a while, and so had asked her mother to babysit. Reluctantly she had agreed; Vanessa's mother wasn't a huge fan of children, including her own. As Kimberley only had an hour for her lunch break and the leisure centre was close to the surgery they had decided to meet there.

As Kimberley chased a cherry tomato around her plate with her fork, Vanessa stared at her.

'So . . . what made you ask?'

'I'm not sure, Ness. I just thought . . . it made sense. He doesn't like his flat, and his landlord is a real pain in the rectum. He's at mine most weekends and at least one other night in the week. It just seemed logical.'

Kimberley stabbed the tomato and put it into her mouth.

'And –' she swallowed and then continued – 'it means instead of paying rent he can help towards the mortgage. It also means I don't have to spend another night in his flat with its . . . odd odours.'

Vanessa laughed. She finished the remainder of her salad, excluding her cucumber and peppers, placed her knife and fork together and pushed her plate a couple of inches away from her towards the centre of the table. As her plate was virtually empty and her cutlery lay side by side, it was obvious that she had finished eating, yet she always felt that this small action of slightly pushing the plate away was the final required act.

Kimberley picked up her glass and sucked up the last dregs of her strawberry-and-mango juice through her bendy straw. As the last drop disappeared she accidentally made a loud 'slurping' sound. Two elderly ladies, who had just finished their aerobics class and were sitting at the next table, looked over at her with disdain.

As Vanessa laughed, Kimberley felt her face redden.

Vanessa then leant in closely to Kimberley.

'I forgot to tell you, I have some news.'

'What about?'

'Well, actually, *I* haven't had the news; Laura69 has!'

Kimberley eyes widened. She also leant in closer. They were now almost touching noses. Realising how ridiculous they looked, Kimberley moved back.

'Well,' said Vanessa, 'as you know, I've had, or rather *she's* had, over a hundred emails since you set it up. But nothing from PP. Until now.'

Kimberley looked surprised. For two reasons.

'You've waited until we've finished lunch before telling me?!'

'I didn't want to spoil your appetite.'

'Go on, what's happened?'

Vanessa pushed her plate further away. There was no doubting she'd finished.

'Well, the last time I checked Laura's emails there was an email from PP, although I didn't know it was from him immediately. He was using a different email address to his normal one – obviously the one he uses for other women. But the photo was him, complete with his usual bad grammar and spelling.'

'So what did he say?'

In her excitement, Kimberley accidentally slurped again.

The elderly ladies looked again. Kimberley ignored them.

'Well, he introduced himself, said he was married, which he spelt with one *r*, and that he had two kids.'

'At least he's honest.'

Vanessa looked at her.

'I mean "honest" in the literal sense.'

Vanessa continued. 'Anyway, he told me the area where he lived and then started telling me about me. Which was weird. And unpleasant. He didn't say my name, thankfully, but apparently I don't want to have sex very often and haven't really wanted to since the children were born.'

'What a horrible thing to write.'

Vanessa looked down at the table.

Kimberley felt a little uncomfortable. 'Is that . . . true?'

Vanessa nodded.

'Well, that happens. But it doesn't justify infidelity.'

'Well, I still don't know if he actually *has* slept with anyone else,' said Vanessa who for some reason had decided to suddenly defend her husband. 'It could all just be online flirting. He hasn't had any text messages from other women.'

'How do you know?'

'I check his phone regularly.'

'Maybe he has another phone,' suggested Kimberley, 'one he uses for . . .' She stopped herself and changed tack. 'Maybe you're right. Maybe it is all about flirting, just trying to give himself an ego boost.'

Vanessa sighed. 'Well, I'm about to find out. He asked

when we could meet. He said he'd try and find a way to get to Leeds if I couldn't get down to see him.' Vanessa laughed at herself. 'Listen to me: "If *I* couldn't get down . . ." It's not me he's writing to. He's writing to someone else . . .' She slowed down as she felt the tears welling up.

'Someone . . . someone he'd prefer to be with instead of me.'

Despite her hardest efforts, she couldn't prevent the tears from rolling down her cheeks.

'Who am I kidding? Of course he's being unfaithful!'

Kimberley stroked her friend's arm. 'I'm so sorry, Ness. Maybe this whole thing was a bad idea. Maybe you should have just confronted him.'

Vanessa shook her head. She picked up a napkin from the table and used it to dab underneath her eyes.

'I . . .' She coughed in an attempt to clear her voice. 'I'm not sorry we did it. And I'm still planning to meet him. I want to see the look on his face when he realises I'm her. I mean she's me. You know what I mean.'

Kimberley nodded. 'So . . . have you replied?'

'No, not yet. I've got to think how to play it . . .' She looked up and, even though she didn't really feel like it, forced a smile.

'And . . . I do have an idea.'

CHAPTER THIRTY

Steve looked through the French windows into the garden. There he was as a three-year-old, running around exploring. Then as a ten-year-old, playing football with his friends and breaking two panes of glass in the garden shed. Then as a fifteen-year-old with different friends, smoking behind the same shed.

'Are you sure you don't want anything to eat?'

Steve turned away from the window and his memories.

'No, thanks, Mum, I'm fine. I had a sandwich on the train.'

'What? But they're so expensive, Steven. Five pounds for a sandwich? It's just two slices of bread. Their mark-up must be something like a thousand per cent!'

She put two cups of tea on the small occasional table. She then sat down on the sofa opposite her son.

'So how's work going?'

'Yeah. Good. Better. It's picked up a lot recently. I've got a couple of new clients, and even the older ones are getting more work.'

'That's good. Oh, by the way, did you hear about Tracy Brown?'

'You mean Tracy Edwards,' said Steve. 'That's her married name. No, I didn't hear anything.'

'Well, it's Tracy Brown again. Her husband left her.'

'Oh. That's a shame.'

Steve drank a sip of his tea. There was too much milk as usual, but as usual he didn't mention it.

'Maybe you should give her a call. You always liked her. And she'd probably love to hear from you.'

Steve put the milky drink back onto the table. 'Well, as delightful as the idea of ringing an ex-girlfriend sounds, especially one who has just been dumped and will no doubt be on the rebound, I'll decline. Apart from anything else . . . I'm seeing someone.'

Steve's mum smiled.

Steve knew that smile. It was the smile he'd seen a thousand times. It was the smile she used every time Steve had a new girlfriend. Or failed an exam in school. Or failed his driving test again. It was the smile that said, 'Don't worry. Better luck next time.'

Steve's mum had seen girlfriends come and go over the years. At first when he brought a new one to meet her she'd be delighted, thinking that this might be the one, the one that would make him forget about the girl from that disco and get on with his life. But it never was. Tracey Brown/Edwards/Brown had been the closest.

'This is the one, Mum.'

The smile again, followed by, 'I'm pleased to hear it.'

'No, seriously. This is the one. The one I've been looking for. The one from the disco.'

The smile was replaced by a look of shock.

'What? Really? Are you sure?'

Steve nodded.

'But . . . how . . . ? When . . . ?'

Steve drank some more hot milk. 'Well, I've actually been seeing her for a few months. I didn't tell you because . . . well, because you've seen so many come and go.'

'I wouldn't say that,' she lied.

'Anyway, I wanted to make sure. And now I am. And

I'm moving in with her, in a couple of weeks' time.'

Steve's mum was still in shock. 'I don't know what to say. I just wish your father was alive to hear this.'

Steve sighed. 'He is alive, Mum.'

'Shhh!'

Steve's mum anxiously looked around the room.

Steve shook his head. 'There's no one here.' He hesitated. 'Which . . . which brings me to a subject you're not going to be happy to discuss.'

'Do I need to sit down?'

Steve frowned. 'You are sitting down.'

'I know. But I was going to stand up. But I won't if I need to sit down. With my back I don't want to be bobbing up and down every two minutes.'

'Either is fine. Maybe sit down. Anyway, the thing is . . . I really like this girl. And maybe, sometime in the future I might like to marry her. And if I did, then I'd like to ask Dad to come to . . .'

Steve's mother stood up and walked towards the kitchen. She stopped in the doorway and rubbed her back. 'I knew I should have stood up earlier.'

***

By the time Steve followed his mother into the kitchen she had already started pouring flour into a bowl.

'Okay. If it happens, if we do decide to get married, then I won't invite him. I obviously don't want to upset you. But he's still my father. And he's alive. And I won't lie to Kimberley – that's her name by the way – and pretend that he's dead.'

Steve's mother started mixing butter into the flour.

'And what am I supposed to say to people? "Oh, you know

I said my husband had died on holiday in Spain and we buried him there?" Well, I lied. He's actually been living in Spain for fifteen years with a girl who's young enough to be his daughter. I just made up that story to save myself embarrassment.'

'You should never have started the lie in the first place.'

'He should have never had the affair in the first place!'

The speed of the mixing increased.

Steve watched in silence for a while.

'Lemon-curd tarts?'

'Roly-poly.'

'Nice. Look, it probably won't even get that far. I mean, we might never get married – which would probably make it easier all round. But I'm not going to lie to her.'

Steve's mum looked at him. 'Like your father did to me.'

For a while Steve watched his mother work in silence.

'So when did you last hear from him?'

'Why?'

'Just curious.'

'I had an email from him last week. Apparently Kate . . .'

Steve's mum turned sharply to her son, her eyes wide with anger.

'Sorry. I mean, "the whore" has started a midwifery course.'

'Oh, I'm delighted for her. It's nice to know she's helping to bring families together, after managing to tear ours apart.'

She wiped her hands on her 'World's Best Mum' apron and switched on the oven.

'So when am I going to meet her?'

Steve looked shocked. 'Meet her? Why would you want to meet her?'

It was his mum's turn to look shocked. 'She's your girlfriend. The one you've been looking for your whole life. Why don't you want me to meet her?'

'Oh. I thought you were talking about Kate.'

'Why would I want to meet *her*?!'

'I know. That's what I thought. Anyway, I was going to bring Kim over one Sunday.'

'Lovely. I'll do a quiche or some salmon. Probably with a salad and new potatoes. Nothing too fancy. Does she cook?'

'Yes. Very well. Although by the time she finishes work she's usually tired so we either go out or have a takeaway.'

Steve's mum shook her head. 'Takeaways? Just like your sister! Your generation doesn't cook any more. So what does she do?'

'She's a doctor.'

Even though Steve had said this many times, he still felt proud. And he still smiled every time he said it.

'Really? A doctor? Very nice.'

Steve's mum bent down, opened the bottom drawer next to the oven, took out an oven glove in the shape of a shark's head and stood up. She rubbed the base of her spine.

'Maybe she can have a look at my back.'

CHAPTER THIRTY-ONE

Kimberley walked into the small flat and closed the door behind her. She grimaced as the smell hit her. She knew she'd never have got used to it. She walked into the tiny living room and was immediately taken aback by the mountain of boxes. Any moment she expected a 1970s' car chase to come crashing through them.

They were all labelled in thick black marker pen and ranged from *VIDEOS AND DVDS* to *MISCELLANEOUS*. However only one box was marked *VIDEOS AND DVDS*. The rest were marked *MISCELLANEOUS*. Kimberley wondered why Steve had bothered with the marker pen in the first place.

She called out: 'Steve?'

'Hi, babe.'

Kimberley could hear him but had no idea where he was. It sounded as though he were replying from inside one of the boxes.

She walked around the cardboard wall.

There was Steve, sitting on the floor reading comics. Jeff was with him.

'What's going on?'

'Well,' said Jeff, 'Spider-Man is about to be unmasked by the Green Goblin and . . .'

Kimberley stared at him.

'Sorry,' said Jeff.

Steve got up and kissed Kimberley. 'We were just finishing packing and . . . we came across some of these comics. I'd forgotten all about them. They're really good.'

Kimberley then noticed a pile of men's magazines. She picked one up.

'We came across those as well,' said Jeff.

Steve and Jeff giggled.

Kimberley sighed.

'How's Daniel?' she asked.

'He's great, thanks,' said Jeff. 'We're still not getting much sleep though.'

He corrected himself; 'Well, *Francine's* not sleeping much. I have a tendency not to hear him in the night. I don't know why.'

'Maybe it's the earplugs,' suggested Steve.

'You know me,' said Jeff. 'If I don't get at least eight hours, I can't do anything. And I'm the only breadwinner at the moment so I have to be on top of my game. Someone has to keep the wolf from the door.'

'Absolutely,' said Steve. 'Those clichés won't write themselves.'

Jeff smiled sarcastically.

'Talking of which,' continued Steve, 'the next time I ask you when you fancy going out and you say, "I'll see when I have a window," I will physically push you through one.'

'Fifty-nine,' said Kimberley.

'Sorry,' said Steve and Jeff simultaneously.

'Jinx!' Jeff shouted excitedly to Steve. 'Now you can't speak until I say your name three times or you'll be cursed!'

Steve and Kimberley stared at him. Kimberley then turned to Steve.

'There are fifty-nine boxes. There's no way you'll be able to keep all this stuff at my flat.'

Steve looked shocked. 'But there was double this amount! I've thrown loads away. I've only kept the essentials.'

Kimberley opened one of the boxes. She took out a pile of video tapes. 'These are Betamax. Do you have a Betamax player?'

'No. Mine broke. But I'm going to get a new one.'

Kimberley stared at him.

'You're right,' said Steve. 'It's unlikely they're bringing out a new model. I'll chuck them.'

Jeff pointed to a small suitcase. 'Oh, by the way, the stuff that's in there is all for you, Kim.'

Kimberley opened the case. 'These are all trousers!'

'Well, apparently you're the one who's going to be wearing them!' Jeff laughed loudly and proudly.

Kimberley looked out of the window.

'Oh, Francine's just arrived.'

Jeff immediately stopped smiling and jumped up. 'Why's she here? I told her that I was going to do some food shopping. What . . . ?'

He stopped and turned to Kimberley. It was her turn to smile proudly.

'Very good. Really. Very funny.' Jeff sat down again.

Kimberley, trying to hide how pleased she was with herself, turned to Steve. 'I'm sorry, Steve, there just isn't the room. Have a look through all these again and see what you can throw away, or maybe keep in the office.'

Steve got up. He kissed Kimberley on the cheek. 'Sure.'

He picked up a box. This was a small box which had wrapping paper and a bow around it.

'I was going to give you this after I moved in, but . . . I can't wait.'

Kimberley looked for somewhere to sit down. She frowned.

'Have you packed your chairs as well?'

Steve sighed. 'No, the landlord took them. He needed them for another flat of his.'

Jeff went down on all fours. 'Allow me.'

Kimberley smiled. She sat on Jeff's back and opened the box. When she saw what was inside, Kimberley's face lit up.

'The earrings! You bought the earrings!'

She bounced up and down.

'Ow!'

'Oh, sorry, Jeff!'

She slid off Jeff's back, ran over to Steve and threw her arms around him.

'I thought they sold them!'

'They did. To me!'

She turned to Jeff to explain. 'We saw them in a shop window last week and I said how much I loved them. I went back to buy them the next day but they'd gone.'

'I bought them,' said Steve.

'Yes,' said Jeff. 'I picked up on that.'

Kimberley kissed Steve and hugged him again.

She then pulled back. 'Well, knowing that you can't keep things secret for too long and guessing that you'd buy me a present, I bought you something too.'

She opened her handbag and took out an envelope. She handed it to Steve.

'Is it a cheque?'

Kimberley smiled.

Steve opened the envelope and took out a small circular piece of paper.

'It's a . . . parking permit.'

'Yes,' said Kimberley proudly, 'it's your own parking permit so you can park outside the flat.'

Steve looked confused.

'You are kidding!' said Jeff. He turned to Steve. 'You haven't told her that you can't drive?!'

'Of course she knows I can't drive!' said Steve. He then turned to Kimberley. 'Which is why this is, you know, nice, but . . . slightly redundant.'

'Oh, silly me,' said Kimberley. 'I gave you the wrong present first.'

She handed a second envelope to Steve, which he quickly ripped open.

'Driving lessons?'

'Yes. A crash course . . .'

She quickly turned to Jeff. 'Don't say it.'

Jeff closed his readily prepared mouth.

'It's a six-week refresher course,' continued Kimberley, 'and I have booked your test date for two months' time.'

'You know he's failed three times.'

Kimberley smiled. 'Yes, Jeff. But he's also failed at finding the right girl – until now.'

Steve took Kimberley in his arms and hugged her.

CHAPTER THIRTY-TWO

Steve, dressed smartly in a jacket and trousers instead of his usual jeans and T-shirt, stood and watched as the mark on the wall – the mark he had been creating since the first day he sat in his office chair and leant back – was erased with one swift brush stroke.

John Queen, having that sixth-sense feeling that he was being watched, turned around to see Steve standing in the doorway.

'Hi. How was lunch?'

Steve smiled. 'Yeah, good, thanks. They want Mike Dutch to host the new series of *When Celebrities Fail.*

'Will he do it?'

Steve nodded. 'Oh yes. Even if they were only offering *half* the money they've suggested.'

'Wow. Looks like I left stand-up at the wrong time. Oh, talking of which, look what I found behind one of the cabinets!'

John Queen wiped his hands on his paint-speckled jeans and picked up a poster. On it was a picture of his own, much younger, yet also strangely old-looking face.

'*For Queen and Country!* I can't believe that's the title I went with!'

Steve grinned. 'I did *attempt* to change your mind but . . . that was never easy.'

'No. I guess it wasn't.' John sighed. 'That's what excessive drink and drugs do.'

He put down the poster, picked up a notepad and looked through what he'd written.

'You've had quite a few calls; there are various names and numbers here, one or two I recognise from the old days. Kevin Summer rang to thank you for sending out his DVD and getting him the gig.'

Steve nodded.

John continued reading. 'Oh, and Chrissie rang! It was so nice to speak to her, I haven't spoken with her in years!'

Steve frowned. 'Who?'

John was surprised by the question. 'Chrissie. Lady Langley.'

'Oh, of course. It's going to take me a while to get used to her real name.'

'We had a nice chat actually. You know we used to have a . . . thing?'

Steve nodded. 'Yeah, it wasn't exactly one of the *big* circuit secrets. Everyone knew.'

'Yes,' said John, 'apart from my girlfriend.'

Steve had thought this, but had decided not to say it.

'It's great that you've taken her on, Steve; she deserves a good agent.'

'Thanks.'

John picked up his brush and continued to paint the wall.

Steve looked around. 'This looks great, John. Really nice. Who knew you had such a hidden talent?'

John smiled as he continued his work.

'Do you ever miss stand-up?'

John didn't stop to answer. He'd been asked this many times.

'I thought I would but I don't. To be truthful I don't know how I ever did it. Well, I do – I was always off my head on something or other. But the thought of going onstage now . . .' He shuddered. 'I couldn't think of anything worse. I still meet up with old circuit friends from time to time, and even hearing about the gigs they've done – trying to get a room full of stag and hen nights just to listen to the material they've sweated over – it makes the hairs on the back of my neck stand on end. Which is tricky when you're bald!'

Steve laughed.

'I'm glad you're doing so well though, Steve. I mean, it's a shame you lost Gareth, but you've got some great new acts.'

Steve smiled. 'Yeah, I guess things could be a lot worse.'

CHAPTER THIRTY-THREE

Kimberley walked into her kitchen, or, as she now saw it, her and Steve's kitchen. Neither of them had lived with anyone since their student days, so they had both expected it to take a while to get used to. They had both been wrong – one of the other many things they were to discover they had in common. Of course they weren't compatible in every way; Kimberley was meticulously tidy, almost to the point of obsession, had no interest in comic books or sci-fi films and loved living in her two bedroomed flat in West Hampstead. Steve was having difficulty with the location. Since leaving Reading, he had always been based in south London. Living north of the river seemed almost foreign to him. But he knew he could, and would, adapt; getting used to the area, learning not to leave his clothes on the floor, remembering to use coasters. Everything.

But they did have many things in common; they had the same taste in food, the same view of religion and the same disinterest in politics, but they also found out that their general day-to-day lives were similar. They both only liked to have a coffee for breakfast, they both disliked all reality TV shows (even though, it could be argued, they actually met because of one) and they both liked to cook – which was occasionally the source of mild disagreement.

Tonight, however, Steve was cooking. Or at least attempting too. He was currently, while dressed in the 'hilarious' naked woman apron Jeff had bought him, wiping the top of the electric hob. The damp cloth sizzled as it hit the hot surface.

'Don't worry; we'll clean it up later. How's it coming along?'

Steve sighed. 'Well, let's put it this way: the guacamole is the only thing that isn't burnt!'

Kimberley smiled. She raised herself up slightly and kissed him on the cheek.

'I'm sure it's all fine.'

Steve stirred the sauce, being careful not to spill any more over the side of the saucepan.

'Try this. Tell me if it's too spicy.'

He scooped some of the sauce onto the wooden spoon, blew it and held it towards Kimberley's mouth. Kimberley also blew it and then tasted it. Steve waited.

'Well?'

'I gan't veel ny licks.'

'Oh, ha-ha. Seriously, is it too hot?'

Kimberley smiled. 'It's . . . a little warm, both temperature and spice-wise, but there's no point in making Mexican food if it doesn't have a bit of a kick.'

'But you know what Francine's like.'

'Yes, but she's not the only one coming, is she? There'll be eight of us. And you can't please everyone. And you certainly can't please her. Do you need me to do anything?'

'Yes, I do. And it's quite important. Can you take one of the beers from the fridge, open it . . .'

Kimberley waited. 'And?'

'That's it. I'll do the rest!'

Kimberley punched him on the arm and opened the fridge. As she did, the doorbell rang. Steve looked at the fridge.

'Nice trick.'

Kimberley looked at the clock on the kitchen wall. She checked the time against her watch. She panicked.

'It's only quarter to!'

'Sorry. It'll be my sister. I forgot to tell you – she's incredibly punctual.'

'Three-quarters of an hour early isn't punctual! It's just as bad as being late! Worse!'

She quickly started to tidy up the kitchen. 'I haven't laid the table, I'm not changed . . .'

Steve put his hand on her shoulder. 'I'll answer the door and then I'll lay the table. You go and get changed.'

Kimberley looked at him. She then ran out of the kitchen and into the bedroom.

Steve looked at the open fridge.

'I'll get the beer myself then!'

He took a bottle of lager from the fridge and walked towards the front door.

'Hi, sis.'

Sheila kissed her brother and held up a pink hydrangea.

'I've got you a plant.'

'Oh,' said Steve. 'Now you've spoilt the surprise!'

Steve held out his hand towards his brother-in-law. Dave took it and shook it with one hand and held out a plastic bag with the other.

'I man. I bring beer.'

Steve took the bag. 'And I have a feeling that tonight we're going to need them.'

'Really? In that case, I'll start now.'

Dave took the chilled bottle of lager from Steve's hand and walked past him into the flat. Steve closed the door and followed.

'So who's coming exactly?' asked Dave.

'Well, apart from the four of us, there's Jeff and his wife Francine – who you met once before . . .'

Dave frowned. 'I don't remember her.'

'Yes, you do,' said Sheila, as she looked around for somewhere to put the plant. 'We met her in Steve's flat. She complained about anything and everything and constantly picked on Jeff.' She went into the living room.

Dave shrugged.

'You'll remember her when you see her.' Steve handed him the bottle opener and started to put the contents of the carrier bag into the fridge. 'There's also another couple. Kimberley's friend Vanessa, who's very nice, and her husband PP. Who isn't.'

'Steve!'

They turned around to see Kimberley walk in from the bedroom.

'Sorry,' said Steve. 'I only said it because . . . I thought you couldn't hear me.'

***

'So . . . can you arrest people without your hat on?'

The other people at the table looked at PP. They then looked at Dave.

'Er . . . if you mean can I arrest them when I'm not on duty, then yes. I always carry my warrant card and badge on me.'

'So, if you like see a fight or something, you could go in and break it up and arrest everyone.'

Dave looked a little awkward. 'Well, it's not as straightforward as that. You have to assess the situation and—'

'Do you know how to use a gun?'

'Er . . . yes, I have firearms training. I obviously don't carry one, but—'

'And if you get caught drunk-driving – which I've never been, by the way . . .'

'What – caught?' suggested Jeff.

This brought slight light relief to the question-and-answer session. PP ignored it.

'If you get caught, right, what's the best way to get out of it? Can you refuse a breath test? Should you offer a urine sample? Can you—'

'Come on,' said Vanessa, smiling. 'Let Dave eat his food.'

PP, annoyed, turned to his wife. 'I'm. Just. Asking.'

'The best thing,' said Dave, in an attempt to end the interrogation, and change the atmosphere, 'is not to drink and drive in the first place. Then you won't have to worry about getting out of it.'

Before PP could start another question, Dave turned to Steve. 'Talking of driving, how are the lessons coming along?'

'Slowly,' said Steve.

'Then maybe you should take it out of first gear!' Jeff grinned and looked around. He was greeted by a couple of forced smiles. He'd hoped for a better response.

'Oooh, tough crowd!'

This got a better reaction.

'This is really good,' said Francine, pointing at her plate and wiping her mouth with her napkin. 'Although it's a little bit hot for me. I don't really like anything too strong.'

'Which is why you married Jeff!'

Steve regretted saying it before the words had left his mouth.

And the fact that everyone around the table – excluding Jeff and Francine – had laughed, hadn't really helped. Kimberley, fully aware that Jeff could easily come back with a comment which could turn the atmosphere, quickly picked up one of the bottles of wine from the table.

'Who'd like some more wine?'

PP finished off what was in his glass – which was more than just a small mouthful – and held it out towards the bottle.

'Yeah, cheers, Kim.'

Kimberley filled up half of the glass. PP waited. She added some more.

PP then turned back to Dave.

'So you helped these two to get together then?'

Dave looked shocked. He looked at Steve.

'No, he didn't,' said Sheila. She slowly turned to her husband. 'Did you?'

'He did one of them police Photofits or something,' explained PP. 'It's nice to know taxpayers' money isn't being wasted!'

Sheila stared at her husband.

'It was nothing really. Just a little thing we knocked up. Nothing worth talking about.'

'Apparently not,' said Sheila.

'It worked though, didn't it?' said Vanessa. 'If I hadn't seen that picture on the programme, then . . . they might never have met.'

'Oh, talking about that television programme,' said Steve, 'they've asked me to go back on.'

They all turned and looked at him. Each of them had a question to ask. As with the wine, PP got in first.

'Why? Are you looking for *another* woman?' He laughed.

Vanessa and Kimberley exchanged a look.

Steve explained. 'They want to do one of those follow-ups. You know, the whole "what happened next" type of thing.'

'Are you going to do it?' asked Jeff. Although, as his mouth was full of spicy chimichanga, only Steve fully understood what he'd said.

'I'm not sure. Although I hated the experience the first

time, I feel as though I owe them something in a way. After all, without that programme, we wouldn't all be here tonight.'

'Well, I think it's a mistake.'

Dave turned to Sheila. 'Why?'

'Well,' said Sheila, 'because those programmes always make people look ridiculous. Oh, and by the way, I'm not talking to you now that I know what you did behind my back.'

PP shouted loudly, 'It's a fair cop!'

He then laughed, on his own.

'It wasn't behind your back,' said Dave, as quietly as he could around a silent table.

'Well, you didn't tell me about it, did you? You kept it from me. Therefore it was behind my back.'

Dave was about to reply when he realised – he didn't know how to. His 'domestic situation' training hadn't prepared him for this.

'Are you really thinking of going back on the programme?'

Steve was surprised by Kimberley's question.

'I'd like to. It's also a good chance to plug the agency. You know, just *happen* to mention it in passing. But if you're not happy about it, then obviously I won't.'

Jeff leant across the table intending to take another handful of nachos. Francine gave him a look. He withdrew his hand before it arrived at the chips 'n' dips tray.

'Well, let us know when the programme is on,' said Jeff, mostly in an attempt to cover the nachos retreat.

'Of course I will,' said Steve.

But he wasn't sure he would.

In fact he suddenly wasn't sure about the whole thing.

CHAPTER THIRTY-FOUR

Charlie Race enthusiastically shook Steve's hand.

'Hi, great to meet you, I'm Charlie Race.'

'Er . . . I know. We met when I was on the programme last time.'

'Oh yeah. Right. You're the guy who married his son's girlfriend.'

'Er . . . no. I'm the guy who found the girl he was looking for – through your programme.'

Charlie Race shook Steve's hand harder. 'Of course! Sorry about that.'

Steve was hoping to get his hand back at some stage. 'That's all right. You probably meet a lot of guests.'

'Yes. But you're all important to me.'

Steve eventually recovered his hand, but was now starting to lose his sense of pride.

'Is the girl not with you?'

Steve had been waiting for this question.

'No, she's very camera-shy.'

He wished he'd worked on a better reply.

'Do you have a photo of her?'

Steve hadn't expected this question.

'Er . . . no. Not really. Don't you still have that Photofit one?'

'Yes, but we need to compare it to the real thing!' Charlie Race sighed loudly and aggressively. 'Bloody researcher! You give them a job because they want to "get into telly", then you find out they're useless. Well, she won't be back for the next series!'

Steve felt awkward, even though it wasn't his fault. 'I . . . I might have one on my phone. It won't be great quality, but—'

'Charlie, can we have you on the floor, please?'

Charlie shook Steve's hand again. This time Steve made sure it was a short shake.

'I'll see you out there. Oh, and remember the show is live now so no swearing!'

As Charlie walked past his young researcher, he said loudly, 'Can you get a photo of his girlfriend from the phone – or do I have to do that as well?!'

The girl looked at the floor.

Charlie then muttered quietly to her, 'Is it really only the *one* thing you're good at?'

***

It was only while he was sitting on the uncomfortable studio chair, with the hot lights causing perspiration to seep through the thin layer of powder on his face, that the realisation hit Steve. He should not be doing this. He had had a genuine reason the first time and it had worked out well. But he hadn't needed to come back. He could have just written a thank-you letter, or planted a tree or something.

Steve watched the other two guests leave their seats to walk backstage. They did look like an odd couple. The guy was forty-five and the girl was nineteen. Steve felt appalled, and, of course, slightly envious. He was surprised and pleased that the man and his son – his girlfriend's ex-boyfriend – had reconciled their differences. He was also surprised that he cared. He had spoken briefly to the couple backstage and could see that their feelings for each other were genuine. For the moment.

'And we're back in five, four, three, two . . .'

The *Charlie Race* title music played. Steve took a deep breath.

The studio audience applauded.

Steve wiped his brow. Some of the powder came off on his finger. He wondered if he'd left a line across his forehead.

Charlie Race spoke to the camera as he read the autocue: 'Welcome back to *Charlie Race*. Now I'm sure you all remember Steve. For literally half his life, he had literally been looking for the girl of his dreams. He had literally given up all hope of finding her – until he came on the *Charlie Race* programme. Because of this programme, and you, our faithful viewers, he found her. And now they're together.'

The audience 'aaawed' and applauded on cue.

'So, Steve, is there something you wanted to say?'

Steve had known he was going to be asked questions, but he didn't know this would be one of them.

'Er . . . Yes. I guess I wanted to say thank you and—'

'You're welcome, Steve.'

Charlie Race turned to the camera. 'And to think there are some people out there who think this programme is of no use or service to anyone! I think we've just proved them wrong!'

The audience went wild with their applause.

Charlie Race turned back to Steve.

'So, Steve, here is the Photofit you brought to the show when you first came on . . .'

The Photofit of the blonde woman showed on the monitors.

'And here is the actual girl herself. Your now-girlfriend, Kimberley.'

The Photofit was replaced by a photograph.

Steve looked confused. So did Charlie Race.

'Er . . . It doesn't look much like her, Steve . . .'

'No,' said Steve. 'That's because she's my sister!'

The *Charlie Race* audience wasn't quite sure what to make of this.

'Er. Okay, Steve. We actually did a similar programme to this last week, so maybe we should just—'

'No, my sister isn't my girlfriend!'

Charlie Race quickly interjected: 'Not that there's anything wrong with that!'

Steve looked at him. He was regretting everything.

He tried to explain. 'I gave your researcher my phone with the photo on it. I told her which one was my girlfriend. She's obviously used the wrong picture.'

Suddenly a new picture appeared on the monitor. This one was of Vanessa.

'That's not her either! These were all taken at a dinner party we had the other night.'

The next photo wasn't Kimberley either. It was Francine. And not a flattering view. The audience laughed. Steve assumed this would all be cut before the show went to air.

He'd forgotten it was live.

CHAPTER THIRTY-FIVE

The pounding music not only made it difficult to hear anything but also made it difficult to focus. It was as though the sound waves were actually distorting the air. Steve only vaguely recognised the song that was playing.

Jeff, or at least someone who looked vaguely like Jeff, came over to Steve and handed him one of the two double whisky and ginger ales he was holding.

Steve looked at him. He couldn't quite work out what was different about him. Maybe it was his hair. Had he always had a side parting?

'So, have you seen her again?'

'Sorry?'

'I said, have you seen her again?'

'Who?'

'That girl.'

'Er . . .' Steve couldn't remember. He couldn't even remember why he and Jeff had gone to . . . wherever they were, in the first place. 'No, not yet. I don't think so.'

Steve then noticed the Spider-Man figurine in Jeff's hand. 'That's mine!'

He tried to grab it.

'You gave to me!' said Jeff, hugging it to his chest.

'No, I did not,' said Steve. 'Wait, I remember. You stole it from me when my mum wasn't looking!'

Steve grabbed the figurine from Jeff.

'I don't want to be friendly with you any more,' said Steve.

'In fact, I thought we'd already stopped being friends.'

Steve walked away from Jeff. He pushed open the large double doors that led to the cloakroom and toilets of the club. As he went through he suddenly came face to face with Kimberley. Although, like Jeff, she also looked different.

'Kim?'

Kimberley looked at him. 'Sorry?'

Steve looked at her again. 'I have a—'

Before he could finish the sentence, Steve was pushed forward. He started falling towards the floor.

'Leave him, he's not worth it!'

'Leave him, he's not worth it!'

'Leave him, he's not worth it!'

As the voice echoed, Steve struggled to get up from the floor. He wanted to argue. He wanted to say that he was worth it. Very worth it. He suddenly sprang up.

'Steve? Steve! Are you all right?'

Steve looked around. He was perspiring and breathing heavily.

Kimberley stroked his arm. 'It's all right – you were having a bad dream. Are you okay?'

Steve tried to control his breathing. 'Yeah. Sorry.' He took a deep breath and forced himself to breathe out slowly. He looked around the bedroom. He wanted to make sure that he actually had woken up and that this wasn't one of those dreams within a dream he used to have.

'What were you dreaming about?'

Steve looked at her.

'Er . . .' He tried to remember. 'Well . . . you, actually.' His breathing had now stabilised. He wiped his forehead with the back of his hand. 'It was just a weird dream. You were there. And Jeff . . .'

'And the Tin Man? The Cowardly Lion . . . ?'

Steve smiled. 'I was back at Angels. The night I first met you. But it was different to how I normally remember it or how I normally dream about it.'

Kimberley looked surprised. 'Do you often dream about it?'

Steve hadn't really wanted to divulge this. He knew how ridiculous it sounded.

'Not so often now. I used to. But I haven't done in a long time. Hardly at all since I met you actually.' He smiled at her. 'Something else I have to thank you for.'

Kimberley leant over and kissed him.

'I suppose I just have things on my mind. And don't forget I've spent the past couple of weeks apologising to you, Francine, my sister . . . everyone.'

'True. Oh, and that reminds me – one of my patients asked me for my autograph yesterday!'

Steve felt the perspiration starting up again.

'Don't worry.' Kimberley smiled. 'It's quite funny really. And at least they showed a nice photo of me. They could easily have shown that one of me at the beach!'

'I've told you before, that's a lovely picture.'

'No, it's not. My hair's a mess, I'm not wearing make-up and I look about twenty years older than I am.'

'It's natural.'

Kimberley looked at him.

'Yeah, that came out badly. But you know what I mean.'

'Anyway, at least it's not as bad as Fran's picture. I still can't believe you hadn't deleted that immediately.'

'I was planning on using it . . . you know, for sexual reasons. It's always handy to have an image that stops you from finishing too quickly!'

Kimberley didn't want to laugh – mainly due to her sense of female solidarity. But she did.

Steve rubbed up and down his face with both his hands. 'The annoying thing is that my sister was able to say, "I told you so." After all, she did tell me not to go on the programme. Oh, and she's still not forgiven Dave for lying to her. Even though technically he hadn't.'

'He lied by omission.'

Steve sighed. 'I didn't tell you that I had an avocado and cheese wrap for lunch at work yesterday. Does that mean I lied to you?'

'That is completely different and you know it. And besides, you *did* tell me what you had for lunch – and it was an egg-mayonnaise baguette.'

Steve thought for a moment. 'Oh yes. Which means I *did* actually just lie to you!'

Kimberley laughed again. She leant over Steve and looked at the clock.

'It's just gone one o'clock.'

'Sorry.'

Kimberley thought aloud. 'Well, I feel quite awake now. It will probably take me quite a while to go back to sleep. So, I suggest . . . we have sex.'

Steve looked surprised. 'Don't I get a say in this?'

'Of course you get a say. If you don't want to have incredible passionate sex with me now, please feel free not to get an erection.'

She put a hand between Steve's legs.

Steve looked at her.

Kimberley gently started to move her hand. She smiled. 'Nice try.'

As Kimberley started to remove his boxer shorts, Steve leant across to the bedside table and picked up his phone.

Kimberley stopped. 'What are you doing?'

'I'm getting the photo of Francine ready!'

CHAPTER THIRTY-SIX

What would you like to do to me?'

Vanessa looked at what she had just written. Even though she knew she'd typed it herself, she was still shocked. She took another sip from the glass of water on her bedside table. Of course she wasn't being herself, she was being Laura69. And Laura was really a bit of a slut.

There was a *ping*.

'I'd love to lick your tits and then go down on you.'

Vanessa shuddered. She'd always hated the word 'tits'. And PP knew that. Not that PP knew he was currently writing to his wife. As far as he was concerned, he was having virtual sex with a woman called Laura who was in Leeds. Had he known that his new *sexting pen pal* was actually his wife, who was sitting in bed upstairs typing on a laptop, he would have been rather surprised. Apart from anything, he didn't know she had a laptop. Kimberley had actually lent her an old one on which to practise her computer skills. It hadn't taken her long to work things out. And it was when she was checking the profile of Laura69, about five minutes earlier, that she had received the first message from her husband – who was downstairs, supposedly working on his accounts. She hadn't known how to react at first. She found receiving a message from her husband who thought she was someone else a bit strange to say the least. But this was what she had wanted. This was her plan. It had just suddenly become real.

PP's first message had been, simply: 'Hi, how are you?'

Vanessa/Laura69 had replied with: 'Gr8 thanks. And u?'

She knew she had to be careful not to write as herself, and one of the things she hated, and PP knew she hated, was abbreviating words.

PP had replied with: 'Yeah, book.'

Vanessa had frowned.

'What are you wearing?'

Vanessa had stared at the screen. Is this what people did? Is this what they asked? She had looked down at what she was wearing. She reckoned that writing 'an old Mickey Mouse T-shirt that you bought me and green tracksuit bottoms' might give the game away.

'Just bra and knickers.'

'Are they matching?'

Vanessa had read this twice. Matching?! Since when did he care if underwear matched?! Did he have an underwear fetish she didn't know about?

'Take your bra off.'

Vanessa froze. What was he going to say next? Let *me* put it on?

She had written back: 'Ok'.

And this is more or less where they were now. She had told him that she had taken off her bra and then her knickers. PP had started to tell her what he wanted to do to her and she had responded.

Vanessa read the last line again: 'I'd love to lick your tits and then go down on you.'

She wasn't sure how to reply. 'Thanks' would sound a bit odd. She thought for a moment. Maybe she didn't have to reply. She put the laptop to one side, got off the bed and walked out of the door.

PP heard her coming down the stairs and clicked to

minimise the page just before Vanessa walked into the room.

'How's it going?'

Her husband sighed and stretched. 'Okay. Quite a bit of work to do yet though.' He pointed at the screen in front of him. Vanessa looked. A spreadsheet of numbers filled the whole screen.

'Are you coming to bed? It's gone one.'

'Yeah, I'll be up soon.'

'All right.'

Vanessa smiled and walked back up the narrow stairs which linked the living room with the small landing.

Back in the bedroom Vanessa looked at the laptop. She read what PP had written in the short amount of time she had taken to walk back upstairs.

'I'd better go. My mates are waiting for me to go clubbing with them.'

Vanessa shook her head. She then wrote back: 'Ok. Nxt time. Xx'

She shut down the laptop, closed the lid and slid it under the bed. She then opened the novel which was lying on the bedside table, unfolded the corner of the page and stared at the words. She couldn't concentrate on reading. She'd had the book for months but was still only on the second chapter, and she'd had to read that twice as she'd literally and figuratively lost the plot.

Moments later PP walked into the bedroom.

'You tired?'

Vanessa looked at him. 'A bit.'

She knew where this was headed. The next thing would be some sort of compliment.

'Dinner was great tonight. Really tasty.'

'Thanks.'

PP got into bed. 'Talking about tasty . . .'

He leant over and kissed her on the lips. She responded with as little effort as possible.

PP then followed his tried and tested routine. He ran his hand over her breasts – making sure he didn't give more attention to one than the other – and then worked his way down her body.

They hadn't had sex in a while, and the truth was Vanessa had missed it. But how could she do it now? She didn't know if he was actually sleeping with anyone else or just having a bit of online fun. As she felt PP touch her – he always knew how to press the right buttons – she knew she wouldn't be able to resist him. In a way, a partially justifiable way, she was actually enjoying the irony. She was about to have sex with her husband because he was feeling turned on by someone he had been talking with online. And that person had been her. She had turned her husband on without him knowing. He was going to be fantasising about Vanessa – albeit with a different name – at the same time as having sex with her. She smiled. PP looked at her and smiled back.

CHAPTER THIRTY-SEVEN

Steve applied a little pressure to the brake pedal. He then put his foot on the clutch and shifted the gear stick from fourth down to second.

The car complained as the needle on the rev counter hit red.

'No, you have to slow down a lot more before making that change. It was a good try though. As I said, examiners do like to see a block-change. Now, at the next roundabout I want you to take the third exit.'

As Steve drove towards the roundabout he could feel the beads of perspiration on his forehead. He had been enjoying the lessons, this was his third, but the pressure had been increasing. The test wasn't that far away.

He stopped at the roundabout and gave way to the right. As he released the handbrake and moved off, the car lurched forward and stalled.

'Shit!'

'It's okay, Steve. Take your time.'

The car behind sounded its horn.

Vernon, the instructor, looked into his rear-view mirror.

'Just ignore him. He was also a learner once.'

The beads had become large pearls. Steve applied the handbrake again, put the car into neutral and then restarted the engine. He started to pull away. Suddenly he found himself testing the resistance of his seat belt.

'Look!'

Steve looked up to see a Range Rover shoot past him.

'You forgot to check what was coming!'

Steve could tell that Vernon, who was normally pretty calm, was a little bit shaken. Although Vernon was always ready, he hadn't been expecting to use his own set of brakes at that moment.

'That vehicle shouldn't be on the road anyway,' suggested Steve. 'There are no farms around here!'

'Have a look around, make sure nothing is coming and then slowly pull off,' suggested Vernon as calmly as possible.

Steve did as he was told.

***

Ten minutes before the end of the lesson Vernon suggested, in light of the earlier roundabout incident, that Steve practise his emergency stop.

'Just drive along, and when I bang my hand against the dashboard I want you to imagine a child has run into the road and I need you to apply your brakes immediately.'

Steve nodded.

He drove along, nonchalantly trying to pretend that he wasn't about to have to 'slam on the brakes'.

From the corner of his eye his saw Vernon's hand tense slightly. This is it, he thought. 'Get ready.'

He saw Vernon's hand leap up from his lap and slam against the dashboard...

***

'Isn't it a bit early? They won't be drunk enough yet.'

Jeff offered one of the drinks in his hand.

Steve looked at it.

'Go on, take it. It's whisky and ginger. That's what you wanted, wasn't it? Or did you want another lager and lime?'

'I . . . I mustn't drink and drive.'

Jeff looked at him. 'I know that. But the good thing is, you're not driving. And as you haven't even started lessons yet you might not be driving until you're in your thirties. If you live that long!'

Steve took the drink.

'Are you okay?'

Steve wasn't sure. He looked around. What was he doing here? Why did everything seem so odd? Had he drunk too much?

'I . . . I think I'm going to get some air.'

Jeff shrugged. 'Okay. Make sure they stamp your hand or you won't be allowed back in.'

Steve nodded, even though he wasn't really listening. As he walked towards the doors that led to the entrance hall and cloakroom he saw his reflection in one of the mirrored columns. He was wearing a blue-and-white striped shirt with a large white collar. He looked at his face. Something wasn't right. He couldn't work out what it was, but it felt as if his face didn't match his clothes.

Michael Jackson's 'The Way You Make Me Feel' played in the background.

He walked out through the double doors of the club and came face to face with a beautiful young blonde girl.

They looked at each other. For a moment he thought he recognised her.

Her friend, almost a polar opposite, grabbed her by the arm.

'Come on – my dad's waiting!'

Steve went to speak but was suddenly pushed forward to the floor.

'Come on, leave him, he's not worth it!'

***

'Steve? Steve!'

Steve wanted to open his eyes, but they were already open.

'Are you okay?'

He blinked half a dozen times in succession. He stared out of the windscreen in front of him. He then turned to Vernon.

'What happened?'

Vernon looked surprised. 'That's what I was going to ask you! I banged the dashboard, but you didn't do anything. I had to apply my brakes again. Then you just sat there staring for a full couple of minutes. That's not going to help you pass your test!'

'Sorry,' said Steve. He wasn't sure what else to say.

Steve didn't know what was going on, but he knew he had to do something about it.

CHAPTER THIRTY-EIGHT

Steve looked over the piece of paper and then handed it back.

'I know what I signed. I'm not planning on suing you. I just need to sort out what's going on.'

'You told me that before you even came to see me, you used to have flashbacks.'

'No, I had daydreams. And night dreams. But they weren't like this. Not as . . . real. And I never went into a trance . . .'

Greg quickly interrupted. 'You didn't go into a trance! All that's happened is that the memories are a bit stronger than before. It's not dangerous.'

'Oh no, falling asleep when he's driving isn't dangerous at all. Tell you what, why doesn't he take you for a spin in the car, maybe near a cliff edge. Let's see how safe you feel then. Or maybe—'

'Okay, Jeff,' Steve interrupted. 'Thanks, you've made your point.'

Greg and Jeff exchanged a look.

'So what can you do?'

Greg looked away from Jeff – which gave Jeff a little sense of achievement – and turned to Steve.

'Well, I could put you under again and see if there's anything we missed. Maybe there's something in your subconscious that is trying to come out. Maybe we untapped a memory, something important that needs to be looked at.'

Steve sighed. 'Will that help?'

'It can't harm.'

'Ha!'

They both turned to Jeff. Even he was surprised at how loudly he'd made the noise.

'Okay, let's do it.'

'I'm going to have to charge you.'

'What?! You're the one who got him into this state; you can't charge him for trying to get him out of it!'

'Jeff, it's fine. Really.'

Jeff went to speak again, but realised there was no point. 'Fine,' said Jeff. 'But don't do the regression thing again. I don't want to find out that he was my great-great grandmother or something.'

'Don't be so stupid,' said Steve. He then covered his teeth with his lips and leant closer to Jeff; 'Now be a good boy and give Granny a kiss.'

***

The disco. Jeff. The drinks. The music. Dancing. But this wasn't like before. Steve wasn't in this memory; he was watching it from outside. And it wasn't the whole thing, just the highlights. It was as though he were watching an abridged version of what he remembered. Like a trailer for his past: *'Coming soon, to a memory near you . . .'*

He saw himself talking to Jeff, saw himself drinking, then he saw himself walking out of the club towards those huge double doors.

Then he was in the memory again.

Then watching it.

And there was the point where he bumped into the girl of his dreams. He was looking at her from two different viewpoints, jumping between them as though it were a film being shot from two angles. He saw her from his point of view, then from above. A two-shot. Him and her together.

Except that he soon realised, whichever angle he was looking from, one thing was certain . . .

'Come on,' said the friend.

'My dad's waiting,' said the friend.

'Leave him, he's not worth it . . .' said the friend.

'Come on . . . Helen.'

It wasn't Kimberley.

CHAPTER THIRTY-NINE

Kimberley wiped her mouth with the corner of her perfectly ironed linen napkin.

'Are you sure you wouldn't like a top-up?'

She smiled and shook her head. 'No, thanks. I'm so full. And those cakes were delicious.'

Steve's mum put the offered teapot back onto the table.

'Well, there are loads left over. You and Steven can take some with you. It's only me here, and I can't eat them all on my own.'

She got up and started to take things from the table. She suddenly stopped and rubbed the base of her spine – a little more dramatically than was necessary.

Steve looked at her.

'Are you okay?' asked Kimberley.

'Sorry?' said Steve's mum as though she had absolutely no idea as to what Kimberley could possibly be referring.

'Do you have a pain in your back?'

'What? Oh, that. It's nothing.'

She lifted up the plate of cakes and sucked the pain in loudly through her teeth.

'Are you taking anything for it?'

Just sympathy, thought Steve. It wasn't that he didn't believe his mum had a pain in her back; he was just amazed at how it came and went depending on whether she had anything else with which to occupy herself. And whether she had company or not.

'I take painkillers occasionally. But they don't really help.'

'What does your doctor say?'

'Oh, you know doctors. No offence.'

Kimberley smiled.

'Anyway, that's enough about me complaining.' She gave Kimberley a big hug. 'Oh, it's so lovely to meet you! You would not believe how long I have been hearing about you. Steven was more or less obsessed.'

Kimberley looked at Steve. She raised her eyebrows. 'More or less?'

Steve smiled. But he didn't feel like smiling.

He watched as Kimberley helped his mother to take the things from the table into the kitchen. What was the matter with him?! He couldn't get his visit to the hypnotist out of his head! He had remembered everything from the regression this time. He hadn't needed Jeff to make notes. He had seen the girl plainly. She hadn't looked like Kimberley. Not even like a younger version of her. And he couldn't stop thinking about it. Why had the girl changed?

Or maybe she hadn't.

Maybe he just had a clearer image of her this time. Or maybe all the messing around with his memories had got him completely mixed up. He didn't know. Greg hadn't known either. It was impossible to tell which memory was real. It was like telling people a lie – if you say it enough times, and with enough conviction, you start to believe it yourself.

Steve knew he shouldn't question anything. He knew he should just accept that Kimberley was the right girl for him now, regardless of anything else. But he couldn't. He had to be sure. What he didn't know was how he'd cope with the result.

***

As they waved their goodbyes and walked away from the house

towards Kimberley's car, Steve's mind was still full of these thoughts.

'Your mum's lovely.'

'Yes, she is. And sorry about the whole back-pain thing. And the "so when's the wedding?" bit.'

Kimberley laughed. 'It's okay. Mine's just the same. As you'll soon find out.'

Steve smiled. Outwardly.

Kimberley opened the driver's door. 'Oh, do you want to drive? I've got the L-plates in the boot.'

'No, it's okay,' said Steve. Although it wasn't. He hadn't driven since he had almost crashed the car in the last lesson. And the way he felt at the moment, he didn't care if he never drove again.

He sat in the passenger seat of the car and did up his seat belt.

'Would you mind . . . having a drive through the town, instead of going straight back. Just for old time's sake.'

'Okay. Sure.'

***

Steve directed Kimberley through the town centre.

'Can you stop here a minute?'

She pulled over.

Steve pointed to a large building.

'Remember that?'

Kimberley looked. She frowned. 'It's a casino. You know I hate gambling. Why would I have ever gone to a casino?'

'It wasn't always a casino. It used to be a nightclub. A disco.'

Kimberley looked at the building again.

'Is that where Angels used to be?'

Steve nodded. Had she known that or was it just a guess?

'How many times did you actually go there?'

Kimberley turned her gaze from the building to Steve. 'I don't really remember. Whenever my friend Sharon and I were bored of Bracknell. Maybe two or three times. No more than that. Why?'

'Just asking.' He stared out of the window for a moment. 'What did Sharon look like?'

Kimberley was a little surprised by the question. 'Sharon? Er . . . well . . . her weight used to fluctuate a lot. Sometimes she'd be quite big; then a few weeks later she'd have lost a lot of weight and—'

'Did you ever wear white trousers when you went there?'

'Okay, Steve, what's going on?!'

'Nothing.'

'Don't lie to me. You've been strange for the past couple of days. And it didn't make meeting your mum any easier!'

Steve looked out of the window.

'So is this nostalgia trip finished? Can I drive on or are there more questions?'

Steve turned to her. 'I'm sorry. I . . . just have things on my mind at the moment.'

'Do you want to talk about them?'

I don't think you're actually the girl I've been looking for and in light of this, I'm not sure how I feel about you any more, was what Steve was thinking. But of course this wasn't what he decided to say.

'It's noth— I mean, there's just stuff going on at work.' He turned to her and smiled. He put a hand on her leg.

'I'm sorry, sweetheart. Honestly, everything's fine. I'm just a bit tired. Come on, I'll show you the pub where I got drunk for the first time.'

Kimberley looked at him. She then smiled and drove off.

As they drove back along the high street, Steve watched the old shopping centre, and his memories, shooting past. He felt they both needed rebuilding.

CHAPTER FORTY

Jeff looked at his reflection in the blacked-out windows. He'd always found the concept of one-way glass fascinating. He then remembered that as this was one-way glass, then the people inside, as he had done himself on many occasions, could now be looking out.

He turned away and looked towards the front door.

'Well?'

Jeff shook his head. 'No. It just . . . I don't know. A part of me wants to – and we both know which part that is – but the rest of me . . . well . . .'

Steve put a hand on Jeff's shoulder.

'This is an important step, my friend. If you do want to go in, I'll go with you like I said. But if you feel ready to walk away, then I'm ready to support you.'

Jeff turned and smiled. 'Thank you, Steven.' He took a deep breath. 'Come on, let's go.'

Steve followed Jeff as he walked past the door of the lap-dancing club. He followed him as he turned the corner and headed towards a cafe. He then followed him as he retraced his steps and went into the club.

***

'No, thanks, Rachel. Not just now.'

The girl, dressed in fishnet T-shirt and hot pants that left only a very small amount to the imagination, smiled as she walked away from Jeff and Steve's table.

In the centre of the room, a naked girl was having an intimate relationship with a silver pole. Most of the men – well, those who weren't currently having their own private dance – were watching her.

Jeff however was staring at Steve.

'I just don't get it. I mean, you love her, right?'

'She's great.'

'Answer the question.'

'It's a ridiculous question, Jeff. You *know* how I feel about her.'

Jeff took a sip of his mineral water. 'Well, Steve, I thought I did.'

'Look, I really, really care for her. It's just . . . what if it's not her?'

Steve had barely finished the sentence when he felt the sting on his face.

'Ow!'

'You're an idiot!'

Steve stroked his face. 'You didn't have to slap me!'

'Yes, I did.'

Jeff spoke quietly. After having lived with Francine for so long he understood that speaking slowly and quietly – without being patronising – was the best way of putting your point of view across.

'Steve, don't be an idiot. Greg said that the hypnosis thing – remembering the name Helen – might not be accurate at all. Your subconscious could be adding things to your memory. That's why he suggested you don't go back to him any more and just move on. These new memories might not be real.' He sighed. He spoke even more slowly and quietly. 'Steve, seriously, you have a great thing here. You are the happiest I've ever seen you. Things are going well at work; you're in a fantastic relationship with a woman you love – even if you don't admit it.'

'I . . .'

'Let me finish. Are you telling me that you are prepared to throw all this away?'

Steve looked at down at his drink.

'Jesus, Jeff – when did you start being the mature one?'

Jeff smiled and shrugged.

Steve picked up his glass and looked up at Jeff. 'You're right. Of course. I'm just . . . tired. I wish I hadn't gone on that bloody programme again. I should have just said no.'

'Well, it's done, so just forget about it.'

Steve nodded. He took a large swig of his lager.

'In fact, Steve, forget about everything in the past. Live for now, seize the day, Nessun Dorma.'

Steve spat back out the mouthful as he laughed.

'It's not "nessun dorma, you idiot",' he spluttered. 'It's carpe diem!'

'Is it? Oh, right!' Jeff laughed too. 'Well, that too!'

They both laughed loudly.

Jeff looked around. Some of the clientele, as well as the naked gymnast, were staring at them.

'Come on,' he said. 'Let's get out of here.'

CHAPTER FORTY-ONE

The noise of the reversing engines together with the sound of the undercarriage lowering and the wing flaps being raised were always worrying for Steve. He didn't mind flying – well, apart from the being in the air thousands of feet above the ground bit – and he didn't mind the taking-off part. But what he really hated was the landing. The thought of a huge, people-packed metal tube, coming down to the ground, however gradually and carefully, made him very nervous. Even though he had flown many, many times, he had still avidly listened to the – he wasn't sure what the correct term was: air hostess? Flight attendant? Cabin-crew person? – anyway he'd listened to all the instructions as to what to do in the event of an emergency. He'd checked to see if his life jacket was indeed under his seat as promised and, as told to, he read the laminated instruction leaflet in the pocket in front of him. He couldn't understand why the people in the little drawings looked so happy as they slid down the yellow evacuation slide. He wondered, as he always did on flights, how he would really react in an emergency situation. Would he calmly put on his oxygen mask as it dropped down in front of him? Would he remember not to inflate his life jacket until he was outside the aircraft? He looked at the little drawing of the life jacket and remembered the number of comedy routines he'd seen about the little whistle attached to the jacket and how pointless blowing into it would be when you're bobbing up and down in the middle of the ocean. He then thought about the ritual ahead of him: queue to get off the plane, queue at passport control, queue at the luggage carousel – it sounded such a fun word – queue at the taxi rank, then, eventually, over an hour later, leave the airport. Yet this was nothing compared to the process he'd already had to go through. Even though he'd arrived the requested two hours prior to departure, he'd still had to wait for an hour in the check-in queue before assuring the depressed check-in-desk person that he had indeed packed his own case, that he hadn't been given anything by anyone and that he wasn't carrying any of the objects on the lovely poster behind the desk. Then he'd queued for the privilege of removing his belt and shoes. All this, together with the landing, was why he hated flying. But at least this time he wasn't on his own. This time he had someone to share his hatred of the experience. Well, he would have done, had they been awake.

He slowly turned his head to Kimberley who, despite the pre-landing noises, was still fast asleep with her head resting on his shoulder. He looked at her for a moment. He then leant over and gently kissed her. He then sat back, looked at her again and smiled. His smile suddenly dropped as the plane hit the runway. The movement of both the plane and Steve's arm caused Kimberley to wake up. She blinked twice and looked around, forgetting where she was for a moment. She sat up and rolled her neck around slowly. She then opened her mouth wide in an attempt to clear her blocked ears.

'Have a good sleep?'

'Sorry?'

'Did you have a good sleep?'

Kimberley smiled, yawned and nodded all at the same time.

The plane slowed down.

'Ladies and gentlemen, welcome to Malaga where the local time is a quarter past six. Please remain in your seats until the captain has switched off the "fasten seat belts" sign.'

As the announcement finished, the majority of passengers undid their seat belts and started removing items from the overhead lockers.

***

'¿Usted quiere la carretera vieja ó la nueva?'

'¿Qué diferencia hay?'

'La nueva es más rápida pero tienes que pagar un peaje.'

'¿Cuánto es el peaje?

'Aproximadamente diez u once euros.'

'Muy bien, vamos en esta.'

'Vale.'

'Well, that was impressive,' said Kimberley, 'unless he didn't know what you were saying.'

Steve smiled. 'There's apparently a new faster road,' he explained, 'but you have to pay a toll. I said to take it anyway.'

'Oooh, Mr Flash. So how far is it from here?'

'Not all that far. You're not going to start saying, "Are we there yet?" every five minutes, are you?'

Kimberley shrugged.

As the taxi drove along the A-7, which was also known as the E-15, towards Marbella, Steve looked out at the calm Mediterranean Sea. He had been to Marbella many times: as a child going with his parents to their newly purchased timeshare apartment: as a teenager with friends to stay in, and almost wreck, that apartment; with his parents to sell the timeshare and then buy their own apartment; and then going there more than once to have some time alone. Steve liked the area, although he would have preferred it to be less, well, British. There were just too many British pubs and restaurants. And they all seemed to be from a former era. You couldn't walk a hundred yards, or, as it was in Spain, 91.44 metres, without bumping into a 'Ye Olde World's End' or 'George and Dragon'. It was as though people needed to be constantly reminded of how proud they were to be British – even though they had left their home country to avoid the weather and/or police.

Steve looked up at the cable cars high above them, which ran back and forth from Benalmádena to the summit of Monte Calamorro. He'd been on the cable car once, but his vertigo had stopped him from enjoying it, although he had been impressed by the incredible view of Gibraltar and the coast of north Africa.

'I'd love to go on that,' said Kimberley.

'I don't think we'll have time,' Steve lied.

His phone beeped loudly. 'Probably another welcome message from the Spanish phone company.' He checked the message. 'No, it's from Mum, asking if we've arrived safely.'

'I thought she didn't want to know anything about this trip,' said Kimberley, smiling.

'Yeah,' said Steve.

***

After paying the cab driver and asking for a receipt – he was hoping to think of a way to claim this whole trip back as a business expense – Steve walked, with Kimberley's hand in one hand and his suitcase in the other, to Villa Aston.

His father, James, had been an Aston Villa fan since the age of eight when an uncle had given him a 1957 FA Cup Winner's pendant. He had promised himself in his early twenties, just before meeting Steve's mother, that one day he would buy a Spanish villa and call it Aston. Steve's mother had hated the idea. She no longer had a say in the matter.

'Kate, they're here!' Steve's dad shouted loudly through the upstairs window of the villa.

'I'm coming down now!' He disappeared from the window, although his voice lingered.

'Here we go,' said Steve quietly.

***

The four of them sat on the *terrazza*. The tiles of the mosaic table in front of them were all but covered with the spread of food and drink, which included a jug of sangria overflowing with fruit and ice, several bottles of San Miguel lager, two bottles of Rioja Campo Viejo, breadsticks and olives stuffed with anchovies.

'So, do you have any famous people on your books?'

Steve opened another bottle of lager and put the Toreador bottle-opener-cum-corkscrew back onto the table. 'No, not really. I had a couple of fairly well-known comedians once, but—'

'Like who?' Kate wanted to know.

'Well . . . I managed Gareth Ice for a while.'

Kate smiled and nodded.

'You . . . don't know who that is, do you?' suggested Steve.

Kate continued to smile and shook her head.

'You're probably too young,' said Kimberley.

Kimberley was surprised by the tone in her own voice. She hadn't intended to be nasty. In fact, she was generally proud of the way she handled herself in social situations. Maybe it had been the wine. And the lager. Maybe it had been the long day. Or maybe it was the fact that Kimberley really liked Steve's mum and didn't like the way she'd been treated.

'I hardly remembered him myself really,' said Steve, attempting to cover, 'but he is probably as close as I've got to having anyone famous. There are one or two I have now who might make it big in the next year or so though.'

Kate nodded. She stood up.

'I've got some potatoes in the oven. I'll just go and get them.'

Steve watched Kate walk towards the kitchen. He really liked her, even though he knew he shouldn't. After all, this was the girl who caused his parents to separate. Yet he couldn't blame her for everything. Of course she had known his dad was married – after all, she was the estate agent who had sold Villa Aston to his parents in the first place and so she should never have flirted with him and then met with him whenever he came to Spain – but she was a pretty twenty-nine-year-old who was lonely and wanted a relationship and a father figure. So she combined the two. If he should blame anyone, it should be his dad. But again he understood – if not approved. His dad had become obsessed by her. And if there was one thing Steve could empathise with it, it was obsession.

'You do know that you drove us mad, don't you?' said Steve's dad, standing up and taking another bottle of lager from the slowly diminishing ice bucket.

'Er . . . sorry,' said Kimberley, who really couldn't tell if he was joking or not.

'If Steve had spent as much time on his studying as he did trying to find you, he would have probably gone to university instead of that crap drama school.'

'Right. Well . . . sorry. Again.'

'Don't listen to him, Kim. He's just trying to be funny.'

'Yeah, Kim, I'm just trying to be funny. Like Gareth Ice used to be.'

Steve sighed. His dad could be a bit trying at the best of times, but he was worse after a drink or two.

'So he tracked you down through a TV programme then?'

'Well, yes, sort of,' said Kimberley, who would have been quite happy, actually deliriously happy, to be discussing anything – irritable bowel syndrome, superhero films, expansionary fiscal policy – anything but this.

'It was my friend who saw the programme and thought the girl was me.'

Even though the Toreador bottle opener was in front of him, Steve's dad placed the neck of his bottle against the side of the table and, holding it tightly with his left hand, slammed his right hand down on top of it.

The bottle cap flew off into the jasmine bush behind him. Steve's dad quickly bent down and sucked at the lager foam which was now trying to escape.

'So, Steve, are you sure she's the right one? I mean, the whole thing could just be a scam. She could be another agent who's trying to steal all your showbiz contacts.'

'Don't worry, James, I'm definitely her,' said Kimberley.

Steve looked down at the floor. The other reason for wanting to get away had been to put his doubts, his uncertainty, his foolishness behind him and to just enjoy being with Kimberley.

'These are called *patatas alioli*. It's potatoes with garlic mayonnaise, and these are *patatas bravas*, which are in spicy sauce.'

Kate tried to find space on the table for the two terracotta bowls in her hands. Steve stood up and moved the bottles of wine onto the floor.

'Thanks,' said Kate. 'So, what have I missed?'

'Well,' said James, 'we're just trying to find out if Kimberley is real or if she's taken on the identity of this girl for financial gain.'

Even though Kate had known James for over five years, she still didn't always know when he was joking.

'Oh, right. So, who wants to try the potatoes?'

***

'Sorry again that I couldn't pick you up, but the car's only a two-seater.'

'I know, Dad, don't worry. The cab was easy.'

Steve's dad took three short puffs on his cigar, tilted his head back and blew the smoke up into the cloudless Andalusian sky.

They sat in silence for a while, which was only occasionally broken by the sound of Kate and Kimberley clearing the table and chatting.

'That new toll road is good, isn't it?' said Steve.

James took another puff and let it out almost immediately.

'Yeah, it's awesome.'

Steve looked at his father. There was no point in commenting on his vocabulary. It was all part of the 'new' package.

'Kim's lovely, son. Well worth the wait!'

Steve smiled.

'Reckon you're going to get married?'

Steve had been wondering how to approach this subject. This was one of the reasons he had come over to see his father. He could have spoken over the phone, but as Kimberley had some holiday to use and as they had wanted to go away together for a while, this seemed an ideal opportunity to kill both proverbial birds.

'Well, I don't know. We might. The thing is, Dad . . .'

'If you do decide to get married, then you'd prefer it if Kate and I didn't come.'

Steve was taken aback. He was a bit disappointed in himself for not having given his father credit for appreciating the situation. He'd actually had nightmares about his wedding in which his father turned up halfway through the vows, wearing a garish suit and driving his prized red Morgan Aero 8 right into the registry office. The only saving grace of the nightmare was that Kate got out of the passenger seat wearing a tiny leopard-print bikini. He knew it was wrong to think of his father's girlfriend in that way, but he couldn't be held responsible for what went on in his subconscious. He did find Kate attractive, but the fact that she could potentially be his stepmother was a little disconcerting, if no less alluring.

'Er . . . well . . . yes. You understand.'

James looked down at the glass of wine in his hand. He spoke quietly. 'Sure.' He smiled. 'Apart from anything else, it would probably be difficult to explain my sudden resurrection.'

'Yeah.'

James held the wineglass to his lips, but then took it away without drinking. 'How, er . . . how is your mum?'

'She's okay. Still got a pain in her back.'

'I bet she loves Kim.'

'Yeah.'

He put the glass back up to his mouth and this time took a small sip.

'It'll be good to see you settled down son.'

'Well, you know, nothing's definite.'

Steve's dad turned so quickly towards his son that some of the wine spilt onto the *terrazza*.

'What does that mean?!'

Steve was shocked by the reaction. He felt like a small child again. He suddenly started to remember, in quick succession, occasions when his father had raised his voice at him. Like the time when, at fifteen, he'd come home drunk at two o'clock in the morning, or when he'd found his dad's porn collection and taken it to school to show his friends, or when he'd put their home phone number on all the 'Looking for this girl' posters he'd stuck up around the whole town.

'I just meant . . . er . . . you know, nothing is ever definite.'

James put the glass of wine onto the floor. He put a firm hand on Steve's leg.

'I don't know how much fatherly advice I gave you when you were growing up—'

'You gave me loads,'

'Okay. I hope so. But I want you to learn one thing from me . . . make sure you don't mess things up.'

Steve was surprised. This conversation was more serious than he had expected.

To lighten the atmosphere, he looked around and grinned.

'Well, you haven't done too badly . . .'

Steve's dad applied a slight yet noticeable pressure to Steve's leg.

'Seriously, don't mess things up.'

***

As Steve and Kimberley walked along the Paseo Maritimo towards their hotel, Steve thought about the conversation with his father. Although he had been over to see his dad quite a few times – sometimes without telling his mother – they had never really spoken at any great lengths. And certainly never so seriously.

'You like Kate, don't you?'

Kimberley's words were slightly slurred.

'Yeah,' said Steve. 'I know I shouldn't, but I do. Do you

know she's studying to be a midwife? She actually wanted to be a doctor when she was younger but then became an estate agent instead!'

Kimberley laughed loudly. 'Maybe that's what I should have done!' She laughed again. As she laughed she lost her footing on the marble stone of the Marbella boardwalk. She stumbled, regained her balance and laughed hysterically. She then stopped laughing and turned to Steve. She frowned as she spoke – to make sure he understood it was a serious question. 'What did you want to be when you were younger?'

'A teacher,' replied Steve, without having to think.

'Really?' said Kimberley. 'You've never mentioned that before!'

Steve shrugged. He was surprised that he'd never mentioned this to Kimberley.

'Wow,' said Kimberley. 'You think you know someone!'

Steve looked at her. He was about to say something, although he wasn't quite sure what, when Kimberley tripped again and laughed again.

Steve usually liked it when Kimberley was drunk. She lost all her inhibitions. She also tended to talk about things she'd normally not discuss – like previous boyfriends, sexual experiences, mistakes she'd made. But Steve really only liked Kimberley being drunk when he was also drunk; otherwise he found it annoying. Like now.

'A teacher, eh! Maybe you can teach me a couple of things back in the hotel!' She giggled as she overly cautiously took a couple of small steps.

Steve didn't respond.

James had invited them to stay in Villa Aston, but Steve had politely declined, as he wanted to stay in a hotel and make more of a holiday of it with Kimberley.

'Do you think you'd ever sleep with someone behind my back?'

Even though Steve knew this was the type of thing she said when she was drunk, the question threw him. He suddenly thought about the times he'd been unfaithful to other girlfriends.

'No, Kim.'

'Would you tell me if you did?'

'I just said I wouldn't do it.'

'But would you tell me if you did?'

Steve knew he was going to get dizzy if he continued going around in this particular circle. Fortunately Kimberley decided to stop the ride.

'Let's promise each other that we'll never hide anything. We'll always tell each other the truth.'

Steve looked at her. He watched her blink twice as often as normal in an attempt to keep focus.

'Okay,' he said.

He put his arm around her, both as a sign of affection and as a subtle way of helping her to walk straight.

CHAPTER FORTY-TWO

Steve picked up the newspaper from the floor at the side of the bed. It was still a little cold from having been sitting, moments earlier, in its cage on the petrol-station forecourt. Steve had always loved his Sunday routine: getting up later than normal, putting the kettle on, throwing on some old clothes, walking to the local newsagent's to buy two, sometimes three newspapers, coming back home, making himself a cup of tea and some toast and then, eventually, getting back into bed with all the items.

One of his slight concerns about moving in with Kimberley was that this Sunday ritual would be changed. And it had been changed. For the better. There were a couple of downsides of course, like he now had to make two cups of tea instead of one, and, as there was no local newsagent to Kimberley's flat, he had to walk ten minutes to the petrol station to buy the papers. But the fact that he was not in bed alone, and was actually with someone he really cared for, made up for these *slight* inconveniences.

'Are you going to read the paper now?!'

Even though she could sometimes be a little bossy.

Steve slowly refolded the paper and put it back onto the floor.

'No. Sorry. Go on.'

Kimberley, propped up by a large heart-shaped cushion behind her back, flicked through the Highway Code book.

'Right, when are you allowed to use your hazard warning lights?'

'When you have to warn other drivers of an obstruction or traffic ahead.'

'Good.'

'Or when you've double-parked outside the newsagent's and you're just popping in to buy a couple of Lucky Dips!'

'Steve!'

'Sorry.'

Kimberley sighed in mild irritation. She looked for another question.

'This is for your benefit, Steve, not mine. You're the one who has their driving test tomorrow. I already know all this.'

'Do you really?'

'What?'

'Know all this?' Steve pointed at the Highway Code book.

'Yes,' said Kimberley, hoping that the confidence in her voice would avoid an interrogation.

'Pass it to me then.'

It hadn't.

'Come on, Steve, I'm not the one . . .'

Before she had time to finish the sentence, Steve had taken the book from her hands and was leafing through it.

'Steve!'

'Right then – what must you do when passing someone riding a horse?'

Kimberley sighed. However, as this was a fairly easy one for her she decided to play along.

'You slow down and don't sound your horn.'

'Correct. You must also put your window down and shout out, "I think you'll find we're in the twenty-first century!"'

'Ha-ha.'

'Look, this is helping me. Right, next question, on a similar topic, when are you actually allowed to sound your horn?'

'Er . . . I know you can't do it after eleven o'clock at night . . .'

'Unless you're a minicab driver picking someone up. But that wasn't the question. When are you allowed to sound your horn? Come on, little Miss *I Know All This.*'

Kimberley managed to hold back her irritation. 'When someone . . . I mean, when there's . . . er . . . to tell someone . . .'

'*To warn other road users of your presence.* Or if you happen to see an attractive-looking girl.'

'For goodness sake!' Kimberley snatched back the book.

The telephone at the side of the bed rang. Kimberley looked at the clock display on the portable television set.

'That's my mum. Don't make a noise.'

Steve bit his lip, literally, and shook his head. He picked up the newspaper again and looked at the front page – although he didn't read it. He couldn't believe, or understand, how his girlfriend – a grown woman – kept the fact that they were living together a secret from her mother.

'Hi, Mum . . . No, I was just having some breakfast . . . Okay, what time? . . . Fine . . . No, I'll meet you somewhere, the flat's a mess because I'm still doing some decorating . . .'

Steve made a point of sitting up straight and, looking around the room, frowned and gave an exaggerated shrug.

Kimberley threw him a nasty glance.

'. . . yes, it was a lovely evening. Steve and I went out for dinner . . . The Thai Castle . . . Yes, I know!'

Steve coughed. It wasn't intentional – well, he had intended to clear his throat, but he hadn't meant it to do it so loudly.

Kimberley stared at him.

'That was the television. Some programme about . . . sea lions. I'll just turn it down.'

Steve put down the paper and quietly applauded her response.

'Sorry, what did you say? . . . er, yes, I think next Friday should be fine I'll check with Steve when I speak to him later . . .'

Kimberley turned to Steve and mimed the word 'Sorry'.

Steve smiled sweetly. He then turned sideways in the bed to face her. She smiled back at him as she spoke.

'So shall I meet you at Franco's?'

Steve moved his hand under the covers and slowly started to caress Kimberley's breasts. She quickly turned to him, shook her head and moved away.

'Okay . . . No, I didn't hear. What happened to her . . . ?'

As Kimberley tried to listen to her mother, Steve moved his hand further down her body.

Kimberley twisted her body in an attempt to stop him.

'Uh, uh . . . oh really . . .'

Steve burrowed his way under the duvet.

'Oh, sorry, Mum, there's someone at the door!'

Kimberley's voice came out higher than she'd expected.

'Yes, it is early. Probably Jehovah's Witnesses. Call you back later. Bye!'

As she lay there and closed her eyes, Steve suddenly reappeared from under the duvet.

'You know they will want to come around to your flat sometime. You can't constantly say that it's untidy or that you're decorating.'

Kimberley sighed. 'I know.'

'And you're going to have difficulty explaining your sudden interest in superhero figurines – unless you expect me to move them from the shelves.'

Kimberley was now getting a little annoyed, and frustrated.

'No, I won't expect you to move them!'

She took a breath. 'I *will* tell them that you've moved in. I'm . . . I'm just waiting for the right moment.'

'It's okay. I know how tough teenage years can be.'

Kimberley looked at him. 'Very funny, Mastermind.'

Steve frowned. 'What do you mean, Mastermind?'

Kimberley looked at him; 'You've started, so you'll finish.'

She pushed Steve's head back under the duvet.

CHAPTER FORTY-THREE

Worried about a small mole on L.H. shoulder. Advised not to be concerned. Referred to Mr Hammer at St Luke's.

As Kimberley finished typing her notes onto the screen, she noticed that her mobile was flashing. She picked it up and read that she'd missed a call. She checked the time of her next appointment, looked at the clock on the computer screen and decided that she had enough time to return the call.

'Hi, sweetheart, I missed your call . . . Oh, I don't mind, whatever you fancy making. You know we need quite a bit of shopping though. . . . Okay, or I can go tomorrow if you prefer . . . Fine, well, don't forget to get eggs and milk and – oh hang on a minute . . .'

Kimberley looked at the display.

'Sorry, sweetheart, I'll have to call you back, Vanessa's on the other line . . . No, she isn't more important than you, but we've kept missing each other today and I have appointments now for the next hour and a half.' Kimberley smiled. 'Yes, I know. I love you too. Bye.'

She switched calls.

'Hi, Ness, sorry I haven't got back to you, and I can't speak long now. I . . . What do you mean you're going to meet PP tonight? And more to the point, why have you been calling all day to tell me that? He's your husband. That's hardly news . . .'

Kimberley stopped as she listened to her friend's reply.

Her eyes widened and her mouth dropped open. If she had been green and squatting at a lily pond she wouldn't have looked out of place.

She closed her mouth slightly to ask the next questions. 'So . . . what are you going to do? Where are you going to go?'

Her mouth dropped open again as she listened to the response. She eventually replied.

'Wow. Wow! Look, Ness . . . are you sure? I mean, are you sure this is a good idea?'

As Kimberley listened again, the phone on her desk rang. An internal call from the surgery receptionist.

'Hang on a sec.'

Kimberley picked up the phone and spoke immediately; 'Hi. Sorry, I was just writing up the notes from Mr Edwards and clearing up. I'll buzz in two minutes . . . okay.'

She put the phone down and picked up her mobile.

'Sorry . . . no, it's okay. Look, just think about what you're doing, Ness. I mean, are you sure it's the right decision? . . . Really? Okay, if you're sure. Do you want me to come? . . . Okay. Well, let me know if you change your mind. Good luck. Call me straight after...'

Kimberley switched off her phone. She looked at the clock on the computer screen once again. She decided that Mrs Green could wait a few minutes longer; it would at least give her something real to complain about. She sat back in her chair.

Was this idea of Vanessa's really a good one? Should she have tried to stop her? She remembered the last conversation she'd had with her. Strangely Vanessa had seemed happier than she had been in a long while. Since discovering that PP had joined the *Dating Yet Married* website and then pretending to be Laura69, her sex life and her married life had both apparently improved. But both she and Vanessa knew she was living a lie. A false happiness brought on by deception. And that's why she wanted to stop it now. Kimberley understood her reason. But she knew the consequences weren't going to be good. And in a way wasn't it better to live a life which was a bit of a sham as long as you were happy? And she still wasn't sure if PP was having an affair – although what Vanessa was now planning would prove it one way or another.

Kimberley pressed the button on her desk.

Outside in the waiting room the name *Dr K. Richardson* lit up.

'About time too!' said Mrs Green as she sprang out of her chair. She then remembered where she was and why she was there. She bent over slightly and slowly shuffled towards the door to Kimberley's consulting room.

CHAPTER FORTY-FOUR

Vanessa sat in her car in the supermarket car park. She looked around to see where the pounding noise was coming from, until she realised it was her own pulse vibrating in her head. Across the road from her was the Travel Hotel. She could have used their car park, but she didn't want to risk PP seeing her car.

She pulled down her sun visor and looked at her face in the small mirror.

'What. Are. You. Doing?!'

She closed her eyes and breathed out. Even though the heating was on in the car, the air was still cold enough for her to see her breath in front of her.

In a way she wished Kimberley could have been with her. This was going to be tough and having a bit of moral support would have helped. Yet she also knew that she had to do this on her own. She looked at the small hotel room keycard in her hand. She missed the old-fashioned keys with the huge hotel name tag attached to them. She then remembered the first weekend she and PP had spent away together. It had been a small B & B in Blackpool. PP had always gone to Blackpool as a child and he wanted to go back and reminisce. As they hadn't had much money, they weren't able to stay in one of the larger hotels so had to make do with the cheapest room they could find. This turned out to be the Friendly Hope Guest House run by a Mr and Mrs Oliver. Well, it was meant to be a guest house, but it was just the Olivers' house, with their one spare room used for guests. Mr and Mrs Oliver – they wouldn't reveal their first names – had insisted on being paid cash up front and had told PP and Vanessa that they had to be out by nine thirty the following morning as there was a family of four arriving. They were also told not to come back too late in the night and not to make any unnecessary noise. Although they had enjoyed their time in Blackpool – even though the 'lights' weren't as magical as in PP's memory – he had taken the guest house key, along with the huge cork ball attached to it, as punishment for the way they'd been treated. It was now in PP's memorabilia-cum-junk drawer in his office.

Vanessa pushed the sun visor back up. That's when she saw him. PP was walking towards the entrance of the Travel Hotel. It was too late now. Well, of course, it actually wasn't. She could quite easily have driven home and no one, save her and Kimberley, would be any the wiser. She contemplated what she was about to do, and what she had already done . . .

***

An hour earlier she had arrived at the Travel Hotel and paid for the room she'd booked a few days ago. Even though she'd paid in cash – as she didn't want any record tracing back to her in case she pulled out – they'd still insisted on seeing some proof of ID.

'It's to do with money laundering,' she'd been informed.

'Just for £55?' she'd asked. 'That hardly pays my own laundry bill!'

She'd been met with a courteous smile and insistence.

Once Vanessa had paid for the room and shown her driving licence, she asked for two keys. She then went to the lift and pressed the button for the fourth floor. She imagined PP doing the same thing in an hour's time. How would he be feeling? Would he be nervous? Horny? Both? She wondered if you could be both at the same time, and decided that you probably could.

She'd arrived at room 403 and checked that both key cards worked. She'd then gone into the room and moved the furniture around a little – for reasons of strategy as opposed to feng shui. She'd moved an armchair away from the window to the wall opposite the door. She'd then taken the upright chair from the desk and put it outside the room – hoping that no staff member would come along and move it. After that she'd then gone back into the room and, using one of the large local guidebooks, propped the door ajar while she removed all the bulbs from the table and bedside lamps and put them into one of the drawers. As in most hotel rooms, there were no ceiling bulbs to worry about. Satisfied, she had then returned downstairs and given one of the keys to the receptionist. She had told her that someone by the name of Phillip Fowler would be coming and that she should tell him the room number and give him the key.

She'd rarely used her husband's real name and found it quite strange, although not as strange as what she was currently doing. She had then handed over an envelope, which she explained should also please be given to him. The receptionist had dutifully accepted the request without question as though it were nothing unusual.

Vanessa had then driven her car to the supermarket car park, which was where she now sat – watching her husband on his way to have an affair. With her.

***

'Hello, my name's Phillip Fowler and . . .'

The receptionist handed over the key card and letter.

'Room 403. The lifts are over there.' The receptionist pointed, smiled and went back to her sudoku.

'Oh, right, thanks.'

Once inside the lift, PP pressed the button for the fourth floor. He felt nervous. And horny. He opened the letter and read the typed note.

'Hi, here's what I want you to do. Go into the room but don't switch any lights on. Take off all your clothes and get into bed. I'll come in with my own key and get into bed with you. I don't want us to speak – we haven't spoken so far so I don't want to do it just yet. I just want us to have sex. Hard, filthy, anything you like sex. Only then, after we've finished, will we speak.

I can't wait to feel you inside me. Xx'

The lift had arrived at the fourth floor yet PP had not come out. He was rereading the note and was holding the doors open with his foot. They attempted to close against repeatedly, but hit his foot and reopened.

PP eventually finished reading for the second time and stepped into the hallway. The doors, relieved, closed behind him.

PP walked to room 403, opened the door and walked in.

Vanessa looked at the heart she had subconsciously drawn in the condensation on her car window. She looked down at her watch and then checked the clock on the dashboard display. They both showed the same time. And they were both five minutes fast. Vanessa always put her clocks and watches five minutes fast in the hopeless belief that this would mean she wouldn't be late for things. Of course all she really did was to look at the time and then subtract the extra five minutes.

She looked towards the hotel again. She took a deep breath in and then added to the condensation. She opened the car door, stepped out, closed it and then locked it behind her. Even though she had seen it lock and seen the lights flashing to confirm it had locked, she still checked the handle just to make sure. She then started to walk towards the hotel.

'Hi, Vanessa.'

For a moment she hadn't heard the voice. Or if she had then she thought it was in her head – a rap going along to the pounding rhythm.

'Vanessa?'

She turned around to see Steve, shopping bags in hand, standing behind her.

'Oh. Hi. Hello, Steve. How are you? What are you doing here? How's things?'

Steve had never been asked so many questions so quickly before. He wasn't sure which one to answer first.

'Er . . . I'm fine, thanks. Everything's good. I'm just, you know, doing some shopping. How are you?'

'Yeah, yeah, I'm good, thanks. Really good. Oh, congratulations on the driving test.'

'Thanks. You know what they say, fourth time lucky.'

'Yeah. Absolutely. That's what they say, don't they? Hahaha.'

Although they had spoken many, many times, Steve was aware this was by far their oddest and most uncomfortable conversation ever.

'So . . . have you done it or are you about to do it?'

Vanessa looked shocked. She couldn't believe Kimberley had told him. Surely their long friendship meant more than her relatively new relationship. She felt stupid and embarrassed. For several reasons.

'No, I haven't done it yet, Steve! I was just about to! Although if you must know, I'm having second thoughts about it now.'

Steve could feel the sudden coldness in her voice.

'I just . . . I just don't want *everyone* to know about it.'

Steve smiled and blew a little laughing noise through his nose. 'Well, I won't tell anyone.'

'Yes, you will, Steve,' Vanessa said nastily. 'You'll tell Jeff. Then he'll tell Francine. Then before I know it everyone will start talking behind my back! I'll look a fool in front of people. I don't want that! So that's why I'm probably not going to go ahead with it!'

Steve could feel his mouth moving involuntarily. It was trying to form words while his brain was trying to work out what words these should be. He knew that Vanessa had a strange sense of humour, but he usually liked it. In fact the two of them sometimes shared jokes that no one else understood. But if this were a joke, then he certainly didn't get it this time.

'No, Vanessa, really, I won't tell anyone. I promise. Although to be honest, I don't really understand the problem.'

Vanessa was shocked. Almost appalled. 'Oh really, Steve. You don't understand the problem?! You don't think that having a husb . . .'

She stopped. She frowned. She thought. She stopped frowning.

'What *exactly* are you talking about, Steve? Have I done what yet?'

'Er . . . your shopping.'

'Yes, that's what I thought,' Vanessa agreed without missing a beat. 'I was just joking with you. You know . . . pretending I was embarrassed about shopping here instead of one of those fancy shopping places. Like the ones Francine goes to.'

'I'm pretty sure Francine shops here as well,' said Steve, who was now wishing he hadn't stopped to say hello in the first place.

'Oh, really? Well, the joke's on me then!' said Vanessa, forcing another laugh.

Steve smiled and also forced a laugh, mainly to give himself time to think of an excuse to get away.

'Anyway, I'd better be off.'

There hadn't been enough time to think of anything else.

'And I'd better do my shopping. In here! See you soon, Steve.'

She kissed him on the cheek. Steve attempted to do the same thing at the same time, but as Vanessa moved away quite quickly he ended up kissing the top of her ear – which only added to what had been a very bizarre encounter.

Vanessa walked towards the supermarket. She then stopped and looked back. She saw Steve putting his bags of shopping into the boot of his car, close the boot and then get into the car. She quickly hid behind one of the pillars near the supermarket entrance, from where she watched him drive towards the exit and then out onto the main road.

She sighed deeply.

In his car, as he drove along the dual carriageway away from the supermarket, Steve was still thinking about his meeting with Vanessa. He ran back over the conversation in his head. It really had been strange; as if they had been talking at cross-purposes. Suddenly there was a loud beeping sound in the car which made Steve think that he had suddenly come up with the wrong answer in a quiz show. He looked at the dashboard and saw the small red 'low petrol' warning light flashing. He looked at the gauges. That looks full, he thought. He then realised he was looking at the temperature gauge. He quickly shifted his gaze to check the road in front of him and then looked down at the petrol gauge. Empty. He tried to think of the whereabouts of the nearest petrol station. There was one near home, but he wasn't sure if he had enough petrol to make it there. Had he been in Kimberley's car, the onboard computer would have given him an approximate indication as to how many miles he had left in the tank. But his own car, a fifth-hand one which he had bought for £750 from a friend of a friend of Kimberley's father, could cut out at any time. He hadn't even known that the car even had a petrol warning light until now.

He decided that the best course of action was to turn back and fill it up at the supermarket petrol station.

***

Vanessa walked through the supermarket car park and crossed the main road, which led to the dual carriageway. She then walked through the car park of the Travel Hotel. She thought about PP. Would he still be there? How long had she been chatting with Steve? Would PP have thought she wasn't showing and now be getting dressed in order to leave? Had he got undressed in the first place or had he just ignored all the instructions? Being preoccupied with these thoughts, she didn't notice Steve drive past her and wave on his way to the petrol station. But Steve saw her, and as he passed her he looked in his rear-view mirror and watched her walk into the Travel Hotel.

***

Inside the hotel, Vanessa walked towards the lift as best she could. The pounding in her head had now moved to her chest and was giving her a slight difficulty in breathing. The lift doors opened and she stepped through. Less than a minute later she stepped back out onto the fourth-floor hallway. She slowly passed rooms 401 and 402. She then stopped and slid her handbag from her shoulder. She quietly opened it and removed the key card. However the perspiration in her hand together with the shiny plastic made it slip from her fingers. As she bent down to pick it up, the contents of her handbag spilt onto the floor. She thought about just running out and leaving everything there, until she realised that the dropped items included her driving licence and credit cards. Although PP wasn't the brightest person in the world, she knew that even *he* would be able to work out who she was from those clues.

She quickly pushed everything back into her handbag and then put her ear to the door of the room – just below the spyhole. She couldn't hear anything from inside. Had PP left or was he lying naked in bed, waiting. She thought for a moment. She then wiped the key card on the leg of her jeans and put it into the slot in the bedroom door. A green light flashed. She pushed down on the heavy handle and opened the door halfway.

The bedroom was in darkness, save for the light now shining in from the hallway. She could hear PP breathing. She was equally delighted and appalled. As she'd expected, knowing PP was a creature of habit, he had thrown his clothes over the chair she had earlier moved from the far side of the room to opposite the door.

She took a breath and walked into the room, opening the door wide behind her.

The light from the hallway now filled the room. She looked at her husband lying in the bed, his lower body covered by the sheets. She could tell he was holding his stomach in.

She smiled at him.

'Hi.'

PP's face went through a range of emotions in less than a second.

'Vanessa! How . . . ? What . . . ?!'

Vanessa looked at him. 'Please don't say, "This isn't how it looks."'

'But . . . how did you know I was here? Did you follow me?'

Vanessa laughed. 'Oh, darling. You are so, so stupid.'

She picked up PP's clothes from the chair.

She then turned back to him. 'And you're also a bastard.'

She started to walk out of the room.

'Oh, and, I've been meaning to tell you, PP is the stupidest name in the world.'

She then walked out of the bedroom, closed the door, took the chair in the hallway which she had removed from the room and propped it under the door handle. She then walked slowly back towards the lift, leaving the sound of her soon-to-be ex-husband banging on the door in the darkness behind her.

CHAPTER FORTY-FIVE

'How can she *not* be having an affair? Why else would someone lie about going shopping and then go into a hotel? I know I didn't study criminology, but I have seen every episode of *Columbo*.'

'You don't have to be sarcastic.'

'I'm not. I seriously have seen every episode. Well, up until the end of the seventh season anyway. I wasn't really interested in the ones made after 1978. Oh apart from *Agenda for Murder* in 1990 with Patrick McGoohan; you know, the guy who was in *The Prisoner*. He won the Emmy for Outstanding Guest Actor in a Drama Series for that episode. It's not one of my favourites, but—'

'Okay. Okay. You've made your point.' Kimberley took a breath. 'But I can assure you she's not having an affair. Look, I've just walked in. You haven't even given me a chance to take my coat off. Let me have a shower and get changed and I'll explain everything.'

She put her briefcase down by the front door next to Steve's shoes and then went towards the bedroom. Steve looked towards the kitchen and tried to decide which bottle of wine would best be suited for this type of conversation.

***

The explanation had taken almost two full glasses of a Rioja they had brought back from Malaga airport. Steve had sat there and listened while his girlfriend told him what had been happening over the past few months. He didn't know if he was more shocked by the events or by the fact that Kimberley had kept the whole thing a secret.

'I would have told you about it before, but Vanessa asked me not to say anything.'

Steve had always been impressed by Kimberley's mind-reading abilities.

He nodded. Apart from nodding, raising his wine glass and occasionally dropping his jaw in shock, Steve hadn't moved or said anything for the past fifteen minutes.

'Anyway, Vanessa phoned me just as I was arriving home to tell me that she had gone to the room, called him a bastard, taken his clothes and then locked the door behind her.' Kimberley rubbed her forehead with the palm of her hand. The weight of everything that had happened to her friend began to sink in. She took a sip from her own almost untouched wine.

'I'm going over to her place in an hour, so I won't have any more to drink. She's in a pretty bad way.'

'Why didn't you tell me?'

Even though he had heard the whole story, and Kimberley had explained why she hadn't told him, this was the only thing that mattered to Steve. Yes, he was sorry for what had happened to Vanessa; he really liked her and really disliked PP. But it wasn't going to affect his life. However the fact that his girlfriend had hidden this from him just might.

'I told you. Vanessa asked me not to.'

'Jeff asked me not to tell you about the lap-dancing clubs. But I did. He asked me not to tell you about losing all that money at the casino, but I did.'

'This is different.'

'No, it's not. It's about trust. It's about priorities. It's about trust.'

'You already said "trust".'

'I know. It's *that* important!'

Kimberley stood up. She was annoyed – with herself more than with Steve. He was right; she should have told him. Yes, she'd promised Vanessa she wouldn't and they had been friends for . . . ever. But she was living with her boyfriend now. The boyfriend who might eventually become her husband. She shouldn't have lied to him. And she was going to apologise . . .

'I'm going to Vanessa's now. I'll see you later.'

. . . just not yet.

CHAPTER FORTY-SIX

'On The Edge is pleased to announce that we are now representing award-winning stand-up Lady Langley.'

Steve reread what he had just typed. He then highlighted it and changed the font. He did that another three times until he eventually settled on *Abadi MT Condensed Extra Bold*. He then changed the font colour to red and saved the document as 'Press Release: Lady Langley'.

Although Lady Langley, or Chrissie, was award-winning, the award had been for a short play she had written eight years earlier which had won the Three Counties Short Play Award. The prize had been a fifty-pound book token and to have the play performed by a local amateur dramatic society. Still an award is an award. And it was more relevant than the Bicycling Efficiency Award or 100 Metres Breast Stroke Award other comedians referred to when they claimed to be 'award-winning'.

Steve always used the taking on of a new client as an excuse to remind people that his agency was still around and to send out an updated client list. This had varied in length over the years, but of late had been around a pretty healthy twenty people, from open-spots to well-established acts. No one was a household name, but he knew that a few had real potential.

Steve looked through his email contacts and bcc'd all the producers and comedy bookers. He then wrote a short note and attached the press release and client list.

He pressed 'send'. He watched the virus scanner check his document – and then send it.

He then, out of force of habit, pressed 'send and receive'. Nothing further was sent, but he did receive something. Something he wasn't expecting at all – an email from *Girl From The Disco*.

Steve had forgotten all about the website. Had the domain not expired? He awkwardly wheeled his chair over to his filing cabinet and opened one of the drawers. He took out the appropriate 'misc' file and looked through it. He then looked at the firemen calendar on the wall – a Christmas present from Jeff (the calendar, not the wall) – and from the date saw that the domain didn't expire for another month.

He wheeled back to his place in front of the computer and looked at the email again. He still hadn't opened it, but didn't know why. He looked at the sender's name once more: 'H. Potter'. The name meant nothing to him – unless of course a fictitious boy wizard was trying to get in touch.

He'd had over two hundred random emails through this site, including the one from Vanessa which had introduced Kimberley, so why was he now hesitating? His hand moved the mouse around the sender's name. He then stopped. Then, beginning to find himself a little pathetic, he moved the mouse again, clicked on the email and read.

'Hi, Steve. I hope you don't mind me contacting you, it's just that the programme you were on a while ago was repeated yesterday and my mother saw it and recorded it for me. Sorry, this sounds like a boring story but it does have a point! Anyway, I watched the programme, and then looked at your website and . . . well, I'm pretty sure I am that girl.'

Steve reread the whole message. Then he reread this last line three times. She must have been referring to the first programme he'd been on. He looked around the room. He looked at the backwards clock, he looked at all the posters, he looked at his filing cabinets, he looked at his Hulk Versus The Thing figurine – he still wasn't sure who'd win that fight – he then looked back at the email. 'I'm pretty sure I am that girl.' He'd received several of these kinds of emails in the past, and he remembered some of the photos he'd received with them. But this one felt different. And as he continued reading, he knew he was right. This was different.

'*I used to go to a disco called Angels in Reading in the late 80s. I don't remember you, sorry, but it was always such a busy place. I am attaching a photo – although I have obviously changed a lot from 20 years ago! Anyway, I just wanted to say hi.*

Love, Helen.'

Steve felt sick. This had to be some horrible practical joke. But who could have done it? The only people who knew the girl's name were Jeff and Greg the hypnotist. Surely it couldn't be Greg. What would be the point? They weren't mates. It wouldn't really be a laugh they could share.

He put his phone onto loudspeaker and rang Jeff's work number.

'Hello, Jeff's phone.'

'Oh, hi, William, it's Steve. Is Jeff around?'

'Hi, Steve. No, he's gone to get some lunch, back in twenty minutes or so. Shall I get him to call you?'

'Yes, thanks.'

Steve switched off the phone.

Steve liked William. He was very quiet and generally kept himself to himself, although on the few occasions he had joined Jeff and Steve for an after-work drink he had been great company and told interesting stories about the world of advertising. William was the art director to Jeff's copywriter and was a bit older than Steve and Jeff – although he would never say exactly how much older. He'd been in advertising almost his whole working life and had had a succession of business partners. However he told Jeff that he was by far the best. Jeff reckoned he'd said the same thing to all his previous partners. William had never explained why he'd stopped working with his previous copywriters, although Jeff did find out that two of them had died – one from a suspected drug overdose and the other one was mugged and stabbed on holiday in Turkey. Jeff had been upset to hear this, but it also kept him on his toes.

Steve looked at the email again. Of course! If this *were* one of Jeff's wind-ups then the attached photo would be something hideous. Or maybe one of Jeff himself.

Steve scanned and opened the attachment.

Holding a glass of wine and smiling at him was a woman in her mid- to late-thirties with blonde hair and blue-green eyes. There was no doubt she was attractive. There was no doubt she looked like the Photofit. There was no doubt Steve was in trouble.

CHAPTER FORTY-SEVEN

Dave looked into the eyes of the people around him. He'd been a police officer for over ten years and would often pride himself on his ability to read people. He could usually tell in a domestic situation or a vehicle collision which party was to blame just by looking into their eyes. He'd watched line-ups and had seen the guilt, or lack of, in the eyes of the suspects.

Yet looking into these eyes, eyes of people he'd known for many years, he was uncertain. Were they lying? Were they hiding something?

'I'll call.'

Dave took a green five-hundred chip from the stack in front of him and threw it onto the pile of scattered chips in the centre of the table.

He turned to his brother-in-law, who was sitting next to him.

Steve looked at his cards. 'Er . . . sorry, just remind me, does a *straight* beat a *flush*?'

There were general sighs and moans from around the table.

Dave, who felt responsible, as he was the one who'd brought Steve along, quickly explained.

'No, Steve. It's a pair, then two pairs, then three of a kind . . .'

'Or trips, as they're more commonly known,' suggested Graham, one of the other poker players, with equal measures of sarcasm and annoyance.

'Then a straight, then a flush, then a full house, then four of a kind . . .'

'Or quads.'

Graham continued, and finished off, 'Then a straight flush, and then a royal flush.'

'Right,' said Steve. 'Thanks.'

He turned to the others around the table.

'Sorry. I do know how to play; it's just been a while. My girlfriend isn't a fan of gambling, so . . .'

Graham mimed the action of cracking a whip and made the sound to accompany it.

Steve smiled. He was a guest and thought it best to play along with the bullying.

Graham was the one who took these games the most seriously. Too seriously for some of the other players. Most of them saw it as an excuse for a catch-up and a chat or at least a break away from their wives or girlfriends – and in some cases, a break from both. But not Graham. Graham was a gambler. He even had a small tattoo of a pair of aces on his shoulder. Like Dave, and two of the other players, Graham was a police officer. But unlike them he was a sergeant and not a constable, something he rarely let them forget about. As he was divorced with no children, Graham was quite happy to spend the majority of his salary on his 'habit'. He referred to his gambling as a habit and not an addiction. After all, as he always explained, an addiction is something you can't stop. 'I could stop gambling anytime I wanted to' was his favourite phrase. Well, that and, 'Shagged another gorgeous girl last night.' Graham was the one who organised these fortnightly poker evenings. To him it wasn't about the social element, it was about the playing and winning. As in work, he liked to show who was the boss. Sometimes it was difficult to organise the games around work shifts, which was why they were sometimes short of players. Hence the reason

Dave brought along Steve – just to make up the numbers.

Steve used to play poker when he was in school. But it had been a different game back then. From what he could remember, you had five cards and were allowed to change up to three of them up to three times. In retrospect it seemed like an odd way to play, but sitting in the school prefects' room had been like being in a casino – or so they had all imagined at the time.

But this game was different. This was Texas Hold 'Em. The game du jour. And he wasn't quite sure how to play it. Which explained why he'd already lost a £160 in less than two hours.

'I'll . . . raise,' said Steve, as he pushed his cards face down into the centre of the table.

'What?' said Graham.

'You mean you'll "fold"?' suggested Dave, who was starting to regret bringing him.

'Oh. Sorry. Yes. That's what I meant. I'll fold.'

The next player also folded, while the one after that called the bet.

As Graham, the dealer for that round, dealt the final 'river' card, Steve asked what he'd wanted to ask all evening. One of the real reasons he'd accepted the offer to play.

'How . . . er . . . how easy is it to run a check on someone? You know, through one of the police computers?'

Dave turned to Steve. He knew his brother-in-law pretty well and knew this wasn't just a random question.

'It's very easy,' said Jerry, who was not only one of Dave's work colleagues and closest friends but had also been best man at Dave and Sheila's wedding – which had upset Steve a little, not that anyone ever knew that.

'As long as you have a valid reason. You can't just look

someone up because you fancy it. Or them. When you log onto the database, a record of your search is registered.'

'Oh. Right. So what type of reason do you need? What if you had a car accident with them and they drove off? Or what if—'

'Look, are we having a chat or playing cards?!'

Steve felt as if he was back in school. Except no one in the prefects' room had been as unpleasant as Graham.

***

'So what made you ask that?'

'Ask what?'

Dave didn't reply. He just looked through the rain-speckled windscreen at the road in front of him and continued to drive.

'Oh, you mean the question about running a check on people?' Steve had forgotten everything he had learned at drama school, 'Nothing really. Just . . . you know . . . curious.'

'Uh-huh.'

Dave watched the wipers as they intermittently removed the rain. He noticed that one of them was leaving a semicircular trail and decided that the following day he would buy a new set of blades.

'Graham doesn't like losing, does he?'

'No, he doesn't. I prefer it when he's not playing really, but as most of the games are at his flat it's quite tricky.'

'Thanks again for inviting me along. I'm not sure how much I really added to the game though – apart from giving everyone a share of my money.'

Dave smiled. 'So, who is it?'

'Sorry?' asked Steve.

'Who are you hoping I'll run a check on? And, more importantly, why?'

Steve thought about making up a story, but realised there was little point.

'I don't want to get you involved. Especially not after the grief Sheil gave you over the Photofit. That's why I asked the others and not you.'

'Oh, believe me, Steve, I won't get involved. I'm just curious.'

Steve knew how this was going to sound. He didn't really want to say it. But he hadn't said anything to Jeff – not after the lecture he gave him last time – and, well, there was no one else he could talk to. And Dave had been a part of this.

'Well . . . I'd been having doubts about Kim being the right girl and—'

'What?!'

Steve, who since learning how to drive had become a very nervous passenger, felt that he shouldn't have started this conversation while Dave was driving, especially in these wet conditions. But he continued.

'I started thinking it a while ago, but then I tried to forget about it. Then I found out that she hasn't been truthful with me about things. She's been keeping things from me and lying to me, or at least hiding the truth from me. And she hides the fact that we live together from her parents and, well . . .'

'I can't believe what I'm hearing! Are you telling me that . . . that . . . that you think Kimberley has made the whole thing up just to catch you!'

Steve realised how stupid it sounded. 'No, of course not. But—'

'Don't flatter yourself, Steve; you're not that great a catch! I honestly don't think any girl would organise such an intricate and elaborate scam just to get you!'

Steve didn't often hear Dave get annoyed. He put it down

to his training – remaining calm under pressure, dealing with situations in a controlled manner – but there was definitely anger in his voice now.

Steve decided to quickly lay out his whole hand.

'It's not only that. There's this girl who emailed me through the website. She had the same name as the girl in my dreams, my flashbacks, whatever they are. And she looks like the girl, like the Photofit. More than . . .' he swallowed and spoke slowly, 'more than Kim does. I think this is the real one.'

They both watched the rain hitting the windscreen and watched the wipers take the majority of it away.

'So you are hoping that someone would be able to check up on this girl who contacted you and see if she's genuine and also check on your girlfriend?'

Steve swallowed. 'Yes. Please.'

CHAPTER FORTY-EIGHT

Steve wondered who all the people milling around backstage actually were. Surely such a small production didn't need this many people working on it.

'I can't believe how nervous I am!'

Steve turned and smiled at Lady Langley standing next to him. 'Well, you don't have to be. But saying that, I don't think nerves are such a bad thing.'

The producer of the programme, which was being filmed as live from the theatre, walked over to them and spoke to Lady Langley.

'So you'll go on after Richie Richards, who's on next. Just do between five and seven minutes – which will eventually be edited down to four – and come off, hopefully to a huge round of applause. Any questions?'

'What about language?'

'Well, preferably English.'

Lady Langley stared at the laughing producer.

'Sorry, I should leave the jokes for the comedians! Don't worry too much about bad language as we can always edit and it's going out post-watershed anyway. Although avoid the C-word. And I don't mean "cat"!'

The producer walked off, still laughing.

Lady Langley turned to Steve.

'*He's* a C-word.'

Steve smiled.

'It's . . . it's been a while since I've done any telly stuff. And

I'm a lot older than the other comics here. I'm sure some of them are teenagers!'

'It doesn't matter. You know a lot of these young comics come and go – they win a competition or stick something on YouTube and suddenly they're the next big thing. For all of two months. Whereas you . . .'

'I've been around forever. Yet most of these kids have never heard of me.'

'Not yet. But after this they will. The demographic for this show is just the age range you need to appeal to. The eighteen-to-thirty-five-year-olds.'

'Most of them will look at me like I'm their mum.'

'Or at least their mum's rather sexy young-for-her-age friend.'

Lady Langley smiled. 'You always know the right things to say. And thanks again for getting me this. I've always watched this show and tried to get on it, but that c . . . producer didn't ever return my emails.' She pursed her lips and breathed in and out three times. It was her little pre-performance ritual. 'Tell me the truth, Steve – how did you get me this gig?'

'Because when I told them how good you were, they insisted on having you.'

She looked at him.

Steve sighed. 'They wanted Mike Dutch but I told them that they couldn't have him unless they took you as well.'

He looked a little uncomfortable.

'And that's why I joined your agency!' Lady Langley smiled.

The floor manager, a girl in her mid-twenties, walked over to them.

'Hiya. Right, Richie Richards is going on now. You can come over and watch through the wings. Once he's finished,

Eric will do about three minutes, get them focused again, and then bring you on. Sound good?'

Lady Langley smiled and nodded.

'Great, come with me then.'

The floor manager walked towards the wings. Lady Langley and Steve trailing dutifully behind her.

'You can just stand here,' she said quietly. 'Have a good one.'

'Thanks,' said Lady Langley, just as quietly.

As the floor manager started to walk away, she stopped and looked at Steve. 'Do I know you from somewhere?' she asked.

Steve was used to this question. He had one of those faces that people seemed to recognise. He had done a little television work – mainly on 'talking heads' programmes about comedy and comedians – but not enough to make him generally recognisable. So even though he was used to hearing the question, he was never sure how to answer it.

'Er . . . I don't think so.'

Anne Blackman, the agent of Eric Bell – the host and star of the show – turned from the wings and looked at Steve. She put her fingers to her lips and pointed towards the stage where her 'talent' was performing.

'You'll have to speak quieter,' whispered the floor manager.

'Sorry,' said Steve, who believed he had been speaking quietly.

He looked at Anne Blackman and mimed the word 'sorry'. Anne Blackman stared back at him. She then turned her head and smiled as she continued to watch her client.

'You stupid bitch,' said Steve almost silently through clenched teeth and lips.

The floor manager suppressed a laugh.

'You're telling me!' she said, just as quietly. 'Anyway, it'll probably come to me where I know you from. If either of you needs anything, let me know.'

Steve thanked her and she walked off.

Steve looked at his client. He could see how nervous she was as she watched the next act being introduced.

'Well, ladies and gentlemen,' said Eric Bell, standing at the microphone in the centre of the large stage, 'we have a real treat in store for you now.' He looked from left to right to take in the whole audience. 'This guy is relatively new but he's been storming clubs up and down the country. Please put your hands together and welcome onstage . . . Richie Richards!'

Twenty-one-year-old Richie Richards walked confidently onto the stage. He shook hands with Eric as they passed each other. Richie then grabbed the microphone from the stand.

'Hello, people! How are we doing?'

Some of the audience mumbled various responses. It was all irrelevant to him. This was always the way he'd started his set as it gave him time to move the microphone stand downstage.

'It's good to be here. Just flew in from doing a show in the States. Well, I didn't fly in myself, I came by plane. I mean, that would be weird, wouldn't it? Having wings under my T-shirt . . .'

Richie Richards then pretended to sprout wings from his back and fly around the stage.

'It could be handy though. Especially if you were being chased by evil goblins, who were trying to fire golden arrows at you . . .'

He then pretended to be a goblin, firing arrows into the sky; 'Damn you, Richards and your special wings of freedom!'

The audience laughed.

In the wings, Lady Langley stared.

'Don't worry,' said Steve quietly into her ear. 'I don't get it either.'

Lady Langley turned and looked at him. 'If they like this type of surreal stuff, I'm going to die on my arse!'

Steve put his hand on her shoulder. 'No, you won't,' he reassured her. 'You have good, strong material. Actual proper jokes. They'll love you.'

Lady Langley smiled. But she wasn't convinced. She turned back and watched the rest of Richie Richard's act. She didn't smile once.

***

'So, Steve, how's the business going? It's had its share of ups and downs over the years, hasn't it?' While she waited for his response, Anne Blackman picked up one of the mushroom vol-au-vents and put it into her mouth whole.

'It's okay, thanks. You know how it is, acts come and go. Mainly to you apparently.'

Anne ignored the comment, swallowed her vol-au-vent and picked up a second one, 'I work hard for my clients. I'm loyal to them and they're loyal to me.'

'That's what you get for making them sign a five-year exclusive contract.'

Steve watched as she chewed on this second vol-au-vent a little longer. He had never really liked Anne. She was known as a bit of a party animal, a fun-time girl – both of which were really just euphemisms for 'slut'. There were very few comedians, agents or producers that she hadn't slept with – or at least attempted to. She didn't agree with arriving fashionably late at a party, as there was a chance that the free drink would have run out. Not that drink was her only vice;

she also had a long-standing cocaine habit. One of her former clients had made it known how unhappy he was to watch fifteen per cent of his earnings disappear up his agent's nose. Steve had once sat next to her at a comedy awards evening and had quickly become irritated by her constant disappearing and regular sniffing. When he had a cold his mother always used to tell him to blow instead of sniff. Anne was doing both. Even though this sniffing had driven Steve mad throughout the awards, he had still slept with her that night. Well, he hadn't wanted to be the odd one out.

'Anyway,' said Anne, after swallowing and reaching for a third vol-au-vent, 'well done on getting Lady Langley. She did well tonight. I've always liked her stuff. And it's good to see she's still doing the same thing.'

Steve turned down the wine refill from the waitress.

'Well, it's TV, isn't it?' said Steve. 'You don't want to waste your best stuff as you can never use it again. Which reminds me, who's writing for Eric now?'

Anne's eyes narrowed. 'What do you mean "writing for him"?! He writes his own material. All my clients write their own material!'

Steve enjoyed the reaction to the nerve he'd just hit. Although it was generally thought, and expected, that comedians wrote and performed their own material, some did have it written for them, usually by other comedians. One of Steve's previous clients had subsidised his income from stand-up by writing for several circuit comics. Of course this was all kept very quiet, and there was an agreement between writer and comedian that neither would divulge the information. Although the comedian never said a word, the writer would occasionally find a way of letting it 'slip out'.

'Oh, sorry,' said Steve. 'I don't know where I got that from.'

Lady Langley, carrying a large glass of red wine, came over to join them.

Anne smiled at her. 'Hey, Chrissie. You did really well out there.'

Lady Langley, her eyes slightly bloodshot from her earlier drinks, smiled overly sweetly.

'Thanks, Anne. Apparently there is still room for a middle-aged woman on the young persons' circuit.'

Anne smiled. 'If you're good, you're good.'

'Maybe. But you still need someone to believe in you.'

She gave Steve a peck on the cheek. She then looked around the room. 'I can't remember the last time I was in a greenroom.'

'Well, after today, I'm sure there are going to be a lot more of them.'

Lady Langley's eyes started to water, which only added to the bloodshot effect.

'Thanks, Steve. Listen, once we leave, what say I take you out for a celebrity dinner?' She laughed. 'Sorry, I meant a *celebratory* dinner. Let's not get ahead of myself!'

Lady Langley laughed loudly and stumbled backwards. Steve caught her.

'Er . . . sorry, Chrissie. I'm . . . er . . . meeting someone.'

'Oh, okay. Not to worry. Another time.'

'You can join Eric and me for dinner if you like,' suggested Anne.

Lady Langley hesitated. 'Er . . .'

'Go on,' said Steve. 'I'm not worried about her trying to steal you away from me!'

Lady Langley smiled and turned to Anne. 'Okay, that'd be great.'

Steve looked at his watch. 'In fact I'd better make a move. Have fun.'

He leant in to kiss Lady Langley on the cheek. She however came forward and kissed him on the lips. Steve had always found lip-kissing from people you weren't dating quite odd. He also found it strange when parents kissed their children on the lips. However, he realised this was neither the time nor place to discuss the matter. He smiled, gave a nod to Anne and walked towards the pile of coats on the chair by the greenroom door. As he rummaged through in an attempt to find his own without dropping the others on the floor, someone spoke to him.

'Hi.'

Steve turned to see the young floor manager standing behind him.

'I've just remembered where I know you from. You were on the *Charlie Race* programme.'

Steve hadn't even thought about this option when she'd said that she had recognised him. He wondered how many people had actually seen that.

'About half a million,' said the floor manager.

Steve hadn't realised that he'd wondered it out loud.

'I was a researcher on it.'

'Oh, okay.'

Steve suddenly remembered her.

'Oh!'

The floor manager, ironically, looked at the floor.

'Yeah, I was the one who messed up the photographs. Sorry, again, about all that mix-up.'

Steve smiled reassuringly.

'Don't worry. It's fine. It was a while ago. Everyone has forgiven me.'

'Well, they didn't forgive me. I was fired.'

Steve suddenly felt guilty, even though it hadn't been his fault in the slightest.

'I'm really sorry to hear that.'

He rummaged through the pile of coats until he found his and pulled it free.

'Don't worry, it's fine. I hated that wanker anyway. He treated me really badly. Anyway, I got this job almost immediately and it's loads better.'

Steve started to put on his coat. 'That's great. I'm glad it all worked out.'

The floor manager smiled. 'Thanks. And I'm glad it all worked out for you too – you know, getting the girl and everything. I didn't see the first show you did, but there were loads of responses to the second one. I remember there was a woman who wanted your number. She said that she was the *real* girl you'd been looking for and not the one you'd found.' She laughed. 'There really are some nutters out there.'

Steve nodded. 'Yeah. There are,' he said.

He thought about the potential one he was about to meet.

CHAPTER FORTY-NINE

Steve had been having email conversations with Helen for the past five weeks. He'd only done this at work as he and Kimberley shared their home computer. In the past week these cyber-chats had become real when, one lunchtime, just as Steve was about to make a start on the packed lunch Kimberley had made for him, Helen had rung the office.

As Steve spoke with her he had gone through the same emotions he had when discovering his father's pornography videos – excitement, nervousness and guilt. He had even put the packed lunch into his desk drawer, out of a sense of shame. They had talked about Reading, about the shops that used to be there and, inevitably, about *Angels* and how it had now been turned into a casino. They spoke for over an hour, until Helen had to get back to her work.

She had called the same time the following day, and then continued on a similar theme. It was during this second conversation that she suggested they meet for a drink.

Steve told her that he had a girlfriend and how going for a drink might be a little awkward. Helen had laughed and explained that she hadn't meant a *date*, but that she understood and so suggested going for a midday coffee instead. Although this had seemed like a good compromise, and one he'd feel less guilty about, the arrangements were difficult to make. Her job was based in Canary Wharf and she usually worked through her lunch break – unless she was chatting with Steve. The weekends were obviously no good, so they had decided that they would meet after work. Just for an hour. So Steve had arranged to meet her after Lady Langley's gig. And he was already twenty minutes late.

***

The moment Steve walked into the bar he recognised her from her photo. Long blonde hair, blue eyes, early forties. There was no mistake – although Steve realised he could be about to make one. He hesitated at the pub door. She hadn't seen him yet, and as she only had his work number and not his mobile, he could quite easily leave and never meet her. He nodded to himself. Yes, he realised, that would be the best thing to do. He'd seen her, he'd satisfied his curiosity; now he should just get on with his life and his relationship with his girlfriend.

'Hi, I'm Steve.'

Helen stood up and shook his hand.

She was a bit taller than he'd anticipated. But then he remembered that the last time he had seen her, he was lying at her feet on a sticky beer-soaked carpet.

'Nice to meet you,' she said, 'again!'

***

At one point during their conversation and second drink, just when Helen was in the middle of telling him about her ex-boyfriend, Steve's phone rang. He knew from the ring tone that it was Kimberley – he had allocated the song 'Can't Smile Without You' by Barry Manilow to her mobile number as it was one of Kimberley's favourite songs. He thought for a moment about not answering it, but the song started playing louder and Steve began to feel slightly embarrassed. For a number of reasons. He thought about rejecting it and letting it go through to voicemail. But he thought that would be rude – although not as rude as lying about where he was; which was exactly what he was about to do.

'Excuse me a sec. I have to take this.'

He picked up the phone and quickly walked out of the pub as the song continued to increase in volume. The moment he was outside he answered.

'Hi, sweetheart . . . Yeah, I'm still at the recording . . . Yes, she's finished. It went really well. I'm just having a chat with her and a couple of producers; you know, essential networking stuff. Bit boring really . . . I'm not sure. Not too late, but don't wait up . . . Yes, there's food here, some vol-au-vents and stuff . . . Okay, I'll come in quietly . . . You too. See you in the morning.'

He blew a kiss down the phone and hung up.

He then looked back towards the pub. There was nothing stopping him from just leaving now. He'd met her, they'd had a nice chat, he should go now and email her the following day, for the last time, just to thank her. He'd lose nothing. Although he would have to buy a new coat.

He sighed and walked back into the pub.

***

'Thanks. So does your family still live there?'

Steve put the newly purchased bottle of wine into the cooler on the table and sat down.

He'd had enough lager – two bottles in the greenroom and two pints at the pub – and had decided to join Helen in drinking wine. He had taken advantage of the 'buy two large glasses and get the bottle free' offer, even though he knew he was only saving a pound or so.

'Yeah, my mum is still there.'

'Not your dad? Or has your dad . . . passed away?'

Steve topped up Helen's glass and then poured some wine into his own new one. This gave him a little time to decide which way to go with his answer.

'My dad . . .'

He spoke quietly and hung his head – for several reasons. '. . . he . . . unfortunately he left us a few years ago.'

'Oh, I'm sorry to hear that.'

Steve held out his glass. 'Anyway, here's to . . . well . . . renewing old acquaintances.'

Helen smiled. 'Absolutely.'

They clinked glasses. Helen took a sip, Steve took a mouthful.

'It really is an incredible story,' she said, 'and . . . well . . . I guess I'm sorry for taking up so much of your life.'

Steve suddenly felt incredibly embarrassed. As if it had all suddenly dawned on him for the first time. Maybe it was the drink. Maybe it was the fact that he was now sitting with the girl he'd been looking for – the real one. Maybe it was the fact that he had just lied to Kimberley. Whatever it was, he felt as if he wanted to cry.

CHAPTER FIFTY

Jeff opened and closed his mouth three times.

Each time he went to say something a new thought came into his head and cancelled out the previous one.

As he thought, he moved his foot back and forth on the axle of the pram next to him. His son, Daniel, contentedly slept along with the movement.

Jeff took a sip of his Lapsang Souchong. He had recently discovered this tea and now couldn't get enough of it.

He looked around the garden centre cafe. There were several other parents with prammed children, as well as an elderly couple with an even older relative, and several children screaming and/or running around. He always forgot how much he hated coming to this place on a Sunday. He used to come to this cafe often when he wasn't working – so, very often – and either read the newspapers or worked on his never-ending book. He didn't use a laptop and always forgot to bring his notebook with him, so had to buy a new one each time – with either birds or flowers on it – from the garden-centre gift shop. He had several notebooks, each with various chapters. One day he knew he would put them all together and then find a publisher for it. He was sure that there would be a great demand for *1001 Dodges, Excuses and Scams*.

He opened his mouth once more. This time he'd go for it.

'So let me get this straight. Since our last chat, when you decided to stop worrying and just enjoy your life, you've had a couple of dates with a girl who you now think is the real one from the disco, lied to your girlfriend and asked your brother-in-law to run a check on both of them?'

Steve, who was sitting diagonally opposite Jeff, thought for a moment. He then nodded decisively. 'Yep, that about sums it up.'

'I see.'

Steve bent his head down to his glass and sucked up some of his banana milkshake through the green bendy straw. He then blew back into the straw and watched the bubbles rise towards the top of the long glass.

Jeff looked at his watch.

'Sorry,' said Steve. 'Am I keeping you from something?'

'Yes,' said Jeff. 'Getting on with my life.'

Steve felt his stomach turn. And it wasn't due to the milkshake. It wasn't often Jeff made a nasty comment to him, but when he did . . . well, it hurt. Really hurt.

Steve looked at the face of his friend. He saw the memories of their times together: forming a friendship in primary school, doing science experiments in Jeff's shed, masturbating back to back over pornograpic magazines, looking at semen under a microscope, going to discos. And then . . . then having Jeff as the only one to support him in his quest to find the girl of his dreams – in their late teens, through their twenties and thirties . . .

Jeff was right. This had not only been a part of Steve's life; it had been a part of Jeff's as well.

Steve felt selfish. Selfish and pathetic.

'I'm sorry. I'm really sorry. I didn't mean to say that. I'm just tired. Dan's been up a lot in the night teething problems—'

'No, Jeff. Don't apologise. You're right. You're absolutely right. I'm . . . I'm the one who's sorry, mate.'

Steve swallowed and coughed. He then pointed at Daniel sleeping in the pram.

'Anyway, tell me, how's he doing? Apart from the teething.'

Jeff looked down at his son. He knew where he was and what he looked like, but just needed a momentary diversion.

'He's great.'

Jeff then looked back at Steve.

'So . . . what does she look like?'

Steve smiled and shook his head. 'It's okay. Really. I'll sort it out.'

He looked at his watch – even though he knew exactly what the time was – and stood up.

'I'd better make a move. Kim is having an early lunch with her parents because we're going to the cinema later.' He took his jacket from the back of the chair.

'Come on, Steve. Please. I said I was sorry.'

Steve started to put on the jacket. 'I know. It's fine.'

'So . . . you think this is really her?'

Steve stopped. He had an arm through one of the sleeves while the remainder of the jacket trailed onto the floor. He stopped, sighed and nodded.

'Come on, Steve, mate, sit down. I'm not staying here on my own. I'll only get hit on. And you haven't finished your milkshake.'

Steve slowly slid his arm back out of the sleeve, replaced the jacket over the back of the chair and sat down again.

***

Steve watched the silver pony-shaped balloon drift up into the cloudless blue sky.

'It's your fault! I told you to hold it tightly!' shouted a bald, bearded, overweight man, unnecessarily loudly.

The little girl next to him sobbed uncontrollably.

'Stop crying,' he continued even louder, 'or I'll give you something to cry about!'

Steve looked at the father and his weeping young daughter. He turned to Jeff, who was walking next to him, pushing the pram.

'I don't get that,' he said quietly.

'What's that?'

'That phrase "Stop crying or I'll give you something to cry about". The girl has just lost her balloon. She already has something to cry about. The problem really isn't the subject matter.'

Jeff nodded. 'Sunday parents.'

'Eh?'

'Sunday parents.'

'Sorry, Jeff, but repeating it doesn't really explain it.'

Jeff handed his son, who was sitting up in his pram and looking around, a set of plastic keys. Daniel immediately stuck them into his mouth and started chewing on them.

'Most of the parents around here work every day and their career comes before everything. The moment they can, they put their children into nursery and they employ a nanny to look after them at home during the week. The only time they really see the children is at the weekend. Saturday is usually taken up with shopping, children's parties, swimming, etc., so the main day they get to spend time together is Sunday. That's when the parents realise they have no idea how to look after their own children. So they just give them anything they want to keep them quiet; they let them scream and run around regardless of where they are. Then they usually bring them here to the park in an attempt to tire them out. These are "Sunday parents", and the reason why most children are so badly behaved.'

'Wow. I didn't know that. So, and don't take this the wrong way, what will stop Dan turning out the same way?'

On hearing his name, although it could have been coincidental, Daniel smiled, gurgled loudly and chewed harder on his teething toy.

'We've decided . . .'

Steve decided not to question the 'we'.

'That Francine won't go back to work until Dan starts school. And then she'll only work part-time initially.'

'Will you be able to afford that?'

'I hope so. William and I have just been headhunted by a really big ad agency.'

Steve stopped walking. 'That's terrific!'

Jeff smiled. 'I know. We won't take the job though.'

'Really?'

'No. Not yet anyway.' He smiled. 'But we will let our boss know about the offer.'

Steve nodded.

As they continued walking, Steve turned up the collar on his jacket. He wished he'd listened to Kimberley and worn his thicker coat. The blue sky was quite misleading, as there was a definite chill in the air.

'So, is she attractive?' Jeff had wanted to ask this question much earlier but had decided to wait for the right moment.

Steve was surprised he'd waited this long. 'Yes, she is, but that's beside the point,' he lied.

'Have you slept with her?'

Steve had actually expected this question first.

'No, Jeff, I haven't. I have a girlfriend. And Helen has recently come out of a long-term relationship. And I don't think sleeping together, apart from being morally wrong, is really going to help the situation, is it?'

'Mmm, morals, you say. Interesting. Perhaps, morally, you shouldn't have met up with her in the first place.'

As Jeff spoke, the plastic keys flew out of the pram and onto the muddy walkway.

He stopped the pram, bent down to pick them up and handed them back to his son, who immediately put them back into his mouth.

'They're all muddy!' said Steve, shocked.

'Isn't that how they build up their immune system?' suggested Jeff, trying to quote from a book or a newspaper article Francine had once read to him.

The keys flew out again. Steve picked them up, looked at Jeff and put them in the basket under the pram.

Jeff opened up the large bag which was hanging from the handles of the pram and took out a packet of banana-chip biscuits. He opened the packet, gave a biscuit to Daniel and offered the packet to Steve. Steve shook his head. Jeff ate one of the biscuits himself and then put the packet back.

'Yes,' said Steve, 'I am fully aware that I shouldn't have seen her, or even replied to her email in the first place. But I did. And now she wants to see me again.'

Jeff was surprised. 'Even though she knows about Kimberley?'

'Yes.'

'I see.' Jeff re-opened the packet and put another biscuit into his mouth. 'Well, you only have two options: you don't see her again and try to forget about her; or you finish with Kimberley and start seeing her instead.'

'Or I stay with Kim and carry on seeing Helen behind her back.'

'As I said, you only have two options.'

'I know.'

'Excuse me!'

Jeff and Steve turned around. A group of young boys was calling over to them.

'Can you pass the ball, please?'

Steve looked around. He saw the football in the longer grass next to a large horse-chestnut tree. He jogged two steps over to it and rolled it away from the tree with his foot. He then dribbled the ball forward slightly, took two steps back and ran forward to kick it. Whether it was just muddier than he'd anticipated, whether it was the fact that he had no grips on the soles of his shoes or whether he was just incapable of kicking a football properly, Steve completely missed the ball, lost his footing and ended up on his back on the muddy path.

The boys just stared. They didn't even laugh.

Jeff, who was in hysterics, picked up the ball and volleyed it hard. The boys watched as the ball went in the opposite direction to where they were standing.

Jeff shrugged apologetically, although the fact he was still laughing made this appear insincere.

One of the boys shook his head and then ran over to retrieve the ball– realising that this is what he should have done initially.

Jeff helped Steve wipe the excess mud from his trousers and jacket.

Not for the first time that day, Steve felt uncomfortable and embarrassed.

CHAPTER FIFTY-ONE

Steve looked at the small but time-consuming contracts on his desk. Over the past few days he'd kept moving them further and further away in the vain hope that they might disappear altogether. Reading and then rereading contracts was the worst part of his job. Each time he requested a change be made, by the production company or broadcaster, he had to reread the whole thing to make sure nothing else had been altered. Most of his clients had given him permission to sign on their behalf so he felt under extra pressure to make sure there were no mistakes. Of course he preferred having contracts to bills, but being behind on either wasn't ideal. And at least bills just involved writing a cheque – and hoping it wouldn't bounce.

Steve pulled the contracts towards him, flipped the pile over and picked up the top one, which had previously been on the bottom. He looked at the date. His eyes widened in shock. He couldn't believe how long it had been sitting on his desk. He sat back and had just started to read it when the phone rang. Relieved, he answered it.

'Hello?' He suddenly realised he'd not made his customary response. And then realised he didn't care.

'Oh, hi, Chrissie . . . Yeah, good thanks. How are you? . . . Good . . .'

As Steve listened to his newest client, he closed his eyes and shook his head. She was asking him about a job for which she was supposed to be auditioning. Steve had forgotten all about it. He opened his eyes and knew he'd have to come up with a pretty convincing excuse.

'I'm sorry, Chrissie. I forgot.'

He wondered if this really would prove to be the best policy.

Just then his mobile rang. He looked at the display. Helen. For a moment he wondered if he should have given her his mobile number after all.

'Sorry Chrissie can you hold on one second I really need to take this other call . . .'

Steve covered the mouthpiece of the landline and answered his mobile.

'Hi, Helen, how are you? . . . Yeah, good, thanks. Sorry, I can't really talk – I'm just on the other line . . . Tonight? Er . . . well . . . er . . . no, nothing planned . . . Yeah, sure, okay . . . Fine. I'll see you later. Bye.'

Steve ended the call and took his hand from the mouthpiece of the office phone.

'Sorry about that, Chrissie. Look, I'll give the production company a call now; I know a couple of people there, and I'll see if I can still get you in . . . I know, and I'm really sorry . . . Okay, call you right back.'

He put down the office phone.

He thought for a moment. Putting the contract back on the upside-down pile, he pushed them away again. He knew what he was about to do and that he was going to hate himself for doing it. Yet he was still going to do it.

Steve looked at the clock; one forty-five. She'd still be at lunch.

He picked up his mobile phone and pressed Speed Dial 1. Within seconds it was ringing.

'Hi, sweetheart . . . yeah, I'm fine. Listen, I have to go to see a potential new client tonight. I'd forgotten all about it, but they just emailed me to remind me. It's just in a small club in town. A bit of a dive actually. You can come if you like but I think it'll be a bit boring; there's a load of open spots on before him . . . Sure? . . . Okay, I hope I won't be back too late . . . Fine, I'll call you later. Bye.'

Steve put his phone back down onto his desk and looked at it. Bloody mobile phones, they caused so many break-ups and infidelities. It was just too easy to call someone or send them a flirty text. Years ago you'd have to go to a call box, make sure you had change, hope the person was in when you called them, have the risk of someone else answering . . . By the time you did all this you'd have had the opportunity to question your actions. Or even to have quelled your libido. But not now. Now the act was done before the thought had properly formed and before the consequences were taken into account.

Like now.

He had just lied to his girlfriend so that he could go out on a date with another girl.

What was wrong with him?

***

He didn't know how long he had been staring at the wall. He guessed it was seconds, but it could easily have been minutes. All he knew was that the knock on the door made him jump – something which was becoming a regular occurrence.

'Er . . . come in.'

These words, which he reckoned Kimberley probably said at least twenty times a day, seemed very alien to him. He rarely had people come to see him, and even when people did, they rarely knocked, they just came in.

The office door opened and a policeman entered the room.

As most people would have done, Steve panicked. Initially he tried to think what he could have done wrong. Then he wondered if anything had happened to any of his family. This thought suddenly became more imperative as he realised who the policeman was.

'Dave! What are you doing here? What's happened? Are Sheila and the kids okay . . . ?'

Dave was used to having people react this way when he went to visit them in uniform. Unfortunately on a number of occasions he had been there to break bad news to them about a loved one.

But not this time.

'Don't worry, they're fine. I just wanted to pop in and say hello.'

Steve sighed. 'Just one "hello", not three of them?' It was the sense of relief that had caused his feeble attempt at humour.

Dave smiled politely.

'Have a seat,' invited Steve, pointing unnecessarily to the only available chair in the room. 'Do you want a coffee or something?'

Dave pulled the chair from the corner of the room to the other side of Steve's desk and sat down.

'I can't stay long. My partner's in the car downstairs and he's double-parked.'

'Naughty.'

'I know. Yet nothing in comparison to what else I've been doing recently.'

Dave removed his helmet and put it on the desk. Steve desperately wanted to ask if he could try it on but stopped himself.

'So, the reason I'm here is to tell you about something I found out recently which is a bit . . . odd.'

Steve had always enjoyed hearing about Dave's unsolved cases. He hoped Dave had come along to ask for his advice so that he could put his *Columbo*-watching training to good use.

'Tell me something – have you been in contact with that girl Helen Potter?'

'No, I haven't been in touch with her at all.'

A loud high-pitched noise was emitted from somewhere near Dave.

'That's a lie apparently.'

Steve looked shocked. 'What do you mean?'

'There's this new portable lie detector all officers are given. If someone's heart rate increases dramatically when asked a question, then it buzzes. Like it just did.'

Steve wasn't sure what to say.

'But . . .' He suddenly felt really stupid.

Dave laughed loudly. 'You would not believe the number of people who fall for that,' said Dave as he took the small device from his pocket. 'It's just a buzzer from a board game!'

'Well done,' said Steve. 'Ha-ha.'

Dave was still laughing.

'Anyway,' he said eventually, wiping his eyes and coughing to calm himself, 'you are obviously still in touch with her – which I guessed you would be. Well . . .' The smiles and laughter abated and Dave became suddenly quite serious. 'The thing is, I don't think she is who she says she is.'

'What?'

Dave sighed. 'I checked Kimberley, who of course turned out to be one hundred per cent genuine. . . and then I checked out this other girl as well. To be honest, it wasn't difficult. I just ran a check on the number plate you sent me – pretended I'd pulled her over for speeding. Anyway, the car is registered to a different name. It's down as belonging to a Rebecca Hughes who works as a receptionist and lives in Finchley.'

'Is that so strange? It might be a friend, a parent . . .'

Dave nodded. 'I know. It could be – well, not a parent as the date of birth would make her too young – but it could be a friend. It just seems a bit odd, that's all. I thought it might be worth you checking. Have you ever seen her ID?'

'Yes, of course. That's always the first thing I ask when I meet someone: "What would you like to drink and may I see your birth certificate, driving licence or passport?"'

Dave ignored the sarcasm. 'Look, you asked me to check on her!'

'I know. I'm sorry. Thanks, Dave – I appreciate it.'

Dave nodded. 'Just be careful, that's all. There's something not quite right.'

Steve felt a small knot in the pit of his stomach. It was the feeling he used to have on exam days in school. Maybe he had been right to check on her. Columbo would have been proud.

'Well, I'm seeing her later so—'

'Steve!'

He'd forgotten that he wasn't going to mention this. It was just the sheer coincidence that had made him blurt it out.

'Er . . .'

'You're actually seeing her?! Behind Kimberley's back?! I thought you just spoke or emailed. Oh, Steve!'

Steve felt humiliated. It was worse than being told off by his mother.

Dave stood up, picked up his helmet and put it under his arm.

Steve knew there was no point in asking to try it on now.

'Look, what you do with your personal life is your business . . .' Dave stopped and thought for a moment. 'Actually that's blatantly not true. But anyway, all I'm saying is . . . be careful. She really might not be who she says she is. Although for the life of me I have no idea why.'

He started to walk towards the door.

'Oh, and if you ever tell anyone that I've done this for you and your sister finds out, then I'll have you arrested.'

'For what?!'

Dave looked at him. 'Oh, don't worry, I'll think of something. And you won't like it!'

***

After Dave had left the office, Steve started thinking about Helen. Or at least the women he thought was Helen. Was he just being paranoid? Was Dave? It made no sense. If it wasn't her, then what could she possibly want to achieve? As Dave himself had pointed out, Steve wasn't that great a catch. Surely no woman would go through all this just to snare him as a boyfriend. He then thought about the proof he had that she was telling the truth. The name was right, she knew about Reading and Angels, she was more or less the right age, the right look. He realised that although he had a mobile number for her, she had never given him her work phone number. Of course he'd never asked for it; there was no reason to. He decided that he would ask for her work number that night. As well as asking to take a quick peek at her ID.

CHAPTER FIFTY-TWO

The Bull and Arrow had more or less become their regular. It reminded him of the film *Brief Encounter*: a couple meeting in the same place, flirting, yet never consummating their relationship.

Yes, he and Helen had flirted quite a lot the last time, but then they had drunk more – or at least Steve had. Helen didn't really drink very much, yet she had been the one who had suggested they went back to her place. Steve had declined the offer, needlessly reminding her about Kimberley.

'Then why are you meeting me at all?' she had not unreasonably asked.

Steve hadn't answered. He hadn't known how. He had thought of telling her that they actually shouldn't meet any more. That's what a part of him had wanted to say but that wasn't what he'd said. Instead he'd suggested they went out for dinner sometime. But he was yet to make those dinner arrangements.

So here he was again, back at their 'usual' pub. As usual he was early, and as usual he was on his second pint before she arrived. Tonight was an important one. Tonight he would find out the truth about her, and then, regardless of the findings, tell her that they couldn't meet up any more. That it wasn't fair on her or on him, but mainly it wasn't fair on Kimberley.

His girlfriend.

Kimberley.

Who was now standing in front of him.

Steve considered himself a logical person who could generally work things out pretty quickly. Yet there seemed to be no logical reason as to why Kimberley was standing there. Why would she have come to this particular pub? As far as he knew, she didn't ever come to this area. What reason would she have? Had she been following him? She would have had to be sitting outside his office all day. Or was there some way of tracking him through his mobile? Was it really just an uncanny, millions-to-one against, coincidence?

'Kim! How . . . ? What are you doing here?'

It was then that Steve saw Kimberley's eyes. There was a look in them which he had only seen once or twice. He'd seen it when they'd watched the film *The Boy in the Striped Pyjamas* and he'd seen it when she talked about her grandfather who had died a couple of years previously.

It was the look she had when she wanted to stop herself from crying.

'Hi, Steve.'

Steve turned and saw Helen, who was suddenly standing the other side of him.

Ah. That was it. He was having a dream. A nightmare.

He closed his eyes, pinched himself and then opened them.

No, they were both still there.

'Er . . . hi, Helen. This is my girlfriend Kimberley – whom I've spoken about loads of times.'

'I know,' said Helen.

'And this is Becky,' said Kimberley, pointing at Helen. 'She's the receptionist at the surgery.'

Steve thought about trying the 'waking-up' thing again – just in case.

He looked at Helen, or rather Becky, as if for the first time.

He had always known there was something familiar about her but assumed it was because she looked like the girl in the flashbacks and the Photofit. But she looked different . . .

Becky then removed a blonde wig to reveal short dark curly hair.

Steve felt as though he had just been grabbed by his own. He looked at Kimberley.

'I . . . This . . .'

He hung his head. There was nothing he could say.

'I'm going to Vanessa's tonight. I'll stay there for two days and then I'll go back to my flat. Please make sure that you – and all your stuff – have gone by then.'

Kimberley and Becky then walked out together.

CHAPTER FIFTY-THREE

Steve struggled around the living room on his hands and knees. His youngest niece, balanced on his back, screamed excitedly.

'Are you sure you're not a bit too old to play horsey?' enquired Steve, who was beginning to feel too old himself and worried that his knees wouldn't hold out much longer.

'Yes, you're right,' said Hayley, who was watching them and who, as the elder sister, felt she should take control.

'I'm not!' protested Lucy, 'Giddy-up!'

As she playfully kicked her heels into his sides, Steve started worrying about his kidneys.

'Yes, you are,' said Hayley, giving her sister an attempt at a wink. 'And anyway, we don't want to make Uncle Steve *angry*, do we?!'

Lucy frowned and then slowly smiled.

Steve braced himself for what was about to happen.

Lucy climbed from his back and both girls started punching and kicking him.

'No,' said Steve, covering his face, 'don't make me angry. You won't like me when I'm angry!'

The girls giggled as they continued to punch and kick him – a little harder than Steve would have liked.

'Noooo!' shouted Steve. He then fell to the floor in silence. The girls waited in scared anticipation. Suddenly he jumped to his knees and growled loudly.

'Hulk not like little girls! Hulk smash little girls. Hulk angry. Very angry!'

The girls screamed as Steve chased them around the room.

He grabbed them, one in each arm, and pulled them to the floor.

The girls squealed and laughed in equal measure.

Lucy then stopped and looked up at her uncle. 'Uncle Steve . . .'

Steve looked down at her. 'Me not Uncle Steve! Me Hulk!'

'Uncle Hulk,' his younger niece corrected, 'where's Kimberley?'

***

While the children ate their lunch in the kitchen, Steve and Sheila sat in the living room with a coffee and a beer respectively.

'You're such an idiot.'

'I know.'

'An idiot.'

'I still know.'

Sheila leant over and put her hand on her brother's arm. 'So what do you think is going to happen, Steve?'

Steve thought for a moment. 'Well, I think that we will all eventually have identity chips injected under our skin, that cars will be able to fly and that dogs will become an endangered species.'

Sheila glared at him.

Steve sighed.

'I don't know, Sheil. She obviously doesn't want to see me again.'

'Can you blame her?'

'No. Although, as I keep saying, I didn't really do anything!'

Sheila put down her beer and leant slightly forward. 'You did do something, Steve. You were deceitful. You lied to her and you saw another girl behind her back.'

'But I didn't *do* anything with her! I didn't sleep with her. Jesus, I didn't even kiss her!'

Sheila quickly looked towards the kitchen and then turned back to her brother. 'Shhh!'

She spoke quietly; 'Look, Steve, she didn't know if she could trust you. She didn't know how you really felt about her or if you were just obsessed by the idea that she was this girl. So she tested you. And you failed.'

'But—'

Sheila continued: 'And whether or not you slept with this girl is almost irrelevant – though of course there was no way she would have let that happen even if you'd wanted to.'

'Which I didn't!'

'The point is, you betrayed Kimberley's trust and you proved that you are more interested in finding this bloody girl – who, let's be honest, might still actually be Kimberley – than you are about your relationship!'

Steve went to speak, but Sheila hadn't finished.

'Do you know what it was like for me growing up?'

Steve frowned. He didn't know when or how the subject had changed.

'Apart from the constant calls to the house when you started putting up those posters – you know, before Mum and Dad got you your own line – I was called *"his* sister". As in: "you know that saddo who's obsessed with looking for that girl – well, that's *his* sister".'

Steve suddenly felt himself getting upset. 'I didn't . . . I never knew about that.'

'Of course you didn't. You only cared about yourself. It was really difficult for me to get a boyfriend, as they were all worried I might start stalking them if they ever broke up with me.'

Steve shook his head. 'I'm . . . sorry.'

'That's why, when I went to uni and Dave asked me out, I couldn't believe it. I'm not saying I didn't fancy him – I did – but he was the first guy to show any interest in me. He made me feel confident again.'

Steve looked at her. 'Is that why you didn't bring him home to meet us for ages?'

Sheila slowly nodded.

Steve had nothing to say. He knew his sister was right and that he was wrong. On every level. He'd messed up and didn't know if there was anything he could do about it.

They sat quietly for a few moments, sipping at their drinks. They could hear the girls bickering slightly in the kitchen.

'By the way, how did Kimberley know the name "Helen?" I assume you hadn't told her.'

Steve sighed. 'No, I hadn't told her. Apparently I called the name out a couple of times in my sleep. She took a guess.'

'Clever girl.'

'Yeah.'

Sheila looked around the room. 'You know . . . you're more than welcome to stay on the sofa. You won't be in the way.'

'Thanks, Sheil, but I'm fine at Jeff's for the moment. It won't be for long. Just until I find somewhere to rent and sort stuff out on the office.'

'You could always move back in with mum.' She quickly added, 'just temporarily.'

Steve stared at his sister. 'Oh yes, that would be a positive move. Going back to live with my mother at this age. I mean . . .'

'Hayley won't give me any of her chocolates.'

Steve and Sheila turned around to see Lucy standing at the door.

'Go and tell her I said to share them,' said Sheila.

Lucy literally turned on her heels and walked back out.

'Don't worry, Steve,' said Sheila. 'It'll be okay.'

'I'm sure it will,' said Steve. 'Hayley won't really mind sharing.'

Sheila didn't say a word or change her expression.

'Sorry. But I know it'll be okay, Sheil . . . I know . . .' He stopped himself. 'Actually, you know what, maybe this time it won't be okay.'

CHAPTER FIFTY-FOUR

'And the winner is . . . Sade Rose!'

The audience, well, those that were listening, not just chatting around the tables, clapped loudly.

Sade Rose stood and squeezed her way through the labyrinth of chairs and tables in an attempt to find her way to the front. The audience continued to applaud, and she was grateful for the soundtrack as she struggled to navigate a route.

She eventually arrived at the three small steps leading up to the stage. She paused for a brief moment and then went up to receive her award.

The host of the evening, Scott Tino – a much-respected comedian who had an incredibly successful career even though he adamantly refused to perform on television – handed over the 'Broken Leg' statuette. Sade kissed him on both cheeks, which threw Scott a bit as he had only been expecting the one. She then walked to the microphone.

'Er . . . wow!'

She read the inscription on the base of the award.

'*Best Comedy Trainee*. Brilliant! Well, I'd like to thank everyone who voted, obviously, and thanks to my agent, Donald, without whom I'd still be working as a receptionist . . .'

Donald Watson, a large balding man with a proportionally large unlit cigar in his mouth, leant across to Steve, who was sitting on an adjacent table, and spoke quietly. Or at least as quietly as his loud drunken voice would allow.

'I know I'm her agent, but to be honest, I've never really found her funny!'

Steve smiled.

'But that never stops us, eh, Steve?!' continued Donald.

'Yeah,' said Steve, humouring the man rather than in actual agreement.

Mike Dutch, who was sitting next to Steve, slowly turned and looked at him.

Steve saw the look. 'Oh, I'm not talking about you, Mike, obviously.'

Dutch's expression remained fixed. 'Obviously!'

'So thanks once again,' continued Sade Rose, 'and . . . er . . . cheers!'

As she left the stage to the audience's applause, Donald leant over again to Steve.

'By the way, Steve, I was sorry to hear about Lady Langley.'

Steve half smiled, half shrugged.

Mike Dutch stood up. He put a hand on Steve's shoulder. 'I'm just going for a piss.' He smiled at Steve and walked away from the table.

Steve found all this a little strange. Not the going to the toilet part – Mike had drunk at least four bottles of lager at the free bar and then most of the wine on the table, so the toilet was inevitable and as far as Steve was concerned long overdue. No, what had surprised Steve was the hand on the shoulder and the smile – little shows of affection, which one would never normally associate with Mike Dutch. In retrospect, Steve should perhaps have realised that it was a sign of loyalty. A sign which said: 'Don't worry, I won't be leaving you.'

'Really, I don't think it's fair,' continued Donald, 'and I don't like the way she's gone around telling everyone that you hadn't been doing much for her recently.'

Steve looked surprised and hurt.

'Really? I didn't know about that.'

Donald attempted to backtrack. 'Well, that's only what I heard. But you know what the circuit is like, all gossip and rumour.'

'Yeah, I suppose,' said Steve. And then, to change the subject, 'Which reminds me, whatever happened to that double act?'

'Apparently Gary Gossip is working as a butcher and Ray Rumour is training to be a plumber.'

They both smiled.

Steve leant closer. 'The thing is, Donald, it's true. I hadn't been doing much for her.'

Donald looked annoyed. 'But you were the one who kickstarted her fucking career!'

Steve shrugged again. He didn't know what else to do.

'And of course,' said Donald, who really wished he could smoke his cigar without having to go outside, 'we both know that she wasn't to blame really. Anne Blackburn had a lot to do with it. You know, with the flowers and champagne and stuff and inviting her to her club and to all those parties. Bit over the top, if you ask me. I mean, Chrissie is a good enough act, but . . . anyway, I think she should have stayed with you. There's no loyalty in this business any more.'

Steve shrugged. His shoulders were beginning to hurt.

'No, Donald, she made the right decision. I really wasn't doing anything for her. I'm not doing anything for anyone. Including myself.'

Before Donald had a chance to respond – which in a way was fortunate for him as he wasn't sure how he was going to – Scott Tino introduced the next award.

'So the nominees for Best Live Act – which should really be me – are . . . Paul Bowman, Ed Husain . . .'

Steve looked around to see if Mike Dutch was on his way back from the toilet yet. This was the category he'd been nominated in, and the main reason they were there – apart from the free drink and socialising.

'Penelope Wilson, Mike Dutch and Eli Chang. And the winner is . . .'

As the envelope was opened, Steve saw Mike Dutch come back into the room.

'Mike Dutch!'

The audience applauded. Mike Dutch looked confused. For a moment he didn't realise what was happening. All he knew was that he'd walked into the room to hear his name being shouted through the speakers. He wondered if this happened to everyone who came back from the toilet. He then saw Scott Tino holding an award and he realised. He made his way through the tables – amidst back-pattings and 'well done's – and onto the stage. Scott Tino shook his hand – and then frowned as he looked at his hand. Mike Dutch whispered an apology, saying that he'd washed his hands but come out of the toilet without drying them. Mike then walked to the microphone, as Scott wiped his now wet hands onto his trousers.

'Er . . . well . . . cheers for this. I only have one person to thank really, apart from myself, and that's my agent, Steve Connors.'

Mike raised the Broken Leg in Steve's direction. Steve raised his wine glass in response.

Donald leant over to Steve.

'Well done, mate. I'm sure that one won't leave you.'

Steve smiled. He then looked back towards the stage at his

client. He was of course delighted about the award, but as he thought about what Donald had just said he realised that if he wasn't careful, Mike Dutch would, like Lady Langley, leave him for another agent. However, the main problem was that Steve just didn't care.

***

The free bar had ended over an hour earlier and therefore the majority of people had left. However, there were still enough people to keep the bar staff and DJ working and irritated. Steve looked at the rows of spirits sitting on the bevelled mirror shelf behind the bar. He didn't know what he now fancied. As far as he could remember he'd so far had beer, wine and three Black Russians. He knew he should have left by now, but he hadn't felt like going; he was drunk but not drunk enough.

'Er, can I get a Jack Daniels, please? A large one. Just with ice.'

The barman, who had hoped to finish work half an hour ago, reluctantly dispensed the drink from the optic.

'I'll get this.'

Steve turned around to see Anne Blackman standing behind him, money in hand. Steve didn't want her to pay for his drink – even though the way things were going with work, money was getting a bit tight.

'I'm fine, thanks, Anne . . .'

But she stopped him and handed the money to the disinterested barman. Steve could see how persuasive and confident she was and how someone could easily be taken in by her. He really didn't blame Lady Langley at all.

Anne lifted her glass of champagne towards him.

'Congratulations on Mike's award.'

Steve nodded and smiled. He then drank from his glass without making the toast.

'Are we good?'

Steve looked at her. What was she talking about? Were they 'good'? Had she been watching too many American films? Nobody actually spoke like that. He wanted to point that out to her. He also wanted to point out how much he hated her. How disgusted he was by the fact she had stolen Lady Langley away from him. How the top she was wearing was at least two sizes too small for her. How the thought that he had once slept with her repulsed him on every level. And how disgusted he was with himself to think, in different circumstances, with a bit more drink, he could even see himself doing it again.

'You know Chrissie really appreciates all you did for her. She—'

'Fuck off, Anne.'

Anne stared at him. Although she had been spoken to many, many times like this in the past, she hadn't expected it from Steve.

'I'm sorry?'

'Seriously, just fuck off.'

Steve took his drink and walked away from the bar.

***

Thirty minutes after his encounter with Anne, Steve was sitting back at his table on his own. The remnants of the evening – empty champagne bottles, invitations, menus etc. – were spread out in front of him. Steve looked around the room. At least he wasn't the last to leave. Yet. There were still a couple of agents – including Anne – a few of the nominated losers from various categories, a girl he recognised but couldn't quite place . . . who was now smiling at him . . . who was now walking over to him.

'Hi, we meet again.'

And who was now speaking to him.

'Hi. Yeah. How are you?'

Steve had attempted to convey that he was genuinely pleased to see this unknown person. All he did know about her was that she was young and pretty. And, in his drunken but not yet paralytic state, those were good enough reasons to have a conversation with her.

'Yeah, I'm good, thanks,' said the pretty young girl. 'Well done on Mike's award. That was a nice thing he said about you.'

Steve had been complimented and congratulated quite a few times since the show had finished and he'd become, if not blasé, just slightly immune to it. He'd seen a similar thing happen when audience members approached comedians after a show. They liked the first couple of compliments as it reassured them that they had done a good job, but after that they more or less switched off and just gave automatic smiles and thanks.

Steve smiled and thanked her.

'So, how's Lady Langley?'

She wasn't to know.

'Er . . . she's fine, I guess. Haven't seen her for a while. I'm not looking after her any more.'

The young girl wasn't sure what to say. She didn't know whose decision that had been and was reluctant to ask. 'Oh. She did very well on the programme, didn't she?'

Steve quickly put all the clues together. Columbo would have been proud.

'Yes, she did,' and then, with more confidence, 'So are you still working as a floor manager?'

The young girl smiled. Steve wondered if he'd been too

obviously pleased that he'd suddenly remembered who she was.

'Yes. But I'm freelance, so I only work whenever a production company needs me. I also work part-time for a friend of mine who's a casting director.'

Steve nodded. 'Well, if you're ever stuck for work, give me a call as I could always use a hand in the office.'

'Really? Okay, I will, thanks.'

Steve smiled, which hid what he was really feeling. What was he talking about? He could hardly afford to pay himself a salary let alone someone else! Why had he said it? Of course, he knew why. Because he was drunk. Because he was feeling down. And because he believed he wanted to sleep with her.

Steve looked around, mainly to avoid eye contact with the girl. He didn't want to say anything else that he'd immediately regret. He saw Mike Dutch standing laughing at the bar. He was about to go over to him and suggest he join them – another excuse not to say anything stupid to the girl – when he saw with whom Mike was talking and laughing. Anne Blackman was putting her hand on Mike's arm as they talked and laughed together. Steve must have been staring for a while, as he suddenly became aware that the girl was looking at him and then following his line of sight.

'Er . . . this is getting a bit crap in here now, isn't it?'

Steve nodded.

'Shall we grab a bottle of wine and go back to mine?'

Steve nodded again.

CHAPTER FIFTY-FIVE

Steve looked at the smoothie on the kitchen table in front of him. He breathed in and out several times.

'Seriously, you should drink it.'

Steve shook his head, and immediately regretted it.

'Honestly, mate, it will bring up your blood-sugar level.'

Steve looked at the smoothie again.

'I know, Jeff, but I really don't feel like it.'

Francine, carrying her son, entered the kitchen.

'Not feeling too good, Steve?'

Steve shook his head again – forgetting how much pain it had caused the last time.

'No, not really.' He then looked at her stomach; 'Have you put on weight?'

Francine didn't smile as she spoke. 'Still so funny. As I've said before, you should be a comedian, not just represent them.'

She turned to her husband. 'I'm going to take Dan for a run in the car to get him to sleep. He's grumpy because he was woken up in the night.'

Steve was too hungover to realise that this was a dig at him.

'Okay. See you later.'

Without saying goodbye to Steve, she left.

Steve waited until he heard the door close – which was done a lot noisier that he would have liked.

'She preferred me when I was seeing Kim, didn't she?'

'Yes, my friend, she did.'

Steve picked up the smoothie. The chill of the glass sent a shiver through his hypersensitive body. He put it down again.

'So, what do you remember about last night?'

Steve thought this was quite an odd question. Surely he remembered everything. He hadn't been that drunk. He tried to remember. He vaguely remembered buying an unopened bottle of wine from the bar and getting into a cab to go back to the girl's flat.

'Would you like me to fill in the blanks?' suggested Jeff.

'Please.'

Jeff stretched his arms out in front of him and cracked all his knuckles.

'Well, you bowled up here at half past two. You noisily opened the door and then fell over Dan's musical walker, setting off a loud rendition of 'Twinkle, Twinkle, Little Star.' Dan woke up crying. Fran thought it was a burglar – albeit a particularly useless one – and woke me up. I came downstairs to find you sitting on the floor frantically looking for the off switch.'

Steve hung his head, which didn't help the nausea.

'I switched it off and took you into the kitchen to give you a glass of water. That's when you told me, a little too loudly, how you'd gone back to some young girl's house, where you proudly turned down her offer of sex and instead caught a cab back here.'

Steve still felt quite proud of himself. He knew how much he would have regretted having sex with the girl and was pleased that his subconscious had taken control in his inebriated state.

'Sorry.'

Jeff smiled and sighed.

'Don't worry. Seriously. It's not like Fran's working. And I had already planned on taking today off.'

'Thanks, mate.'

Steve forced himself to take a mouthful of the mixed fruit mush in front of him. Even though he'd cleaned his teeth twice, the mix of flavours in his mouth made him feel even more sick.

'Listen, Steve, though. Er . . . now we have the new baby on the way, well . . . pretty soon – not immediately – but soon, you won't be able to stay here any more. The baby will be going into the spare room and . . .'

'It's okay, Jeff. Seriously. I really appreciate all you've done.'

'So, what are you going to do?'

'I'm not sure yet.'

He took another sip of the smoothie and regretted it.

'I'll make you some toast.'

Steve couldn't be bothered to protest.

Jeff stood up and raised the hatch of the breadbin. He took two slices from the cut cottage loaf and put them into the toaster. Steve was surprised that people of their generation used breadbins. He always kept his own bread in the fridge. When he had his own bread. And his own fridge.

Jeff looked at his friend sitting at the table. He was reminded of the many times they had sat at kitchen tables together over the years and chatted at various ages about cartoons, comic books, bullying and girls. Only girls had remained a constant.

'I dreamt about Kimberley last night.'

And continued to do so.

Jeff smiled and hoped it didn't look patronising. 'I don't suppose you've spoken to her at all?'

'No. I did email her a couple of weeks ago, but she didn't

reply. She didn't even acknowledge the receipt request.'

Steve sighed and looked back at his drink.

'It's all a bit of a mess, isn't it, Steve?'

'Oh, I don't know. I think the colour of the strawberries mixes nicely with the banana.'

Jeff looked up at him. 'What are you going to do, mate?'

'Well, obviously I'm just going to put it all behind me and move on.'

'Really?'

'Of course,' said Steve. 'You know me – I never let things hold me back . . .'

CHAPTER FIFTY-SIX

Kimberley looked around. As she'd assumed would be the case, the majority of the clientele in the bar were couples. In her slightly drunken state she imagined going over to each table in turn and asking whether either of them had been unfaithful to their partner. She imagined the look of surprise on their faces and then . . . then . . . well, what would happen? Would either of them admit to it? Would one person say a categorical 'no' while the other hesitated, just slightly, before also denying it? Maybe one of them had been unfaithful. Maybe they had admitted it in a moment of guilt and shame; 'They meant nothing to me. I was drunk.' 'I've never done anything like this before and I'll never do it again.' 'I love you and I'm so, so sorry.' Maybe their apology was sincere and maybe their partner had agreed to put it behind them and move on. But would it ever be forgotten? Really forgotten? Or would there always be that little bit of doubt, that feeling of insecurity every time they went out on their own?

'Fancy a long multiple orgasm?'

Kimberley looked up and smiled. 'You have *no* idea!'

Vanessa put the cocktail down in front of Kimberley. She then put down her own drink, a large glass of dry white wine, sat in her seat and put her purse back into her handbag.

'Are you sure you don't want to try some?' asked Kimberley, offering her glass.

'No, thanks. Remember, I don't drink spirits. Not since Poland.'

Kimberley nodded. 'Of course.'

Three years earlier Vanessa had gone on a hen night to Krakow. There had been twelve girls altogether, although Vanessa had only known the bride-to-be, Diane, and her maid of honour, Christine. They were the only schoolfriends with whom Vanessa had stayed in touch. She hadn't enjoyed the weekend as she had little in common with the other girls and she was the only one, including the hen, and her mum, who was not looking to 'get off' with anyone. So Vanessa had drunk, a lot. Mainly vodka. What she hadn't known was the potency of Polish vodka. On one night she'd drunk three large vodka and cranberry juices – which she'd normally manage fairly easily – and discovered that she was unable to walk. It wasn't that she felt all that drunk; it was just that when she attempted to stand up to go to the toilet, she literally could not feel her legs. She had to pick each one up manually, put it on the floor, raise herself up onto them and then move them one at a time towards the toilet – something which the rest of the group, in their pink 'Diane's Hen Weekend' T-shirts had found hilarious.

It was only the following day, after a night spent shaking and vomiting, that Vanessa was told about Polish vodka and how it apparently made you drunk from the legs up. From then on she vowed never to drink vodka, or any spirit, ever again. So she just drank wine and the occasional pint of lager, even though Kimberley constantly pointed out how unladylike she found it when women drank pints

Vanessa raised her glass towards Kimberley. 'Happy Valentine's Day.'

Kimberley picked up her glass and tapped it against Vanessa's.

'And to you, my dear. And I've just put some songs on for us.'
They each took a sip of their drink.

'So, go on...' said Kimberley, 'you were going to tell me something about Sarah before you went to get the drinks.'

Vanessa looked around and then moved in closer to Kimberley. 'She swings.'

'Sorry?'

Vanessa pointlessly spoke even more quietly. 'She swings. They do – her and Robin. They're swingers.'

Even though Kimberley understood everything Vanessa was saying, there was still a part of her that thought, or maybe wished, that she'd misheard.

'What are you talking about?'

Vanessa laughed; 'I'm serious, Kim. She told me. There's a house they go to, a friend of a friend, who has regular swingers' evenings. She's actually invited me along.'

'But . . . but . . .' Kimberley tried to think logically, 'but you don't have anyone to swap!'

Vanessa laughed loudly. 'I know. I was thinking of taking my old microwave!'

They both laughed. Some of the couples, clearly wishing they'd chosen a quieter, more romantic venue for this evening, turned and looked at them.

'But it's not only for partner-swapping,' Vanessa went on, attempting to keep her voice down. 'Apparently you can just go and watch if you want to. That's how Sarah started. She and someone from her work went along and . . . just watched. They didn't take part. Not at first anyway. Then the next time, she went with Robin and . . . well, they did take part. They chose people, went to a room, and slept with them.'

'Eurgh!'

'I know. That's what I thought!' said Vanessa.

She picked up a wooden cocktail stick and used it to push an olive stone around the bowl in front of her.

'Maybe we should go with her!' suggested Kimberley.

Vanessa looked at her.

'Are you serious?'

'No!'

They both laughed loudly.

'Look at us,' said Kimberley. 'Valentine's day, and we're on our own talking about going to a swingers' night. Where the hell did it all go wrong?!'

She shook her head and smiled.

Vanessa didn't.

'I'm sorry about the whole Steve thing,' said Vanessa quietly, almost to herself.

'I've told you a million times it wasn't your fault!' said Kimberley.

'It *was* my fault, and I'm sorry. If I hadn't emailed him after that programme or—'

'Ness, that's enough! I'm not a child. I made my own decisions. It wasn't your fault. That's like saying it was my fault that you found out about PP – you know, if I hadn't helped you create that website profile, everything—'

Vanessa sighed. 'You're right, Kim . . .' She looked down at the empty olive bowl. 'It *is* your fault!'

Kimberley looked at her.

Vanessa laughed.

Kimberley picked up a beer mat and threw it towards her. Vanessa quickly moved out of the way and Kimberley watched as the mat continued through the air until it hit the forehead of a young man on the next table.

The man looked up. Kimberley thought about hiding but realised it was a little pointless as the man was looking directly at her.

She held up her hand. 'Sorry. It was an accident.'

The young man smiled. Kimberley was surprised by the flirtatiousness in the smile. She wondered what his girlfriend (she reckoned he was too young to be married), sitting in front of him with her back to Kimberley, would think about that look. A moment later Kimberley found out, as the person turned around to reveal that they were in fact also a young man – with surprisingly long hair.

This second young man also smiled.

Vanessa turned around to see the recipient of Kimberley's thrown beer mat and came face to face with the second, longer-haired man. She smiled, more out of surprise than anything else.

'Hi.'

Vanessa didn't know why she had expected him to have a higher-pitched voice, maybe it was the hair, but she was pleasantly surprised.

'Hello.' She spoke over him to the first man: 'Sorry about my friend. She wasn't allowed to have a Frisbee when she was a child.'

'I understand,' he replied. 'I'm the same with swings and slides. Never allowed to go on them as a child. Now at least once a week I go sliding or . . . or *swinging.*'

Vanessa looked at him. 'You've been listening to our conversation, haven't you?'

'Sorry, but we didn't really have a choice,' said the deeper-than-expected voice of the second young man. 'You were speaking pretty loudly. Oh, and just to let you know, we think you should go!'

***

Kimberley looked at herself in the large wall mirror. She didn't have that many wrinkles – she'd moisturised from a young age – and although the long work hours and a few nights of crying had caused bags under her eyes, her make-up covered them up. She turned and looked at herself from a few different angles. Yes, she could pass for a couple of years younger . . .

Vanessa came out from one of the cubicles. She was still laughing.

'This is ridiculous, Kim! We have nothing to talk to them about!'

'I know!'

They both laughed.

Kimberley looked back at her own reflection. 'Where's the harm though, Ness? I mean, it's not like we're going to do anything with them.'

Kimberley waited for her friend's concurrence. The silence was so long that for a moment she wondered if she had actually said her last sentence out loud.

'Ness?'

'No, of course not!'

***

The young man with the long hair brought a tray of drinks to the table. 'Are they still not back yet?'

The one with the short hair shook his head. 'No, they've been gone ages.'

'Must be having a dump.'

His friend nodded in agreement.

The young man with the long hair put the drinks onto the table, put the tray down on the empty table next to him and sat down. 'So, have we decided yet, or are we going to continue arguing?'

'Well, as I said, as I made first contact, I have first choice. And I'm going with the doctor.'

The shorter-haired young man sighed.

'Fine. But you owe me one.'

They reached across to put their empty glasses onto the tray on the next table and then picked up their new drinks.

'To be honest,' said the young Man with the longer hair, 'I think yours is going to be the filthiest. She looks like she's up for anything.'

They smiled, tapped their glasses together and then both drank.

The one with the shorter hair spoke under his breath.

'MILF's returning at two o'clock.'

Kimberley and Vanessa arrived at the table.

'So, you've finished powdering your noses then?'

'And having a poo?'

The other three turned and looked at the young man with long hair.

He shrugged. 'I'm just guessing . . .'

Vanessa picked up her drink.

'So', said the man with short hair, 'we were thinking, let's finish these and go to the Scarlet Lounge.'

The song 'Holding Back the Years' by Simply Red faded out in the background and was replaced by Duran Duran's 'Girls on Film'.

'Oh,' said the young man with the long hair, turning his head slightly as though this would help him hear the music, 'I love this song.'

'I'm surprised you know it,' said Vanessa.

'Are you kidding?' continued the young man. 'My mum plays it all the time.'

Vanessa turned and looked at Kimberley.

Without saying a word, they both stood up and put on their coats.

'What . . . what's going on?' asked the young man with the short hair.

'Thanks for the drinks,' said Kimberley. 'Enjoy the rest of your night.'

And she and Vanessa turned around and walked out.

CHAPTER FIFTY-SEVEN

Steve and Mike Dutch had been sitting in silence quietly in Steve's office for just under a minute – although it felt longer to both of them. Steve looked at the space on the wall where the backwards clock used to hang. He'd forgotten that the clock, like the majority of the smaller office items, was packed away in one of the banana boxes stacked on the floor along the wall under the window ledge.

'I'm sorry, Steve . . .' said Mike, '. . . but I don't want to go with another agent. I want to stay with you.'

Steve leant forward in his chair and smiled. 'I know, Mike. And I appreciate it, I really do. But I'm giving it all up. I haven't enjoyed it for a long time. You need to be with someone who can devote the time and energy you deserve. You're going to be big, Mike. I can see it happening . . .'

'And most of that is because of you. You're the one who had faith in me. You're the one who put me forward for things when everyone else ignored me. No one else really liked, or got, my act.'

Steve looked down at the ingrained interlocking coffee stains on his desk. He wondered if he would lose any of his office rental deposit for that.

He looked Mike straight in the eyes. 'To be honest, Mike . . . I wasn't so keen on your act either.'

Mike frowned.

Steve realised how incredibly vulnerable Mike suddenly looked. Like a child who was being told off by the headteacher.

'What . . . what do you mean?'

Steve hated what he was about to say.

'When you sent the DVD into the office, I didn't like it. No, more than that, I thought it was absolute shit. One of the worst I'd seen. The reason I recommended you for that first corporate job I sent you on was because the client was a knob and I wanted him to suffer. In a way I guess I wanted you both to suffer. Him for being an arse and you for having such a crap act.'

Although he was known for his quick retorts, Mike had no idea what to say.

'I'm sorry, Mike. Of course, my opinion did change eventually. Of you at least. I'm still not a *huge* fan of your material. But I know how talented you are. I'm just not interested in representing your talent, or anyone's, any more.'

Mike stood up.

For a moment Steve thought he was going to be punched.

Mike held out his hand. Steve also stood up, and shook it.

'Well, Steve, I still owe you a lot. Thank you. And good luck with everything.'

Steve smiled. 'You too, Mike, although you won't need luck.'

Mike Dutch looked around the sparse office and then walked out.

Steve watched him leave and then continued to stare at the now empty doorway.

Steve bent down, picked up an empty shoebox from the floor and put it onto his desk. He then took out the small bottom drawer of the desk, tilted it slightly so as to bypass the hinges and pulled it completely out. He lifted the lid off the shoebox and started emptying the contents of the drawer – pens, paperclips, envelopes, empty CD covers and an assortment of business cards – into it. As he did, the phone rang. Steve continued with his task. He heard his voice unnecessarily telling the caller whom they had just dialled. Like most people, Steve didn't like the sound of his recorded voice, much preferring the voice he could hear when it resonated in his head.

As he heard the caller enquire about representation, he finished replacing the drawer and sat back in his chair. He rested his feet on the lip of the desk and laid his head back against the wall. He stared straight ahead and, as the call finished, he closed his eyes.

CHAPTER FIFTY-EIGHT

Steve opened his eyes. The poster of John Travolta and Olivia Newton-John smiled down at him. Although slightly yellow around the edges and with one torn corner as a result of a sibling argument, the iconic *Grease* poster was in pretty good shape. When he was younger he used to think that John Travolta was taunting him, as if to say, 'Look who I'm with and you're not.' He used to have a postcard of this picture as well and had once cut out his own face from a photo and put it over John Travolta's.

He looked at the rest of the items on the walls: a poster for *Scarface*, three framed certificates – one for swimming, one for speech and drama and one for a charity fun run – a 1996 Reading FC pennant from when they were promoted to the Second Division and an album cover of Prince's *Sign O' The Times* held up by three drawing pins.

In the distance he could hear the bell-ringers practising for whenever the next local wedding might be. He had always loved this sound. It reminded him of lazy Saturday summer afternoons, when he'd stay in bed until lunchtime and then go for a wander into the town centre with Jeff. Then, later, after having a shower and getting changed – jacket, shirt and tie – going into town again, but this time by bus or, if they were late, taxi, and going to a disco.

He stared up at the ceiling and watched a small cobweb gently moving in the draught from the window.

It could have all been so different. The slightest change

and his life could have been altered beyond recognition. He and Jeff would often talk about any regrets they might have. Jeff was usually the one who regretted most things. Apparently that had now changed. Jeff now believed that his whole life had led to him being a dad. That was something neither of them had expected to happen.

Steve had rarely regretted anything, apart from a one-night-stand on a holiday in Turkey, and he had paid the price for that. Literally. Pharmaceuticals in Turkey weren't cheap.

But generally, even though he wasn't the happiest or most positive of people, he didn't regret things. Until now. Now he regretted everything from the age of eighteen onwards.

What if he hadn't gone to Angels that night? What if he'd stayed with his girlfriend Debbie instead? Maybe they would have married young, had children early, and now their children would be away at university and he and Debbie would be travelling the world together. Maybe he would have had a different career altogether. That was likely. He would probably never have gone to drama school but would have passed his exams and studied to be a teacher instead.

He could have done anything.

And anything would have been better than this.

'Steve, your breakfast is ready.'

He hadn't heard that for a long time. Even though he knew his mother's voice had changed over the years, it still sounded the same as it had when she used to call him for school.

'Coming!'

He threw back the sheets and blanket – his mother had never made the change to duvets – and got out of bed.

***

'Seriously, Mum, I couldn't eat anything else.'

'But you've only had one slice of toast.'

Steve looked across the table at his mother. 'And a bowl of cereal. And a croissant. I normally have . . . well . . . *nothing* for breakfast.'

Steve's mother shook her head in disappointment. Something Steve was quite used to.

'You know it's the most important meal of the day?'

Steve nodded. 'So I've heard. Although I prefer dinner myself. And if you eat late enough you don't need breakfast.'

Steve's mother didn't respond to his comment. She just took another slice of toast from the toast rack, wiped some margarine onto it and put it on Steve's plate.

Steve resigned himself to the fact he was going to have to eat it, and took a bite.

'Did I tell you that Sheila and the kids are coming down tomorrow?'

'Yes, Mum. Three times.'

'Really? Sorry, it's old age, you know. I keep repeating myself.'

'I know. You told me that too.'

Steve's mum smiled. She looked at the pile of boxes currently taking pride of place in the breakfast room. 'Are you going into London today? I think I heard something about a problem with the trains . . .'

'No, I'm not going in today. I'm going in tomorrow to see about getting my deposit back for the office. And I don't have to worry about trains so much; I can drive now.'

Steve's mum smiled. 'Oh yes, I keep forgetting! You see, you *have* achieved something!'

Steve looked confused and disappointed. 'I didn't say I *hadn't* achieved anything.'

'No. Of course not!' said his mum quickly, 'And you'd have no reason to say that!'

She stood up and started to clear away the breakfast dishes. She spoke, trying to sound as nonchalant as possible. 'So, are you . . . going to try to see Kimberley when you're in London?'

Steve swallowed his toast, which he already regretted agreeing to eat. 'What?! No. Why would I do that?'

His mum opened the fridge and put the margarine and cheese inside. 'I don't know. I just thought . . . it might be nice to have a chat.'

'It's nice to have a chat with a friend, or maybe someone at a bus stop; not with your ex-girlfriend who dumped you.' He took a mouthful of tea to help the toast down.

His mother suddenly slammed the fridge door closed, which made Steve jump and spill his drink.

'Well, you shouldn't have had an affair behind her back, should you?!'

Steve didn't know what to say. He'd tried to explain to his mother what had happened and how he hadn't even kissed Helen/Becky, but as far as she was concerned, for obvious reasons, she still saw him as being unfaithful.

'Why did you do it, Steven?'

Her voice dropped to almost a whisper as she repeated herself: 'Why did you do it?'

Steve looked down at the crusts on his plate. 'I . . . I don't know, Mum.'

***

Steve couldn't remember the last time he'd walked around Reading town centre. He'd seen it from a distance every time he caught the train to see his mum – which was usually once a month – but he hadn't walked around it for years. Some of the shops, the ones outside the shopping centre itself, had been there since his childhood. He remembered going into Parkson's the shoe shop with his mother and sister and being scared of the foot-measuring machine, which he thought was going to squash his toes. As he thought about this he became aware of the fact that most of his childhood memories excluded his father. He wasn't sure of the reason for this. He knew his father had worked long hours most days, but he was sure he had been around at weekends, and he didn't leave his mother until Steve was much older. Yet there were hardly any memories that included him. Steve realised that, in a way, his mum had been a single parent long before his dad had left.

Steve suddenly noticed that he had been staring at the window of a pharmacy for quite a while. He felt like a teenager trying to find the confidence to go in and ask for a packet of condoms. Looking at the reflection in the window, his eyes changed focus. Now, behind him, he could see the tinted glass front of the casino. He turned around and looked at it. Even though it was daytime, the word 'CASINO' was lit up. A large poster in the window displayed two scantily clad women about to throw a pair of dice onto a craps table.

'Immediate Membership! Join now!'

Steve remembered how difficult it used to be to join a casino. Two proofs of identity and then a month to wait for your membership to be accepted.

Not now. Now it was on a whim. No pre-planning required. Of course this casino hadn't been there when he was younger. No, this was where Angels had once been. The disco that changed his life – or at least set it on its downward course.

Steve turned back to the chemist's window.

'Steve?'

The uncertainty in the voice made Steve question if the person was addressing him.

He turned and saw a fat middle-aged man standing next to him. Steve thought he recognised the man but couldn't think from where. Maybe it was one of his dad's friends? Although Steve smiled, he couldn't hide the fact that he had no idea who this person was.

'Ross, Ross Davies,' said Ross, Ross Davies.

Steve was even more confused. He'd gone to school with a Ross Davies, but this wasn't him. Ross Davies was a skinny good-looking bloke with shoulder-length brown hair. Ross Davies was the answer to Jeff's drunken question of: 'If you had to shag one of the blokes in our class, who would it be?'

Maybe this was Ross's dad. Maybe the Ross he'd known was really Ross junior.

'We were in school together.'

No, this wasn't Ross's dad. This was Ross.

'Sorry, Ross. I was miles away.'

Ross smiled. 'I can see that. Don't worry – I know how daunting buying your first condoms can be!'

Steve smiled, mainly at the fact Ross had read his mind.

'I was just going to get a toothbrush,' Steve needlessly explained.

'Ah. Even more daunting! I mean, think about it. It's at least a two-month commitment, and you don't want to make the wrong decision. It's not like you can use it once or twice, realise you've made a dreadful mistake and then try to take it back.'

Steve laughed. He'd forgotten how funny Ross could be.

'I mean, I don't know much about statutory rights, but I don't think "the soft bristles are too soft" is really grounds for a court case.'

Steve had also forgotten how Ross had the tendency to push a joke to its extreme.

'Members of the jury, in the case of Steve Connors against Total Toothy Toothbrushes, how do you find the defendant?'

To push it until it was just no longer funny.

'How are you, Ross? It's been . . . years.'

'Yeah. The last time I saw you was at the school reunion. And that was almost seven years ago.'

Steve looked uncomfortable, although he really needn't have done. 'Er . . . I didn't go to the school reunion.'

Ross frowned and scratched his head. Steve hadn't realised that people actually did that.

'Then I wonder who the hell I was talking to?' Ross shrugged. 'Anyhoo, what brings you back to the centre of the universe?'

'Oh, I've . . . come back to visit my mum. What about you? Are you also on a quick visit?'

Ross looked surprised. 'No, I live here. I never left.'

Steve just stopped himself from saying that he was sorry to hear that. After all, there was nothing wrong with living there. Steve personally had wanted to leave as soon as possible to go and live in London. But he now realised that London wasn't the be all and end all. Whatever that meant.

'Do you remember Alison Costa?'

Did Steve remember Alison Costa? Of course he remembered Alison Costa. Alison Costa was the first girl he kissed. Properly kissed with tongues and everything. It had happened in the coach on the way back from a school trip to see *Joseph and the Amazing Technicolor Dreamcoat*. Steve had hated the show – he hated all musicals apart from *Grease* – yet the journey back had more than made up for it.

The following day he couldn't wait to go to school, thinking that Alison Costa was now going to be his girlfriend. However she completely ignored him, as though the previous day's encounter hadn't happened. This taught Steve a big lesson, which, like most of the lessons he learnt at school, he subsequently forgot.

'Er . . . yes, I think so.'

'Well, I married her.'

There was no hiding the pride and cockiness in Ross's voice. Steve wondered if she had ever told her husband about their snog.

'Well done.' He didn't quite know how else to react. Giving Ross a round of applause seemed a little out of place.

'Yeah. We've got two kids, five and seven. Strange names I know!'

Ross looked expectantly at Steve. Steve obliged by smiling widely, even though he had heard this joke, ironically, about twelve times.

'We keep having to change their names every year,' he pushed.

'So... what do you do?' asked Steve, who felt he needed to carry on the conversation a little longer before making his excuses to leave.

'I run that ol' place over there, for my sins.'

Steve followed Ross's thumb indication.

'What? The casino?'

'Yeah. I was a croupier there for a while. Then a pit boss. Now I manage it.'

'Wow.'

Steve was genuinely impressed, although he wasn't sure why.

'The place used to be Angels. Do you remember it?'

'Er . . .'

Ross interrupted. 'Oh, of course you do!' He laughed. 'That's where you met that girl you ended up searching for.

Did you ever find her? Skids said he saw you on some TV show or something a while ago . . .'

Steve felt as though he had gone back twenty years. Here was his old classmate – albeit an aged version – referring to another classmate by their nickname as though it were completely normal. Steve was a little envious. This was someone who was obviously happy, yet who was still subconsciously living in the past. Or maybe there was no past or present for him; maybe time just remained a constant.

'No. No, I didn't. I . . . er . . . gave up on that.'

Ross laughed. 'Do you remember the posters you put everywhere?'

Steve shrugged. 'Vaguely.'

Ross continued as though he hadn't spoken. 'That was the funniest thing ever!' He then remembered. 'Oh, that's right, we were all talking about it at the reunion. That's why I thought you were there. I bet your ears were burning that day!'

Steve wasn't in any way a violent person. He'd only ever had one fight in his life and that had been in the school playground when he was fourteen. He'd lost badly. But then the girl *had* been a lot taller than him. But although he wasn't a violent person, the one thing he really wanted to do now was to punch Ross. He imagined himself putting all the pain and upset of the past couple of months and all the wasted time of the past few years into one huge punch, which would send Ross flying backwards through the chemist shop window.

'I bet you feel a bit of a dick, thinking about that now!'

Just one punch. Straight on the nose.

'Oh, and do you remember Jeff Richards from our class?'

Steve knew he had to interject immediately,

'Yes. I'm still friendly with him.'

'Nice guy,' said Ross.

Steve realised he would never know if this was what Ross had intended to say.

'Yes, he is. He's happily married, with a baby.'

'Really?' Ross laughed. 'Isn't that illegal? Shouldn't he have married someone a bit older?!'

Maybe just a quick sharp knee in the balls instead. Pretend it was an accident.

Ross looked at his watch. 'Anyhoo, I'd best be making a move. No rest for the wicked!'

Steve smiled and nodded.

'Oh, by the way, Steve, I was sorry to hear about your dad.'

'Thanks.'

'Still, I guess there are worse ways to go than passing away on holiday!'

Steve smiled. 'Absolutely.'

They shook hands and Steve watched Ross walk away. He then looked at the casino. For a moment he actually thought about going in. Then he realised: he'd already gambled too much of his life away in that building.

CHAPTER FIFTY-NINE

Mrs Green hesitated at the door. She knew there was something else she had wanted to say, she just wasn't sure what it was. She'd mentioned her left arm and her right leg, she'd spoken about the ulcers in her mouth and she'd asked about the large mole on the back of her neck – which had turned out to be a mosquito bite.

'Oh yes, I get nasty pain here every time I breathe.' She pointed towards the left-hand side of her abdomen. 'It could be appendicitis.'

Kimberley swallowed her sigh. She looked at Mrs Green's notes on the screen in front of her.

'Well, Mrs Green, it's unlikely it's appendicitis as you had your appendix taken out thirty years ago. And even then it was on the other side.'

'Well, maybe it's one of those phantom appendicitises. Like a phantom pregnancy.'

Kimberley resisted the urge to hand over a leaflet on euthanasia.

'Well, let's see how it is in a couple of days, and if it gets worse, come back and see me.'

Mrs Green reluctantly agreed and walked out.

Once the door had closed, Kimberley blew into her cheeks and let the air out slowly.

She turned to her computer screen and wrote up the notes. She was aware that she'd written more notes on this patient than most of her others put together.

She finished writing, opened the top drawer of her desk and took out a bottle of water. She unscrewed the cap – which took more effort than she anticipated as she had a tendency to over-tighten ever since the soggy handbag incident – took a mouthful, re-screwed it too tightly and put it back into the drawer. She then pressed the button on her desk to let the next patient know she was ready for them.

She briefly looked at her computer screen. A new patient. She wondered if this one would be as annoying as Mrs Green.

There was a knock at the door. She was so used to hearing this sound now that she sometimes heard it in her head before going to sleep at night. Steve had told her, on several occasions, that she said the words 'come in' when she was sleeping.

'Come in.'

She assumed it was because she was momentarily thinking of Steve, but as the new patient walked in, he actually reminded her of Steve.

'Hi.'

He even spoke like him.

'Sorry, Kim. I hope you don't mind. I just—'

'Steve?! What the hell are you doing here? How are you a new patient?'

'Well, it was fairly easy really. Jeff knows someone who lives in the area and I used their address for a temporary residency form.'

'That's illegal!'

'Probably. Certainly unethical. But I knew if I had rung you wouldn't have taken my call. And waiting for you outside the flat would be borderline stalkerish . . .'

'And you think this is better?!'

'Until a few seconds ago I did, yes.'

Kimberley stared at her ex-boyfriend.

'So what do you want?'

'Er . . . well,' said Steve 'I have a small rash I'd like you to check, and . . .'

Kimberley didn't react.

'I just wanted a chat, Kim. That's all. I wanted to say . . .'

Steve paused for a moment. He'd practised this conversation several times while walking around his mum's garden. He didn't want to forget any of it. He'd even thought about writing down bullet points on the back of his hand in case he forgot anything. And he knew he had to start the conversation well. He'd seen enough stand-up comedy to know that the opening line was the most important – you had to get your audience's attention, show them you knew what you were doing and put them at ease. He needed to do this now with Kimberley. He knew he didn't have much time and would only get one chance. He didn't want to blow it.

'I love you.'

Damn, he thought. He should have started with a gag.

'I'm so sorry, Kim. I know what I did was stupid . . .'

He paused briefly in the hope Kimberley would interject. She didn't.

'But you have to understand something . . . I'm an idiot. A stupid, pathetic, puerile idiot.'

He paused again.

No, he was still performing a monologue.

'Look, Kim . . . sorry, can I sit down?'

'No, the chairs are for patients.'

'Okay. Anyway, the thing is, I've only ever really been happy, really happy, twice in my life. Once was when I was seventeen and Jeff and I used to go out drinking, dancing, playing pool and meeting girls every night, and then the other time was when I met you.'

Kimberley laughed. But not in a good way.

'Are you telling me that you were unhappy for over twenty years?!'

'Well, no but . . .' Steve thought and changed his mind. 'Well, in a way, yes . . .' He did it again. 'Well, not unhappy but . . .'

Steve sighed. He saw the past twenty years flash before his eyes. He wondered if he was about to die. If he were, he realised that there were worse places for it to happen.

'You don't love me, Steve. You loved the idea that I was the girl you met all those years ago.'

'But you probably are her!'

Kimberley stared at him.

'Not that that's important,' continued Steve. 'Look, I know I've obsessed about this for over half my life and I know how pathetic it is – in the true sense of the word. But when I met you, well, it all changed.'

'Then why did you meet with Becky?'

Steve had expected this question and he'd worked hard on his answer. He'd given it a lot of thought, in fact. He wanted to say the right thing – not too much, but something concise and explanatory. Something that would put everything right.

'I don't know.'

It was the best he could do.

Kimberley slowly shook her head.

Steve knew he was about to blow his only chance.

'I'm so sorry, Kim. Of course I shouldn't have met with her.' He than added quickly, 'But you know we didn't do anything together . . .'

Kimberley opened her mouth to speak but Steve

continued: 'Which I know is irrelevant as I still lied to you . . .'

Kimberley closed her mouth.

'But you have to understand that I'm . . . an addict.' Steve stood up straight; 'My name's Steve Connors and I'm addicted to a memory.'

He looked at Kim. There was no reaction. Steve thought it was a shame she hated gambling so much as she'd be an amazing poker player.

'Unfortunately there are no support groups for this type of addiction. I've checked. There's no *Obsessed with girls from discos twenty years ago Anonymous*. Or *OGDTA*.'

He knew he'd missed out some letters in the acronym, but assumed the point had been made.

For a moment, a brief wonderful moment, Steve thought he saw a glimmer of a smile in Kimberley's eyes.

'I know I've messed things up, Kim. But don't walk away. You are the best thing that has ever happened, or will ever happen, to me.'

He knew there were other things he'd wanted to say, he just couldn't remember any of them. If wished he could shout into the wings to ask for a 'line'.

Kimberley looked at the clock on her computer screen.

'It's time for my next patient. Who I'm assuming will be a real one.'

'Okay.'

Steve stepped towards the door and opened it. He was about to walk out when he suddenly remembered something else he'd planned on saying. But he realised the moment and the opportunity had passed.

CHAPTER SIXTY

Jeff looked around. He smiled when he thought how the room hadn't changed much over the years. Of course the wallpaper was different, at least different to the brown and beige oval pattern they'd had in the seventies. And the furniture had changed from the hard leather three-seater sofa to two comfy armchairs. But the smell was still there. And it was a good smell. All his friend's houses had had their own smell, but Steve's was the best. It smelled of cakes; unlike their friend Nick's house which always smelled of cabbage, even though no one in that house ever ate it. Jeff thought about those thirty-odd years and he realised how his and Steve's lives and their relationship had changed. He'd always been secretly jealous of Steve. Well, maybe not so secretly. In fact, as he had once told Steve, 'I'm really jealous of you,' he'd more or less stripped away any secrecy. Steve had always been the one with the good looks. Although girls said that 'a good sense of humour' was the most important attribute they looked for in a bloke, Jeff knew this was crap. He was far funnier than Steve and always had the girls laughing, yet Steve was the one who ended up sleeping with or at least snogging them. But, thinking how their lives had panned out, Jeff knew that his was the life that had turned out the better. Yes, he was married to someone who could be a pain in the arse a lot of the time, but they did love each other and they were relatively happy. And after years of living off his parents' and the state's money, Jeff was now the main breadwinner for his wife, son and child to come. Steve on the other hand . . . well, even though in school he'd been voted the most likely to have fame and fortune, he had ended up living an existence instead of a life. Now he was the one with no job. If they hadn't been such good friends, Jeff would have allowed himself to gloat. Or at least gloat a little longer. But he really hoped that things would pick up for Steve soon. And he knew, if tonight went to plan, they would pick up sooner than later.

Steve's mum walked in with a pot of tea and a cup and saucer on a tray. She put them on the table next to Jeff.

'Are you sure you don't want something to eat?'

'No, thank you. I'm fine, really.'

'Are you ? Just a sandwich or something?'

Jeff smiled. 'Honestly I'm not hungry. I had a big lunch before I left.'

'I've got some of those lemon-curd tarts you used to like.'

Jeff was about to politely decline again when the memory of the flavour came back.

'. . . with the sprinkles?'

Steve's mum smiled. 'Of course.'

'Well . . . just one.'

'That's a good boy!'

Steve's mum excitedly went back into the kitchen.

Steve entered the room. He was dressed in what would be described as *smart casual*.

'Okay, I'm ready.'

'Just a sec, mate. I'm having some tea and tarts.'

'What? But you were the one who said they wanted to go out early!'

Steve's mum came in, carrying three of the lemon-curd tarts.

'Are you two boys playing nicely?'

'Yes,' they both replied automatically.

She put the plate down in front of Jeff, picked up the teapot and started to pour.

'So how's your baby?'

Jeff smiled. 'Not a baby any more. He's walking now.'

She stopped pouring. 'You're joking!'

She shook her head and continued to pour. 'It's like only yesterday that you two were playing here as children yourselves. Now you have kids of your own. Well, *you* do anyway.'

She didn't make eye contact with her son.

Steve decided to change the subject, and tone. 'I still can't quite understand why you wanted to come here tonight. I mean, it's nice of you to surprise me but . . . since when have you been so nostalgic?'

Jeff picked up one of the tarts and took a bite. 'I don't remember.'

Steve pointed to Jeff's top lip. Jeff licked it with his tongue and dragged the sticky sprinkles into his mouth.

'Like I said, mate, I hadn't seen you in a while and I thought it would be nice to go around our old haunts.'

'But you're driving. You can't even have a drink.'

Jeff finished off the tart and swallowed. 'You know me, I don't have to drink to have a good time.'

'The first part of that sentence cancels out the other.'

'So,' interjected Steve's mum, 'how are they?'

'Delicious, just as I remember, thank you.'

Steve's mum smiled proudly. She then picked up the plate with the rest of the tarts and offered them to Jeff.

He didn't bother arguing. 'Oh, go on then, one more. Just for old times' sake.'

Steve was still bemused by the whole thing. 'And Francine is fine about you coming here, on a Saturday night?'

'Absolutely. I'm surprised you're surprised.'

'And I'm surprised you're surprised I'm surprised.'

'Are you sure you don't want to stay the night, Jeff?' asked Steve's mum, more as a way of stopping the conversation than anything else. 'I could easily make up Sheila's room for you.'

'No, thanks. Although, to tell you the truth, if you had asked me twenty years ago if I wanted to sleep in Sheila's room, my answer might have been different.'

Sheila's mother and brother stared at him.

'Yeah, that should have stayed as a thought really.' Jeff dragged in another lip-line of sprinkles and swallowed.

Steve's mum topped up Jeff's teacup even though it was half full, or, as Steve saw things, half empty.

***

The sound of the coins hitting the metal tray at the bottom of the fruit machine immediately reminded Steve of Las Vegas. He and Jeff had gone there to celebrate Jeff's thirtieth birthday. They'd had a good time even though Jeff had actually lost the whole day of his actual birthday due to his partaking of the free drinks the night before and subsequently suffering from the worst hangover he'd ever had. He'd spent the entire day in bed, leaving Steve walking up and down the Strip on his own. Steve hadn't minded really, as it had given him the chance to visit most of the hotels. Although each of them had a different theme, the constant electronic tunes and the noisy and surprisingly frequent payouts of the machines made them all sound exactly the same and therefore blend into one.

Although Steve had enjoyed Vegas, he wasn't enjoying this.

'You okay, Steve?'

'Not really, mate. I thought you wanted a nostalgic evening. You can't really be nostalgic about a place you've never been.'

'I know. I just wanted to see what it was like. We won't stay long. A couple of games of blackjack and we'll leave.'

'You play, mate. I'll have a go later. I'm going to the bar.'

Jeff nodded and walked to the tables to look for a free seat.

Steve made his way towards the bar. As he did, he looked around the room. He tried to fit the look of it with what he remembered of Angels. He frowned as he attempted to work out where the dance floor would have been, where the DJ would have sat, where the cloakroom would have been, where the doors leading from the entrance into the club would have been. He suddenly realised that he could be standing in the exact same spot as he had been when he saw the girl.

Although not a flashback – he hadn't had those for months now – he naturally remembered that evening once more.

The doors, the girl, being pushed towards the floor, hearing the words 'leave him, he's not worth it', then looking up from the floor and seeing that she'd left.

Thinking about Kimberley reminded Steve of the last time he'd seen her. It had been almost a month since he had gone to the surgery. A part of him, the optimistic part he never knew he had, had expected her to call later that week. By halfway through the following week, and not having received a call, his natural pessimism had returned.

'What can I get you?'

Steve looked at the barman, who, dressed in his lime shirt and brightly coloured waistcoat, wouldn't have looked out of place at a children's theme park.

'A pint of lager, please.'

The barman nodded. He turned, took a small metal bowl, dipped it into a large pack of assorted salted nuts and put it onto the bar counter in front of Steve.

'Thanks. Oh, by the way, is Ross in tonight?'

'Mr Davies? Yes, he is. Would you like me to get him for you?'

Steve thought for a moment. He then shook his head. 'No, it's fine, thanks.'

He realised that he wasn't really in the mood to speak to him. He took a handful of nuts and put them into his mouth. As he chewed and swallowed he felt thirsty and hoped the barman wouldn't take too long with his drink.

***

Steve and Jeff sat two seats away from each other at the full blackjack table. This was their fourth hand and so far the House had beaten them both every time. Steve was getting annoyed with the person sitting to his right. The point of blackjack was that everyone played together against the dealer – but most people didn't realise this. In the previous hand the dealer had 12. Any good player would stick with almost any hand they had, in the hope that the dealer would draw a ten or a picture card – with the value of ten – and therefore go bust. But the man next to Steve had drawn on 15 and been dealt a picture. The one the dealer should have had. He then went 'bust', and although everyone else had decided to 'stand' on their respective 13, 14 and 16, the dealer had drawn an eight and won. They had all glared at the guy, but he was completely oblivious.

Over the next five hands Steve won twice, although as one of the wins was by splitting aces which both beat the dealer, he technically won three times.

Steve saw Jeff look at his watch. He assumed Francine had given him a curfew and that he would soon be leaving.

Jeff spoke to Steve behind the back of the annoying player between them. 'So, what are your plans for this week?'

Steve found both the question, and the timing of it, odd. They were in the middle of a game! Couldn't they chat about this later?

'Er . . . I'm not sure, Jeff. Looking for a job, I guess. I'll let you know.'

'Okay. It's just that Francine and I would like you to come over for dinner.'

Steve frowned. It was as though he and Jeff had just met for the first time and had to make small talk.

'Er . . . okay, mate, thanks. I'll . . . let you know.'

He turned back to the table.

He looked down at the cards he'd just been dealt. A king and an 8. He looked at the dealer's hand; a 7 and a 6.

Steve looked up.

'I'll . . .'

Jeff wished he'd been allowed to take a camera into the casino. He'd thought about asking Ross, but as he was already doing them such a big favour, he didn't want to push his luck. So Jeff decided he would mentally remember the image instead. Maybe one day he'd go back to the hypnotist with Steve so that he could describe his expression to him perfectly.

Steve wasn't quite sure what was happening. Was it another flashback? But how could it be? This had never happened. Was he drunk? No, he'd only had a pint. Was he dreaming? Unlikely, especially as he remembered the whole day. Then what other explanation was there? What other possible reason could there be for having a change of dealer – and for this new dealer to be his ex-girlfriend?

'Kim?!'

Kimberley, dressed in the same theme-park outfit as the rest of the staff, was standing across the card table smiling down at him.

'Tell me about it, stud.'

The hair on the back of Steve's neck stood up. This was his favourite quote from the film *Grease*, and Kimberley knew it. It was one of the last lines of dialogue spoken by Olivia Newton-John.

Steve didn't know what to do. He then stood up and leant towards Kimberley. As he did, Kimberley also leant forward and met him halfway over the table.

As they kissed, Jeff, and the rest of the people at the blackjack table, smiled and clapped.

***

'So . . . you organised the whole thing?'

Jeff and Steve were sitting on their own at a small coffee table at the back of the casino. Jeff hadn't stopped grinning since the card game. Steve, who was still in shock, had hardly smiled at all.

'Well. Yes. Sort of. Kim and I planned it together really, with Ross's help of course. Kim had rung me to ask for your number – she'd deleted it, but still had mine, which was nice.

'Very.'

'Anyway, she told me that she had been thinking about you since you went to see her. And, well, she missed you. That's when I thought about this, especially after you told me about bumping into Ross. So I rang the casino and spoke with him and, well, you know the rest.'

Steve went back to looking shocked.

'I can't get over it.'

Jeff leant forward. 'One thing, Steve. Please, please, please . . .'

Steve put his hand on his friend's shoulder.

'Don't worry. I won't. Not this time.' He felt the emotion welling up inside him.

'You know . . . you're a good friend, Jeff.'

Jeff smiled. 'Yeah, I know. It must be great to be mates with me.'

Steve was about to reply when he saw Kimberley, now dressed in her own clothes, walking towards them, accompanied by Ross. Ross was halfway through a conversation with her.

'. . . and I mean it, if you ever feel like giving up medicine, let me know. You'll always have a job here!'

Kimberley smiled.

'Thanks, Ross.'

She sat down at the table next to Steve.

Steve looked at her.

No, he wasn't going to mess this up again.

CHAPTER SIXTY-ONE

Steve, Sheila and Dave stood at the open front door of the flat. The customary two small round balloons with a long balloon separating them, which had been stuck to the outside of the door, were already starting to deflate.

The party was coming to an end. Steve hadn't really wanted to have it in the first place. He'd never been a huge fan of birthdays. But Kimberley had insisted. They had initially looked into holding it in the function room of the pub near his old office, but Steve decided that if he *were* to have a party then he'd want a more intimate event. There was also the fact that, even with his new friends from the teacher training course, Steve wouldn't have had enough guests to even half fill the room. So they had decided to hold it in their flat.

'Thanks for coming.'

Steve kissed his sister and shook Dave's hand. Dave and Steve exchanged a look. Although it was quick, Steve knew that look meant a lot. To Steve, the look meant, 'I'm glad things worked out. I'm pleased I was a part of it.' What Steve didn't know was that Dave's look actually meant, 'I've drunk so much I can hardly focus.'

'Listen, Steve,' said Sheila, 'I didn't want to tell you earlier; I didn't want to spoil the party. But I have to tell you something. It's about dad.'

'He hasn't died again, has he?!'

Steve and Sheila turned and stared at Dave.

'I'll wait in the car,' said Dave, and walked in as straight a line as possible out of the door.

Sheila continued speaking with her brother.

'The thing is . . . he rang me earlier . . . Kate has left him.'

Steve wished he felt more surprised. In truth the only thing he was surprised about was that their relationship had gone on this long.

'So is he going to move back to this country – which would cause a few problems, unless he's changing his name to Lazarus?'

'No, Steve, he won't be moving back, he—'

Steven interrupted. 'So why did she dump him? Was it the age thing?'

'In a way, yes. He'd been sleeping with a younger girl behind her back and now he's moving in with her.'

Steve looked at his sister. He then opened his mouth and laughed and laughed and laughed.

'It's really not funny, Steve!'

'I know!' spluttered Steve through the laughter. 'I know . . . it's pathetic! What an idiot.' He continued to laugh loudly.

Sheila shook her head. 'I'll call you tomorrow!'

She walked off, leaving the sound of laughter behind her.

***

Steve was still smiling as he walked into the living room. The walls were decorated with balloons and 'Happy Birthday' banners. Birthday cards stood on the shelf unit, each one separated by a superhero figurine. Steve had commented earlier that although each year the quantity of the cards had decreased, the importance of each remaining sender had proportionally increased.

'What was all that laughing about?'

'Nothing really, hun. Something I really shouldn't have

laughed at – and probably won't find in the least bit funny tomorrow.'

He sat on the sofa next to Kimberley. Vanessa was on the chair opposite. Jeff was sitting on the floor.

'Jeff was just telling us about the new baby,' said Vanessa.

'He's very sweet,' said Steve.

'Getting broody Mr Connors?'

Steve smiled.

'I can't wait to meet him,' she continued. 'And Logan is such a lovely name.'

Steve and Jeff gave each other a quick look which they assumed no one else would notice.

'What was that look?' asked Vanessa, who obviously had.

'Er . . .' Steve and Jeff looked at each other again. This time more blatantly.

'What is it?' asked Vanessa, slightly more impatiently.

Jeff allowed the drink to offer the explanation. 'Well, I chose the name and Francine loved it. Especially as she said it wasn't the name of a superhero!'

Vanessa nodded.

'So, I've decided,' continued Jeff, 'to wait until he's about five before telling Francine that Logan is actually Wolverine's real name!'

Vanessa laughed, even though she felt she shouldn't.

'Did you know about this?' she asked Kimberley.

Kimberley nodded. 'And I'm sorry to say I also laughed.' She then turned to Jeff. 'By the way, don't you have any new photos of either of them?'

'No,' said Jeff. 'Only the ones I sent you.'

Steve and Kimberley frowned.

'I didn't get any.'

It was Jeff's turn to frown. He then realised. 'Oh, do you

know what? I bet I sent them to your old work email address. But you still have access to that, don't you?'

'Yes', said Steve. He then knew what was coming next.

'Oh, go and get them, Steve!' said Kimberley.

'Yes, I'd love to see them,' added Vanessa.

Steve, who didn't feel like starting up the computer, knew there was no point in arguing. He stood up.

'I'll come with you,' said Jeff, who felt he'd spent enough time with Vanessa and Kimberley while Steve had been saying his goodbyes to various guests.

The moment Steve and Jeff left the room, Kimberley leant closer to Vanessa.

'So, I haven't had the chance to ask you, how did the date go last night?'

Vanessa smiled. 'He was really nice. You know he's a bit younger than me, but he's fine about that. And he loves kids too, so . . . we'll see.'

'Ooooh, how exciting!'

Vanessa looked worried. 'You haven't mentioned anything to Steve, have you? Not yet anyway.'

'You asked me not to,' said Kimberley.

***

In the kitchen, Steve was typing in the address of his old email account.

'So Vanessa met him on the internet?' said Jeff.

Steve nodded. 'Yes, ironically. But please don't say anything – she asked Kim not to tell me.'

Jeff shrugged. 'Okay.'

'Ah, here's your email,' said Steve.

Steve clicked on one of the attached photos and the face of a baby filled the screen.

'Aaaw,' said Steve, 'he's . . . sweet.'

'Yeah, I never know what to say either,' said Jeff.

Steve smiled. 'I'll print them all out. Oh, I've got a couple of other emails on here as well . . .'

As the printer started up, Steve scanned down the other emails. He then stopped.

He spoke quietly.

'Jeff. Look at this.'

Jeff looked. There was an email from a Helen Sanderson.

Even though he had felt warm from the alcohol, Steve now suddenly felt a chill.

'*Dear Steve,*

I have wanted to send this for a long time but kept putting it off.

I saw the programme you did ages ago about a girl you met in a disco in 1988. I knew the minute I saw the programme that the girl was me!

I thought about getting in touch at the time but, as I was with someone, I didn't think it was the right thing to do. Then I saw the second programme when you said you'd met the girl. Ever since then it's been playing on my mind, as I know she's not the right girl. I am. I even remember the night it happened like it was yesterday; that's because it was the night my boyfriend and I split up. We'd been going out since we were 15 and although we argued a lot and had broken up a few times, that was the night it all finished. We'd had a huge argument before we even got to Angels and then, when we were there, he ended up getting into a fight with someone. That's when I knew I'd had enough. I even remember my friend Sally telling me he wasn't worth it....'

Steve looked at Jeff. Jeff was still reading the first couple of lines – Steve had forgotten how slow a reader he was.

Steve suddenly saw it all again in his mind.

The disco, the doors, the fight . . .

He could see the friend speaking. But now, for the first time, he realised that she wasn't looking at him; she was looking at the boys fighting on top of him.

And he'd never mentioned this part of the memory to anyone.

He continued reading.

'I hope you don't mind me getting in touch. I know the website that you mentioned on the programme is no longer there, but as you said you were an agent and mentioned the name of the agency, it wasn't difficult tracking you down.

Anyway, let me know when you'd like to meet up for a coffee or a drink – and see where it takes us. I'm attaching a picture which I hope will bring back memories, even though I've no doubt changed!

Look forward to hearing from you.

Helen x'

Steve stared at the email. For quite a while.

'Shit!' Jeff had eventually finished reading.

Steve looked at him.

'Yeah.'

'What are you going to do?'

Steve turned back to the computer.

He took the mouse and moved the cursor towards the photo attachment. Jeff watched as Steve kept the cursor going, beyond the photo until he reached the delete button.

Without hesitating, he pressed it.

'Are you sure you want to delete this message?' queried the computer, giving him the optional squares of 'yes' and 'no'.

Steve clicked on the word 'yes'.

The email was deleted.

Steve shut down the computer and gathered up the pictures of Jeff's children from the printer.

'Come on; let's show these to the girls.'

Jeff started to follow Steve out of the kitchen. 'I wouldn't have minded seeing what she looked like,' he said.

Steve stopped and looked at him.

'I'm just saying!' He put a hand on Steve's shoulder. 'Anyway, happy birthday, mate.'

Steve smiled at his friend. 'Thanks, Jeff.'

As they walked out of the kitchen, Steve switched off the light.

THE END